Jane Hill w[illegible]irstly as a journalist and then as head of programming for an award-winning group of local commercial radio stations. She is now a freelance writer and broadcaster and is also pursuing a career as a stand-up comedian.

Praise for Jane Hill:

'A fine read. A writer to watch' *Observer*

'You are rewarded with clever twists' *Telegraph*

'Jane Hill is making a name for herself in psychological suspense fiction . . . *Can't Let Go* combines sustained tension with a clever delineation of a damaged young woman . . . It's sit up all night stuff.' *Daily Mail*

'With a plot that keeps the reader guessing and a portrait of obsession that is by turns comic and deeply sinister. Hill's is a welcome new voice, confident and sassy, and, most importantly of all, she tells a great story.'
Mark Billingham, author of *Death Message*

'Like Jane Hill's two previous psychological thrillers, *Can't Let Go* is riveting and completely impossible to put down. It comes armed with a final twist that will make even the most canny readers gasp. I absolutely loved it'
Sophie Hannah, author of *The Point of Rescue*

'Prepare to be sucked in and swept along by this chilling white-water rapid of a thriller'
Cosmopolitan

'A sensational new addition to the psychological thriller shelves'
Daily Record

'By turns playful and poignant, sexy and sinister, Hill's darkly comedic portrait of a woman scorned packs a captivating surprise'
Booklist

'A thrilling tale' *The Lady*

Also by Jane Hill

Grievous Angel
Murder Ballad

can't let go

JANE HILL

arrow books

Published in the United Kingdom by Arrow Books in 2009

1 3 5 7 9 10 8 6 4 2

First published in the United Kingdom in 2008 by William Heinemann

Arrow Books
The Random House Group Limited
20 Vauxhall Bridge Road, London, SW1V 2SA

Addresses for companies within The Random House Group Limited can be found at: www.randomhouse.co.uk/offices.htm

The Random House Group Limited Reg. No. 954009

www.randomhouse.co.uk

A CIP catalogue record for this book is available from the British Library

ISBN 9780099571070

The Random House Group Limited supports The Forest Stewardship Council (FSC®), the leading international forest certification organisation. Our books carrying the FSC label are printed on FSC® certified paper. FSC is the only forest certification scheme endorsed by the leading environmental organisations, including Greenpeace. Our paper procurement policy can be found at www.randomhouse.co.uk/environment

MIX
Paper from responsible sources
FSC® C016897

Typeset by SX Composing DTP, Rayleigh, Essex
Printed and bound by CPI Group (UK) Ltd, Croydon, CR0 4YY

Prologue

When I was eighteen I killed a man and got away with it.

I've never said those words out loud. I hoped I'd never have to. But now the time has come. The axe has finally fallen. And very soon I will have to say them to you.

I'm sitting on a bench in Princes Street Gardens in Edinburgh, waiting for you to make everything okay. It's early in the morning on a chilly late-August day. From time to time there's a hint of drizzle in the grey sky. My jacket, my favourite green velvet jacket, the one I've been wearing all night, is not designed for weather like this. I pull it tighter around me and do up the silver buttons.

Edinburgh's old town looms above me like an illustration from an old-fashioned book of fairy tales, from an era when it was acceptable to terrify children. Tall, crooked, pointed grey buildings huddle around the giant's castle. It's a city from a nightmare: a city of ghosts and goblins and witches, of dark alleys and whispers and hauntings. Looking up at it makes me dizzy. I feel I might fly away on a broomstick or on the wings of a bat.

I must look like a zombie. Maybe I'm about to reach a place beyond fear. I had almost no sleep last night. I spent the night running and hiding: running and hiding from shadows, from shapes; running and hiding from someone unknown who plans to kill me. This morning I have been creeping around the city looking for a quiet place to sit and think, and hide. And now I'm hiding in plain sight, sitting here with my phone in my hand, plucking up the courage to call you; waiting for you to make everything okay.

But you won't be able to make everything okay. Nothing can ever be okay again because today I have to say these words to you: when I was eighteen I killed a man and got away with it.

I look at my phone. I look at your name and your number on the screen. I look at your name and I feel a warm rush of love when I think of our friendship and everything it's meant to me. I never intended to get involved with anyone. Bad things happen to the people I love. And very soon our friendship will be over too: there's no way you'll be able to go on caring for me (and you do care for me, I know you do) after what I have to tell you.

Just before I call you, before I tell you my awful secret, while I'm still sitting here in the stasis of this pre-confession moment, I reach into the deep back pocket of my jeans. I pull out the piece of paper I've been carrying since last night. My hand trembles as I straighten out the creases. There's blood on the paper, blood from my fingers. I read it over again to myself.

'You murdering bitch,' it says. 'Now you know what it feels like.'

One

There he was again, my own personal ghost. I could see him out of the corner of my eye. My own personal ghost, sitting at a table in a motorway service station, drinking coffee. He was there, somewhere over to my left and a little in front of me. If I had turned to look at him full on he would probably have disappeared as if he'd never been there. But that night I didn't want to risk it. I didn't want to look. I knew he was sitting there, his hands wrapped around a mug of coffee, grinning at me with that familiar twinkle in his eye. My own personal ghost: the man I killed. It wasn't the first time I'd seen him. I knew that it wouldn't be the last.

Leicester Forest East Services was a strange place to see a ghost. It's one of those old-style motorway services, built into a bridge over the M1. You need to remember where you are and where you're going at Leicester Forest East, because if you were to lose your sense of direction and come down the wrong staircase, you could work yourself into a panic searching the wrong car park in vain, looking for your car amongst the northbound vehicles when in fact it was right across the motorway in the southbound section. Leicester Forest East has a Burger King, a KFC and a Coffee Primo, but late at night – the time I sometimes found myself there – the only food available was from the hot counter at one end of the restaurant. There was usually one greyish coiled Cumberland sausage sitting alone on a stainless-steel platter under a heat lamp, and maybe the remains of a chicken curry and a single pepperoni pizza.

I was on my way home from a weekend at my sister's house, theoretically to mark the fact that I had turned thirty-five a couple of days earlier. My sister Sarah was four years older than me and I loved her house and the way she lived. Maybe I was envious. She lived in Sheffield, miles further north than anyone else in our family had ever ventured. She owned a Victorian red-brick three-bedroom terraced house with stripped floorboards and original fireplaces. She had a cluttered kitchen with photos and postcards attached to the fridge door with magnets. Every time anyone opened the fridge another photo would flutter to the floor. The house was at the top of a steep hill. From the front windows, if you peered hard enough, you could catch a glimpse of the Peak District in the distance. At the back, the house overlooked dramatic grey industrial chimneys and the M1. Sarah lived there with her bright, charming teenagers Josh and Katie. Her husband left her six years ago for another woman. Or maybe Sarah threw him out when she discovered he was cheating – the story would vary with the number of glasses of wine she drank. Either way, she was doing fine without him.

I had arrived late on the Friday evening and we cheek-kissed on the doorstep. Then I looked at her to see what was different this time. Sarah always had something new about her appearance every time I saw her, probably because I only saw her a couple of times a year. She would be a few pounds lighter, or have a different fringe or a new way of doing her make-up. This time, it was the colour of her hair – blonde and golden streaks lifting the light brown. 'You look great,' I said, like I always say.

She laughed. 'And you look . . . the same.' She always said that too and she was always right. I had found my look, my unnoticeable, blend-into-a-crowd style, and I was planning to stick with it.

Later we sat out on her tiny patio drinking cold *cava*, enjoying the sudden warm spell, watching the sky darken and the lights of the lorries on the motorway. We talked about family stuff: how our parents were enjoying their retirement and whether our younger sister Jem would ever grow up and stop getting tattoos. We talked about Sarah's kids – Katie choosing her GCSE subjects, Josh applying for university. The next morning we all went shopping at Meadowhall, then stopped for a KFC on the way home. That evening Josh stoked up the barbecue in the back garden and we ate burnt sausages and big bowls of salad. It was fun. Until it wasn't.

Saturday night. I was on the road and it was only Saturday night. I had been planning to stay at Sarah's until Sunday afternoon. But it was still only Saturday night and I was on my way home. I walked away. That was what I did, a lot. I would walk away, especially from my family. It wasn't because of arguments or disagreements or anything like that. There would just come a moment when things got on top of me, when the conversation danced too close to subjects I didn't want to talk about, and I felt the need to disentangle myself before it all got too deep. In this case? We were all sitting around in the garden when my sister said to Josh, 'You should ask Aunt Lizzie all about her gap year.'

Sarah still called me Lizzie. She and her kids were pretty much the only people who did. She was married and had left home by the time I got back from my summer in America aged eighteen and announced that my name was now Beth.

'I didn't have a gap year,' I said, hoping I sounded spiky enough to warn her off the subject.

'Yes, you did. You went to San Francisco.' It had always rankled with her that her own godmother had invited me, not Sarah, to stay with her in California.

'I only went for the summer. It wasn't a gap year.'

Sarah made a noise with her lips, a kind of raspberry, as if to say 'whatever'. Then she said to Josh, 'Your Aunt Lizzie went off to San Francisco after she left school, and she came back all grown-up.'

For that was the family myth. Of course I couldn't have told her, I had never been able to tell her, what had really happened: why it was that I went to California as a loud, flirty, flamboyant, full-of-myself teenager called Lizzie and returned home as a sombre, quiet woman called Beth.

Josh wanted to know more, so I walked away. I could feel the mood come over me. I knew it so well. I got itchy. I would feel it in my extremities. I would feel myself wanting to scream, to let it all out. Not straight away, because then it would be obvious, but a little later, during a lull in the conversation, I said: 'Listen, Saz . . .'

'Lizzie, don't . . .'

'What do you mean?'

'You're going to do it, what you always do. You're going to say something like, "Look, the thing is, I need to get back. I've got loads of marking to do."'

'I have.' Marking: it was such a useful excuse. Everyone knew that teachers had marking, and it sounded so dull that they never asked any more questions, and then I didn't have to go into details and get caught out in a lie.

'Well, piss off, then.' Sarah made a joke of it but I could tell she was upset.

She gave me a hug on the doorstep. 'You're weird,' she said.

'I know. Sorry.' I hated myself for leaving.

And so there I was, sitting at a table facing north up the M1. I was watching the white lights of the southbound carriageway and the red lights of the northbound one until they became a blurry abstract pattern. I was picking at the chewy pepperoni slices and stringy cheese from my pizza. I was drinking a can of Red Bull and I was trying to pretend that I was somewhere – anywhere – else. That was when I saw him.

He wasn't there and then suddenly he was, as solid and stocky and dark and vivid as he ever had been when he was alive. He was sitting in the smoking section, just under the big screen showing BBC News 24. From what I could see, looking obliquely at him out of the corner of my left eye, his chin was resting on the knuckles of his right hand, and he was looking straight at me, a half-smile on his face. I could feel his gaze. I knew that the little dimple to the right of his mouth was twitching, the way it used to do when he thought that he knew what I was thinking. Rivers Carillo, the man I killed. Why wouldn't he just leave me alone?

I ignored him, as much as it was possible to ignore him. I tried to concentrate on my pizza, picking off the pepperoni with my right hand, my left hand held up to my temple to cut off my view of Rivers Carillo. In a moment I would try doing what usually worked for me. I would start counting. I would count to four, eight, sixteen, maybe as high as sixty-four – and then I would turn suddenly, to face him full on. And he wouldn't be there. He'd disappear. His image would break up and I'd know that it had been nothing, just my imagination, just the ghost of an idea disturbing my vision.

Deep breath, start counting. And then, hands firmly poised on the edge of my table, a sudden turn of my head in his direction – to face him, to make him disappear.

But he didn't.

He was still there; still sitting there with his coffee, solid and dark and smiling. And he winked at me.

My chair clattered and fell over. A table slammed into my right hip as I raced out of the food court. I nearly lost my footing as I ran down the stairs. I made it out to the car park, breathless and scared. I didn't dare look behind me. I found my car, pressed the key fob and heard the comforting *beep* as it unlocked the door. As I got into the driver's seat I automatically checked the back seat. I didn't even know what I was looking for – a bomb; a booby trap; a bloody horse's head, perhaps – or maybe for the now-adult offspring of the man I had killed, brought up by their grief-crazed mother to exact bloody revenge on me, and lurking in the back of my car with a jagged-edged hunting knife in their teeth. But there was nothing there. Of course there wasn't. There never was.

I put the key into the ignition and tried to start the car. It didn't work. The steering wheel was locked, from where I had made a sharp left to get into the parking space. I could feel my palms sweating as I rocked the wheel to try to release it.

The knock on my window made me jump so much that my chest hurt. Trying hard to control my breathing, I turned to my right. There was a face at the window, a pleasant, solid-looking face surrounded by dark curly hair, a face I had never seen before. No. A face I *had* seen before, drinking a cup of coffee upstairs. I felt very stupid: this was the man I had run away from. He made a gesture to tell me to wind down my window, and I did. 'You left your bag, duck,' he said in a soft northern accent, and he held up the carrier bag that contained the bottle of water and bag of wine gums that I had bought earlier at the motorway services shop. I must have left it behind when I ran out of the café.

I took it from him, and managed to thank him.

'Are you all right, love? You ran off a bit sudden, like.'

'I'm fine. Thanks.'

'It wasn't because I winked at you, was it? I'm sorry about that, duck. You looked a bit worried and I wanted to reassure you, like. You know, because we were the only customers there. I winked at you to let you know I was all right, that I wasn't a perve or anything to worry about.'

'It's okay. Don't worry about it. I just thought you were somebody I knew. Thanks for bringing me my bag.'

He gave me a thumbs-up. I wound up the window, managed to get my car started, and pulled out of the space so quickly that he had to step back sharply to avoid being knocked over. My tyres squealed on the tarmac and I ground my gears as I headed back towards the M1, berating myself as I drove. *Stupid, stupid, stupid.*

I thought you were somebody I knew. I thought you were somebody I killed. I thought you were the ghost that I keep seeing. I thought you were Rivers Carillo.

I drove down the M1 in a daze, my heart still beating hard. I told myself it was the caffeine from the Red Bull. Why had I been so scared of a normal, friendly bloke sitting quietly and drinking a cup of coffee? Why had I thought that he was my ghost? It was a trick of the light. I was tired. I'd had the southbound headlights flickering in my eyes. It was my brain playing games with me, sending me false messages.

I had seen him so many times before, you see, the ghost of Rivers Carillo, when I was tired or stressed or hormonal, or visiting a strange place. Sometimes I would see him in the crowd at a parents' evening, or in the corner of a busy pub, just sitting there, somewhere near the back, a smirk on his face that said: *Go on, then – pretend you haven't seen me*. Always, I would glimpse him out of the corner of my eye and always, always, he would disappear as soon as I turned to look at him. Sometimes seeing Rivers Carillo would presage a migraine, and then I would wonder if there was a scientific explanation, if I could explain him away as a mere visual disturbance, the kind you were supposed to get just before you have one of those appalling sick headaches. But I didn't let him bother me. Not much, anyway. I had come to the conclusion that he was never going to stop haunting me. Seventeen years he'd been at it. Why would he stop now?

But tonight had been different. Tonight it had been a real person. I had run away from a real person, a harmless guy, a nice thoughtful bloke drinking coffee at Leicester Forest East services. The whole thing had become completely irrational. It had gone too far. It had to stop.

By the time I had spent several minutes driving around the area near my flat in King's Cross looking for a parking space, the next day was already dawning, catching up on me before I was ready for it. Even on a warm day, dawn can chill you to the bone. It panicked me sometimes, and it did that morning. The light was never sharper or colder – sharp and cold and hollow like hunger – and the streets around King's Cross were never emptier than they were at three and four o'clock in the morning. I felt exposed by the weird light. The shadows were in the wrong places. It was disconcerting, disorientating. My head ached from the metallic clash of caffeine and exhaustion. I was pretty sure I was about to have a migraine. I felt sick and empty.

I walked back to my flat with my keyring clutched in my fist, keys sticking out between my fingers: a do-it-yourself knuckleduster. I made myself put my shoulders back and walk with a confidence that I didn't feel. I walked past the shuttered pub, past the internet café with its tables and chairs folded and leaning, padlocked, against the café windows, past the shadowy entrance to the neighbouring block of flats. I counted my steps, as if that would ward off the fear I felt. Of course, it was perfectly logical for a woman – for anyone – to feel scared walking in King's Cross in the early hours of the morning. But my fear had a different tone, a different flavour. It was my own personal, irrational fear. I knew it well. I knew the shakes it gave me. They were familiar – not quite old friends, not exactly old enemies either, but like someone I'd known for years and didn't much like but had learned to live with. I had learned how to control those shakes. Counting was good; counting kept everything under control. Every sixteen steps I stopped, stood still for a moment, held my breath and listened hard – my normal routine, but that morning my heart was thumping harder and louder than usual.

At the end of the street the turrets of St Pancras twisted Gothickly out of a façade of boards and scaffolding, like Sleeping Beauty's castle emerging from the thicket of thorns. I reached my block of flats: Edwardian red brick, solid white stonework; charitably built for low-income workers in the early part of the last century, now colonised by those of us who wanted to live relatively cheaply in central London. I pushed open the big wooden door, turned on the light and stood for a while in the cool, echoey white entrance hall. I looked upwards at the six flights of stone stairs stretching dizzyingly to the top of the building. All seemed empty. My footsteps echoed on the white stone floor as I walked towards the lift and pressed the button to summon it to take me to my flat on the fifth floor. I stepped in, stood in the corner and waited for the doors to close. I was nearly home.

I walked along the stone walkway, looking down at the inner courtyard far below me: a few beds planted with despondent trees and dreary shrubs, casting weird shadows on the grey concrete. Finally I reached my front door. My hand shook as I put the key in the lock. Inside, I locked, double-locked and bolted the door. I checked the rooms (force of habit). A glance to my left: the bathroom, empty. To my right: no one in the kitchen. The bedroom: clear. And at last I made it to my sitting room, with its huge window overlooking the London skyline, the Post Office Tower a sharp grey outline against the increasingly bright sky. There was a cheap Ikea sofa, a stereo, a few CDs, a desk, a laptop. A small pile of books on the floor by the settee. White walls, no pictures, no photos. A place of safety. I put the kettle on, made a mug of tea, swallowed a couple of extra-strength ibuprofen and sat on the sofa, shaking.

It was ridiculous. Most women I knew who got frightened travelling home alone at night were scared of rapists and muggers. I was scared of the ghost of a man called Rivers Carillo. And I didn't even believe in ghosts. I sat there early on that Sunday morning and thought about the state my life was in. I thought about the man I had run away from, the man who wasn't a ghost. I thought about my sister, and how I had walked away from a happy, warm, family weekend. I thought about my life, and about how much fear and how little joy was in it. And I told myself this: *I can't live my life like this any more. This has got to stop. It's time to let go.*

Two

The sound of a package being pushed through my letter box and dropping onto the doormat woke me up with a start. I looked at my alarm clock. Ten o'clock. I panicked for a moment, worried that I had overslept, and then I remembered that it was Sunday. I sat up in bed and moved my head slightly from side to side to test my headache. It felt okay, not much worse than a mild hangover. Not too bad. It would pass. I pulled on my dressing gown and padded down the hallway in bare feet. There, on the doormat, was a small white box.

It was a cardboard package, flat and square, about the same size as a CD. It lay on the doormat, passive yet threatening. I stood and looked at it for a while, and then I picked it up gingerly, weighing it in my hand. It was quite light and it didn't rattle. There was no stamp, no address. I turned it over and what I saw on the other side made me go cold. I had to put one hand against the wall to steady myself. I was expecting an address label, or maybe a handwritten address. But instead there were words and letters torn out from newspapers and magazines, stuck onto the cardboard. They looked jagged and dangerous against the white of the package. It was Sunday. It must have been hand-delivered. Someone had just pushed this through my letter box. Someone had been at my door, just a few feet away from me, to deliver this. I felt sick. I made myself read the words: 'To the mysterious brunette in Flat 519. Belated Happy Birthday.'

I could feel my heart beating hard. There were goose pimples forming on my forearms and the backs of my hands. Holding the small container by one corner, I took it into the living room. I sat on the settee and looked at it, as if it was an unexploded bomb and I had to work out how to defuse it. And then, all of a sudden, I realised. It wasn't just a CD-sized box, it actually *was* a CD. I opened the box, fingers shaking, and sure enough that was what it was: a CD, a home-recorded compilation with a white inlay card full of words, no pictures. A compilation CD: a mix tape, as we used to call them in the days before digital technology. Nothing but a harmless CD. Therefore it could only be from Danny, my musical neighbour. He did this a lot. He was forever making me CDs and giving them to me, and then waiting eagerly for feedback. There was already a small pile of them next to my stereo. There was nothing odd or unusual about Danny making me a mix tape, except for the fact that he normally just handed them to me. He'd never pushed one through my door before. He'd never sent me one anonymously. And there was one other thing that didn't make sense.

'How did you know about my birthday?'

I was standing at Danny's front door with my hands on my hips, wearing yesterday's clothes that I had just pulled on. Danny leaned against his door-frame, dressed in a scraggy T-shirt and jeans. 'Oh my God,' he said, a look of mock horror on his face. 'Have I inadvertently breached the protocol of your witness protection scheme?'

I blushed and stammered an apology. The witness protection scheme was Danny's little joke, his way of explaining my oddities. 'I don't do relationships,' I had told him soon after we'd first met, when he'd kissed me goodnight after an evening in the pub with slightly too much enthusiasm, not to mention tongue. And another time, when he had looked around my flat, one of the few times I had ever let him in, and he'd mentioned how spare and empty it was, I'd said, 'I don't really do possessions.'

'Blimey,' Danny had said then (and I thought, 'Blimey – I love that word'). 'No relationships, no possessions. What are you, on the run from the police? The mob? In some kind of witness protection scheme?'

I'd blushed then, too; deeply. And then I had laughed loudly, as if it had been the funniest thing I had ever heard.

Danny Fairburn was an intense, clever, socially awkward guy with the makings of good looks, almost handsomeness. He was about my age. He was tall and quite slim, a bit gangly. He had dark brown eyes and thinning dark hair that he wore shaved close to his skull. He had good bone structure and a very gentle way of talking. And in spite of myself, I had become very fond of him. Not in a relationship way, of course. But he was a good neighbour and a good friend. I didn't want to upset him. Now he looked at me with those dark eyes, and said, 'So, did you like your present?'

'Yes. Thank you. I did. I haven't listened to it yet, but thank you. It was very kind of you. Sorry, that sounded rude earlier. I was just confused. Not many people know when my birthday is.'

'The postman knows.'

'What do you mean?'

'I saw the postman at your door on Thursday. He was giving you parcels. And at least one card in a pink envelope. Ergo, I guessed it was your birthday. Sorry. I didn't mean to creep you out or anything.'

Birthdays had never been a big deal in my family. The parcels and card that Danny was referring to consisted of a cheque for thirty-five pounds from my parents, tucked inside a card in the pink envelope, a couple of chick-fic paperbacks with pink covers from Sarah (she always liked to send me something to arrive on the day itself, even if she was going to see me the next day) and a DVD of some Japanese animated film from my kid sister. I hated cartoons, but at twenty-eight Jem was still the baby of the family and we cut her a lot of slack. If she asked about her present I would humour her and tell her how much I had enjoyed it. It hadn't been a bad set of birthday presents, all things considered. And now there was Danny's CD.

'Okay. Sorry. Thank you. It was really thoughtful of you. I shall enjoy listening to it.'

I started to walk back to my flat and Danny was still standing there, looking at me, when I opened my front door. 'Beth,' he called.

'Yes?'

'This whole paranoia thing is getting a bit annoying, you know? You should learn to trust people. Like me. I like you. I like spending time with you. You're my friend. And friends are a good thing, okay?'

'Okay,' I said doubtfully.

'Beth,' he said again, and this time he was looking down at the ground, stubbing the toe of his trainer into the edge of his doormat. 'Would you like to come to a gig with me some time?'

'As friends, yeah?'

'I don't know. We could see what happens.' He looked at me again, a hopeful look on his face.

'Oh God, Danny, I don't know.'

I pushed the door open and stepped back into my flat. He called after me, a jokily pleading tone to his voice. 'Oh, go on, Beth. What are you scared of? What's the worst that could happen?'

I didn't answer that.

I put Danny's CD on the stereo and went into the kitchen to make coffee. The first song hit me with its perky, percussive guitars. I could identify a steel guitar, and I thought there was at least one slide guitar in there too, and a distinctive female voice, slightly nasal and twangy; hard as nails but vulnerable with it. Lucinda

Williams, of course. A song called 'Can't Let Go'. I couldn't help smiling to myself.

Danny worked for a local authority in some no doubt terribly important and worthwhile capacity to do with housing. But when he wasn't doing that, he reviewed albums and gigs for a music website. Earlier that year he'd been to Austin, Texas, for a music festival called South by South-West, and he had learned to do a dance known as the Texas Two-step. The thought of serious, buttoned-up, thoroughly English Danny dancing was so surprising that I kept asking him about it. So one evening he had tried to teach me. He played this Lucinda Williams song as we tried to dance around his tiny living room, as he called out instructions: 'Step. Step. Step, hold. Step, hold.'

'Danny, it's the wrong rhythm. You can't dance that to this. Are you sure you've got it right? Maybe you've got the wrong number of steps. That dance sounds like it needs three beats. Or six-eight? This song is four-four.'

He stood still for a moment and I could tell that he was mentally counting out the steps. He pulled a face. 'Oh, what the hell. Let's dance anyway. It's a great song.'

So we bobbed around the room awkwardly and unrhythmically, laughing like idiots, as Lucinda sang her song of jaunty pain: a song about a relationship that was over, a man whom she couldn't forget, couldn't let go.

I had my left arm around Danny. His right hand was pressed reassuringly into the small of my back. Our other hands were clasped together. Our hips started swaying together. There was an instrumental break in the middle of the song, as two or more guitars duelled with each other, and Danny took the opportunity to swing me around and dip me over his knee. Back together again, tighter clinch as the song ended, and he picked up his remote with one hand and clicked it to replay the song.

And I found myself remembering another clinch, another dance: slow-dancing with Rivers Carillo in the cabin of that tiny cramped houseboat in Sausalito as the afternoon sun poured in through the big windows. Round and round we danced to Bob Dylan, or whatever it was that was playing on the stereo, repeatedly knocking our shins on the low bed. He nuzzled his stubbly chin against my cheek and held me close. How easy it was to let yourself go, to fall into the warmth of a man's arms when you were dancing with him.

'Can't let go,' Lucinda Williams sang. But that night with Danny, as we clumsily two-stepped around his living room, I was thinking that those words could mean something entirely different. I said to myself: *I can't let go; I can't let myself let go. I can't succumb.* It would be so easy to fall in love with Danny, so lovely and warm and comforting, but I couldn't let myself go. I couldn't let myself fall in love. Not again. Not after what had happened last time. Bad things happened to people I loved. If you made sure you had no one in your life then there was no one who could hurt you. And no one you could hurt.

But it got so lonely. Maybe now was the time to risk it. Maybe now was the time to change.

Three

'What are you scared of?'

Danny had meant his question as a sort of joke, a cliché. It was what you said to people in those circumstances. 'Come on, what are you scared of?'

And the usual answer, the expected answer, the answer most people would give was, of course, 'Nothing.' But not me. What was I scared of? I could have given him a list. I had a list, an actual written list.

I knew all about fear. I lived with fear the whole time, and it was manageable, mostly. It wasn't much fun, but that was okay. I killed someone: I couldn't expect my life to be a bed of roses. But I could cope with the fear, most of the time. I could live with it. I had it down to a fine art.

The best way to manage fear was to analyse it; to divide it into categories and to deal with each little bit of it separately. I did this quite often. I would sit down and I would make a list – a physical list, pen and paper. I wrote down what I was afraid of, and I wrote down reasons why I should or shouldn't be afraid, and what I could do about it. I would keep the list. I would fold it up small and carry it about me somewhere: in the back pocket of my jeans, in the zipped compartment of my handbag; in the inside pocket of my jacket. Sometimes when I needed reassurance I'd pull it out and read it. I would usually keep it until the paper was falling apart, and then I would write a new one.

The list usually fell under three major headings. The first thing I was afraid of was Rivers Carillo; or, more correctly, his ghost – his apparition. That one was easy to deal with, to neutralise. I knew he was dead because I had killed him. The dead didn't walk again except in my imagination. I could usually make the apparition disappear. Sure, it was off-putting. Sometimes it was downright frightening when he would suddenly spring up in front of me. Sometimes, like I've said, he would presage a migraine, but that was okay; that was just something I had to live through. But no actual harm would come to me from seeing Rivers Carillo. It was just a reminder of what I once did.

The second heading, the second thing I was afraid of, was that someone knew what I had done and would come and find me. That was a tougher fear to deal with, because it was both more realistic and more amorphous. It had been seventeen years and no one had yet tracked me down. That didn't mean that they wouldn't at some point in the future. On my list I had three subsections under that heading; three ways of controlling that particular fear. The first was information, the second was disguise, and the third was the ability to run away.

I had gathered as much information as I could about

Rivers Carillo. I had made a sub-list of anyone and everyone who might have known about Rivers Carillo and me; who might have known that we were seeing each other and therefore might, somehow, for some reason, unlikely as it seemed, associate me with his death. I had all the newspaper clippings that I had ever been able to gather on the subject. I had every single thing that I'd been able to find anywhere on the internet that related in any way to the subject: tidal patterns through and around the Golden Gate, for example; the names of second-hand bookstores in San Francisco's North Beach; a list of universities in the state of Indiana. I kept all this information in a manila file, stored between *The Times Atlas of the World* and the *Collins Complete DIY Manual* on the bottom shelf of my bookcase. I knew that having the file in my possession constituted a risk in itself, but I didn't think that anyone would be able to put the information together to make any sense of it. And besides, I hardly ever invited anyone into my flat.

The next tactic was disguise. The woman – the girl – who killed Rivers Carillo had been a pretty, vivacious, annoying whirligig called Lizzie Stephens. On the plane back from San Francisco I killed her too. I supposed I should have changed my whole identity. I should have found a graveyard and a child who had died young, born the same year as me. I had a vague idea that it was possible: I'd seen it in a film or read it in a book. But I was eighteen years old and very, very scared. I wanted to go home to see my mother and father. I needed them. I wanted to be at home. So I compromised. I killed Lizzie.

'I've decided I'd like to be called Beth from now on,' I told my parents as they met me at the airport.

'Oh, I am pleased,' said my mother, who'd never liked the abbreviation Lizzie. 'I'd prefer Elizabeth, but at least Beth sounds like a proper grown-up name.'

Beth was altogether a different person. She looked different. She seemed shorter, although she wasn't. Her hair was straighter and her clothes were much more discreet – jeans, a white shirt, a plain T-shirt, a simple trouser suit for work. There was, I'd discovered, an art to being unobtrusive, to slipping through life without making so much as a ripple. There was great skill involved in keeping your head down and not leaving traces. And just occasionally I worried that I had taken the art of unobtrusiveness too far, that I had become so unobtrusive, so secretive and hidden as to be positively noticeable, almost intriguing: a mystery to be solved. That seemed to be the case with Danny. He was intrigued by me, and that was dangerous for both of us.

That was why my ability to run away was so precious to me. That was why I had so few possessions. I remembered Robert de Niro in the film *Heat*, playing a master thief who kept nothing in his life that he couldn't leave behind with just a few minutes' notice. That was the way I tried to live. That was why I had a car, the height of eccentricity for someone who lived just a stone's throw from the public-transport hub that was King's Cross: because, if all else failed, if I got discovered, I could just throw my life into my car and drive away. I could go to Cornwall, or to Scotland, or to the wild west of Ireland, or

I could drive to Kent and catch the shuttle and head anywhere in Europe. My trusty little Polo could one day be my best friend.

The third heading on my list, my third great fear, was that I would tell someone what I had done. Of all my fears, this was, I thought, the most likely to come true. It ought to have been the easiest to control but sometimes it felt like the most difficult. I usually subdivided this section into three sub-headings, three circumstances under which I might have spilled the beans. The first was when an apparently innocent conversation skirted too close to the subject: the chat at my sister's house about my summer in San Francisco, for example. Any casual chats in the pub with friends or in the staffroom at work that touched on subjects like student life, or memories of past summers, or favourite songs from the late 1980s could be risky. I would walk away from those conversations, using a variety of excuses. 'Marking' worked well, but only with non-teachers. I had lost count of the times that I had suddenly remembered somewhere else I had to be. People expected it of me now.

And then there was the risk of big emotional heart-to-hearts, the sort you had in relationships and in close female friendships. There was a simple solution to the problem: I didn't do relationships. It was that old cliché: I had a skeleton in the closet. I supposed in my case that it was close to being literally true. I imagined sometimes that it was. Rivers Carillo's skeleton was there, in my wardrobe, stuffed into an old suitcase that was pushed to the back, behind the winter coat that I hardly ever wore. Something it was just about possible to ignore, even though I could see part of the suitcase every time I opened the door. But sometimes, when I was sorting through my clothes, I would have to get it out. And then sometimes I'd open the suitcase, hoping that I had made a mistake, that I had dreamt the whole thing and that there was nothing there at all. But there always was. And to push an already overstretched metaphor even further, my fear was that if I were to get involved with someone, sooner or later they were going to want to go rooting around in my stuff, and one day I would find them sitting on the bed with the open suitcase in front of them and a horrified look on their face – a look that said, 'Oh my God, I'm in a relationship with Bluebeard.'

So I didn't do relationships. And I was particularly cautious about close female friendships, too. Guys were okay. You could be great friends with a bloke and yet know almost nothing about each other. I had that kind of friendship with Danny. Sometimes I'd go round to his place and we'd have evenings of playing CDs and watching DVDs, and exchanging names of favourite films and bands, the kind of night that I enjoyed because it represented warmth and friendship rather than intimacy and involvement. That was something I really didn't want to spoil. But I steered clear of close women friends usually, because they would always ask questions about my personal life. Because I was scared that if I let myself get close to people, then one day there would be the inevitable exchange of innermost secrets after a few too many drinks and out it would come: I would reveal the whole, terrible truth. Blokes were safer. They weren't interested in that kind of conversation. They just wanted to know what sort of music you liked.

And, finally, there was the fear that one day I would just blurt it out. That perverse desire to confess was perhaps the thing that scared me most. 'Blurt' – what a strange and specific word that was. The dictionary definition was 'to utter suddenly or unadvisedly'. The word had no roots, nothing Latin or Old Germanic or anything of that sort. It seemed to be imitative, onomatopoeic: a word that made the sound of what it meant. Blurt – the sound of someone revealing the awful secret that they had kept buried for seventeen years. It was like the urge to press a big red emergency button or pull the cord on a train. The more you told yourself not to do it, the worse the urge became. There was no way to control this particular fear except to spend as much time as possible alone.

So that was my life. That was why I lived like that. That was why on that Sunday afternoon, listening to Danny's CD, I was staring out of my open window at the roofs of London below me, trying to ward off a headache that felt like someone inside my head was intent on pushing my eyes out of their sockets. That was why I was just beginning to let myself wonder if I should lighten up a bit; if maybe I was safe now. Seventeen years on, nothing I feared had happened. Maybe I should let myself start living again. Maybe I had served my time. Maybe it was time to reconnect with the human race.

Four

'Miss Stephens?'

I had my back to my class of year tens as I wrote on the whiteboard and I couldn't immediately tell who was speaking, since all the girls spoke in pretty much the same way: confident middle-class with a hint of affected Estuary. I turned and saw that it was Chloe – Chloe T., rather than Chloe P. In other words, the class daredevil, the one who asked the questions that the other girls wanted to but didn't. I looked at her and raised my eyebrows, waiting for the question. I was pretty sure I knew what it was going to be. I would get asked this question, or something like it, at this point every year. In fact, I probably encouraged it. I led the class discussion around to it. If we were going to study that story, the story that seemed to have been written about me, then I knew that I might as well brace myself for the question. I almost laid a bet with myself to guess which of my year ten GCSE English set would ask it, and on what day; and I had my bland, non-committal answer carefully prepared.

'Miss Stephens, do you really think it's true? Do you really think that if someone killed someone and got away with it, they'd be desperate to tell someone?'

Chloe T. put her head on one side after asking the question, a self-satisfied smile on her face. She was a clever girl and a funny girl and I had always liked her a lot. And I had often wished that she wasn't in my class. I looked at her as evenly as possible, and I said, in my brightest voice, 'I don't know. What do *you* think?'

It was probably my catchphrase as a teacher: 'I don't know. What do *you* think?' The kids probably did impersonations of me, using that question. I used it all the time. It worked on almost any occasion, for almost any question a pupil might ask. And it worked that time, too. Chloe narrowed her eyes and started to think, and then the others girls joined in, all calling out with their thoughts; and I stood there with my gaze fixed on the far wall, on a point where the paint was peeling off, half-listening to a bunch of teenage girls imagining that they were murderers, hoping that the conversation would drift away soon. One of them, Bella, was suddenly struck by something. 'Listen, think about it. Imagine the worst thing you've ever done, like, maybe, shoplifting? Or telling a whopping great lie to get out of doing something, but you're really proud of it because it was, like, a really clever lie? You'd be *bursting* to tell someone then, wouldn't you?'

They liked that idea. They all started discussing the worst things they had ever done. There was a confession from one girl about borrowing her older sister's leather jacket and then losing it, and the elaborate lie she had told her sister. Another owned up to breaking her mother's favourite vase and blaming it on her two-year-old brother. I was feeling on safer ground. And then, out of the blue, Chloe T. piped up again. 'Miss Stephens, what's the worst thing you've ever done?'

I felt myself start to blush. I wasn't prepared for that question. I turned back to the whiteboard. I tossed the marker pen in the air and tried to catch it, but I missed and it clattered against the rubbish bin. I took a deep breath, turned back to the class and smiled sweetly: 'Well, Chloe. Funny you should ask. A few years ago I throttled one of my pupils with my bare hands when she kept asking annoying questions.'

The sound of several sharp intakes of breath. A few sniggers. I was getting into my stride now. 'I chopped her body up into tiny pieces and posted it to her parents.'

Some giggles, then a wave of laughter. I could almost see what the girls were thinking: 'Good old Miss Stephens – she's not as dull as she looks.'

I wondered what would have happened if I'd told them the truth, if I'd answered Chloe's question with complete candour. 'When I was just a few years older than you I killed a man. I looked him in the eye and I killed him. I got away with it, and I've never told a soul – until today.'

Probably their response would have been the same: the same sharp intake of breath, the same sniggers and giggles, the same assumption that I was joking. Because how could Miss Stephens, with her neat brown hair and her cheap black skirts and trousers, and her plain, mannish shirts in shades of white and cream and grey, possibly have been a killer?

*

The reason for that intensely, horribly apposite discussion? And the reason why I had to put up with it almost every year? Blame Edgar Allan Poe.

It had been bad enough having to teach *Macbeth* every year, with the hand-washing scene, and Lady Macbeth going to pieces because of her guilt about the murder, and a class full of girls debating whether they could carry off a killing without going mad. But what bright spark decided to put the short stories of Edgar Allan Poe on the GCSE syllabus? Of course, his tales of death, disease, imprisonment and burial alive were hugely popular with fourteen- to sixteen-year-olds. Call it Goth, call it emo, whatever name you gave it, the dark side always held a powerful allure for that age group. And most of the tales were fun to teach: 'Ligeia', 'The Fall of the House of Usher', 'The Premature Burial' – the kids lapped it up. But there was one story that I wished had never been written, and certainly never added to the syllabus. It was called 'The Imp of the Perverse'.

The narrator of the story had committed a murder, a very clever murder for which he would never be suspected. He had got away with it. But something was eating away at him – the perverse desire to confess. Sound familiar? In the Edgar Allan Poe story, the narrator did confess, and it all ended badly as he awaited his death on the gallows. Imagine me having to teach that story every year to a class of inquiring girls.

*

I became a teacher because it seemed the safe, unobjectionable thing to do. I got my degree, did my teaching certificate, kept my head down, didn't make waves. Despite everything, I discovered that I was good at it. It was one of the few things in my life that I enjoyed. I felt safe and normal when I stood in front of a class and communicated with them. Three years earlier I had moved to a fee-paying independent North London girls' school. A teacher's dream, you would have thought. Classes full of bright, attentive girls: Louisas and Amelias, Ellies and Ellas, Alices, Freyas and Floras. Great parental support, a warm and exciting atmosphere in the school and a willingness to encourage pupils to go beyond the syllabus. But, oh, the questions. The school encouraged inquiring minds. And it wasn't just the lessons the girls liked to inquire about. Why wasn't I married, did I have a boyfriend, had I got any action at the weekend, was I a lesbian, why were my clothes so dull, why didn't I try to do something more interesting with my hair? What was the worst thing I had ever done?

School was quiet that day. It got like that in May and June. Year Elevens and the Upper Sixth were no longer in lessons. Exam season was under way. I had taught them all that I could. Now it was down to them. The rest of the pupils, the ones who didn't have big exams, were getting a bit demob happy. It was the time of year when they liked to push their luck and ask outrageous questions.

It was a very warm day, the third one in a row, and people were already beginning to predict a long hot summer. Outside it was glorious. But it had become almost unbearable in the creaky, un-air conditioned Victorian building where I taught most of my classes. The girls had already abandoned their uniform of thick black tights or trousers in favour of skirts, the shorter the better. The bell went, and Year Ten packed up their bags and filed out, still giggling at the thought of Chloe T. chopped into tiny pieces and posted to her parents. 'Nice one, Miss S,' said a couple of the girls as they left the classroom.

It was lunchtime, and I had no classes for the rest of the day. I ran my hands over my face, feeling the sweat that had pooled on my forehead and in the dip above my top lip. I rummaged in my bag for a ponytail band, and pulled my hair back off my face and neck, enjoying the instant if fleeting sensation of coolness. I walked across to the window and climbed onto one of the desks so that I could stick my head out of the open part of the window and feel the fresh air on my face. Outside, I could see a cluster of A-level students sitting on the wooden bench in the shade of the huge old tree in the playground. They had open books on their knees, as if they were doing last-minute revision, but from where I was standing it looked as if they were goofing around instead.

I wandered down to the staffroom feeling uncharacteristically relaxed. I'd had a couple of sleepless nights after Saturday's encounter and Sunday's headache. I'd been lying awake thinking about Danny's invitation, too. But on a beautiful bright day like that day I felt as if I could put everything out of my mind. The weather was making me feel light and excited, almost as if I was on holiday. I made plans for the afternoon. I'd walk home instead of taking the Tube. I'd take my marking with me, and I'd stop in Regent's Park on the way home and do it there. And I guessed it was my happy mood that knocked me off guard and led me to do something I rarely did: I accepted a social invitation from one of the other teachers. Lesley, probably the nearest to a friend I had at the school, invited me out to a comedy night in a pub in North London. I figured that maybe someone had pulled out and she had a spare ticket. Otherwise I couldn't imagine why she would have invited me; I had turned down many overtures of friendship in the past. Because the invitation coincided with the beginning of my change of heart – that half-formed decision that perhaps it might be time to rejoin the human race – I found myself saying yes. Various people in the staffroom reacted with double takes. It had seemed like a simple decision. I had no idea what it would lead to.

I walked home still feeling happy. It wasn't long until the end of term, and I was feeling that mildly euphoric mood I sometimes got on the first truly hot day of summer. If you had asked me exactly what I was feeling, I'd have said that the worst was over. The weather was beautiful. It would soon be the summer holidays, I had survived the toughest question I could possibly have been asked, I had decided that the ghost of Rivers Carillo could just get lost and not bother me again. London felt alive. People were sunbathing in Regent's Park. They were smiling; I was smiling. The time had come to relax, to make friends, finally to put everything behind me. I was actually looking forward to spending time socially with a group of people from work. Maybe I would even say yes to Danny's invitation. Whatever had come over me?

Five

Did I bump into Zoey or did she bump into me? Whose fault was it? Was it fate or just a clumsy collision? The woman with the yellow T-shirt was in front of me at the bar, her back to me. She turned around and she didn't see me. That was nothing unusual. I had spent my adult life perfecting the art of being unnoticeable. She stumbled into me, or I knocked into her. Anyway, one way or another, I found myself standing at the bar with most of her pint glass of Coke dripping down my T-shirt and jeans.

'Jesus, I'm sorry,' she said in an American accent. She had wild frizzy hair and an offhand way of speaking. The words spilled out, seemingly without any thought beforehand. 'Christ. Look at you. You're soaked. My God, I'm sorry. Look, listen, I have to run. I'm doing this – this thing. Upstairs. It's my first-ever headliner. I'm nervous. What can I say? I didn't see you there. I'm sorry. Can you wash it out? Will it stain? Will you be okay?'

She patted me on the shoulder somewhat absently and then darted off before I could say anything in reply. I went into the ladies' toilet at the back of the pub and splashed water onto my T-shirt to wash off as much Coke as I could. I was glad it was such a warm night: it would dry quickly. I was a bit annoyed but not unduly so. It happened. I got bumped into, had things spilled on me. It happened a lot. I never made a fuss.

The next time I saw her was an hour or so later, and she was on stage. Her name was Zoey Spiegelman and her hair was now even wilder. It exploded from her head in dark henna-tipped Medusa spirals. Her bright yellow T-shirt had some kind of logo on it, and she was wearing it with low-slung khaki combat trousers and a pair of red trainers with elaborate soles that looked like they were springs. She wasn't particularly young, not as young as you might have thought from her clothes. I thought perhaps she was my age or a couple of years younger, maybe early thirties. She was lean and athletic-looking, and she prowled the stage, microphone in hand, with the barely suppressed bouncy energy of a gymnast about to do the final vault that could snatch the gold medal. American, of course, possibly a New Yorker; with a crisp don't-mess-with-me tone to her voice. She was very funny.

Not brilliantly funny, not earth-shatteringly funny, but very funny; the kind of funny it was a relief to find on a Friday evening that had been a bit of a damp squib until then. I was sitting at a table in a sweltering hot smoky room above a pub in North London with a bunch of people, only two of whom I knew even slightly. Lesley was there with her husband Mick, of course, a lovely salt-of-the-earth bloke, a painter-decorator by trade; I'd met him before. Then there was a thirty-something couple who lived a few doors down from them, Gemma and Phil. They seemed nice enough. There were a couple of Mick's mates, and an old school friend of Lesley's, Jackie, who she seemed not to have seen in years. And then there was Andy, the available man who had been assigned to me for the night. I hated it when people did that. I had told people so often that I wasn't interested in being set up. But there I was again, making small talk to a well-meaning but dull bloke who worked in IT and had the vaguely creepy air of a man who still lived with his mother. I should have felt happy that I was out for once on a Friday night, like a normal person. Left to my own devices, I would have been at home in front of the television with a glass of red wine and a bar of chocolate. But in fact I felt as if I was being coerced into having a good time.

I didn't know whose idea it was to go to a comedy night. Up till then, until Zoey arrived on stage, it hadn't been a huge success. We had sat through nearly an hour's worth of knob gags and limp jokes about George Bush and Tony Blair, we'd sweated buckets and poor old Andy had been picked on by one young comedian who'd asked him what he did for a living. Andy had made the mistake of giving an honest answer – cue a host of unfunny jokes about IT stereotypes: anoraks and nerds and *Star Trek* conventions. So by the time Zoey Spiegelman bounded on stage we were ready for something at least halfway decent. And we were in luck. There was something special about her. You could almost hear the audience fizzing.

She had stage presence, that was what it was. You felt confident watching her: confident that she was going to be funny; ready to laugh. She talked about marrying a British guy, coming to live in London, the marriage breaking up. She did jokes about being an American in England and knowing the art of when to say 'sorry'. ('Pretty much at any point in any social encounter,' she said. 'You can never go wrong with "sorry".') You wouldn't have wanted to be her ex-husband, that was for sure. She told us that the marriage broke up because of his stiff upper lip, 'which made cunnilingus a painful experience for me.' Her facial expression cracked me up. I let loose a huge explosive laugh, a few seconds too late, that nearly made me choke on my drink. Beer spurted out of my nose and dripped onto my already stained T-shirt. I struggled for breath and Andy thumped me on the back. As I got my breath back I noticed that everyone – including Zoey Spiegelman – was staring at me. I felt myself blush and I wanted to sink into my seat and disappear. I hated drawing attention to myself like that.

After the show Lesley nabbed a table downstairs in the pub and got a round of drinks in. I fought my way to the back of the pub again to go to the loo, in the squalid graffiti-covered hole of a bathroom where I had earlier attempted to clean my T-shirt, and I found myself once again standing behind Zoey Spiegelman. She turned to me and did a double take. Then she smiled. I opened my mouth to say something limp, like 'I enjoyed your act,' but at that moment a cubicle became free. Zoey said dramatically, 'Stay here! I mean, don't go. If you get out before me, wait for me. I want to talk to you.'

I didn't dare disobey an order like that. I emerged from my cubicle expecting to see her waiting, but there was no sign of her. I washed my hands and then discovered the hand-dryer was no longer working, and that the pile of paper towels that had been there earlier had now gone. Instead, I rubbed my hands dry on my jeans. I looked at myself in the mirror and frowned at my reflection: tidy brown shoulder-length hair, greyish eyes; a face that once upon a time, seventeen years earlier and five thousand miles away, had been described as 'elfin' and 'piquant' and even 'pretty'. It now looked tired and ordinary and shiny with heat, and seemed to bear the mark of every single day of its thirty-five years.

There was still no sign of Zoey. I started to feel stupid about waiting. She probably only wanted to apologise again for spilling her Coke all over me. But just as I was thinking that I should head back to my friends in the pub she burst out of her toilet cubicle. She pointed at me and said, 'Yay! You waited!'

She headed for the basin to wash her hands and then she shook them dry. She peered in the mirror and plumped up her wild hair. Then she came over to me, put her hands on my shoulders and said, in what seemed like one breath, 'Listen, thank you for laughing so loudly. I really appreciate it. I feel so bad about nearly ruining your night with the drink-spilling thing. I was nervous. I was a klutz. Stupid of me. What can I say to make it better? Can I buy you a drink?'

Stunned, I looked at her for a few seconds, trying to

work out how to frame a reply. 'Jesus, have I been too American again?' she said. 'What should I have said? "I'm awfully sorry, but might I purchase you a cold beverage?"'

Her English accent was so bad that it made me laugh again.

'You're ignoring your boyfriend,' Zoey said with an evil grin on her face as she settled into the seat next to me.

I looked at Andy and then back at her. I lowered my voice. 'He's not my boyfriend. He's the guy they're trying to set me up with.'

'OK. And let me guess – you don't like being set up?'

She had green eyes and a very intense gaze, and the body language of someone who was genuinely interested in hearing the answers to her questions. She was sitting very close to me, her shoulder touching mine.

I fidgeted with my beer mat. 'I've kind of opted out of the whole relationship thing, to be honest. But no one ever gets the message.'

Zoey raised her eyebrows and gave me a twisted smile. She played with one of her corkscrew curls: winding it around her finger, stretching the lock of hair so that it was straight and then letting it spring back. 'You know, a couple of years ago, in another life, I would have said, "Why? My God, do you know what you're missing? What are you scared of?" But now I say, "Honey? Join the club."'

'Because of your marriage?'

'Tell you what, let's not talk about it. Don't ask me about my marriage and I won't ask you about whatever it is that put you off dating. Your secret heartbreak. Whatever it is. A pact, yeah? Let's shake on it.' She put her hand out to shake and I took it. She grinned at me, and all at once I felt safe. I felt like I'd known her for years. She felt like a friend. It was an unusual feeling for me.

I don't do relationships and I don't do close female friendships. That was what I would have told her if she had asked me any more questions. 'I've kind of opted out of the whole relationship thing': that was just one of the phrases I used. Others included: *I'm very single. I like being single. I enjoy living alone. I like my independence. I don't need anyone else in my life.*

So what on earth was I doing sitting there chatting to an American female comedian who I had only just met? People talked about falling in love but there was no equivalent phrase for falling in friendship. That was what it felt like. It was so unlike me. I recognised something familiar in Zoey. Her mind seemed to run along the same track as mine did. I was enjoying talking to her. I wanted to talk more to her and to tell her things, and to hear her tell me stuff too. I told her about being a teacher, what it was like, how much I enjoyed working with the teenage girls, what I found frustrating about the job. She told me how she was studying for a PhD in Victorian architecture and was working part-time as a barmaid – lunchtimes only, so she could do comedy gigs in the evening – and how exhausting it was, 'having, like, three jobs,' but fun too. I liked the way she pulled at her springy hair and watched it zing back into shape. I liked the way she took up lots of room at the table, the easy way she rested her elbows on the table and fitted right in. She made me laugh. For a little while on a hot Friday night she made me enjoy myself and she made me forget myself and everything that was wrong in a life.

And there was something else. She reminded me a bit of Lizzie, the girl I used to be. The buzz I had got from watching her on stage: maybe part of that was imagining myself – or at least my other self, my old self – up there in her place. If I had still been Lizzie, maybe that's what I would have been doing: standing on a stage, showing off, having fun, making people laugh, not giving a shit.

And then, out of nowhere, I ruined the atmosphere. I asked Zoey this: 'Where are you from?' It sounded abrupt, almost rude, but I had a sudden need to know.

She seemed surprised at my question, and I braced myself for her answer. I was suddenly convinced that she would say San Francisco, the answer I was dreading. But she didn't. 'Boston,' she said. 'What about you?'

'Oh, here,' I said vaguely. 'Well, sort of. Not far from here. What's Boston like?'

'It's okay. Very historic. British people seem to like it. You've never been?'

I shook my head.

'Ever been to America?' Zoey looked at me directly with those green eyes that were striking against her tanned skin. There was a thin film of sweat on her upper lip. I was very aware that I was sweating like a pig, a broad band of dampness making its way from the small of my back up towards my shoulder blades. Did she mean something particular by her question? Despite the heat, I shivered and I could feel the coldness of my sweat against my skin. She was staring at me. Did she mean anything by that stare? The conversation was taking a direction that I didn't like; a direction that made me nervous.

'No.' I lied badly, and I could only hope that she mistook my inevitable blush for the flush of a hot face. Rudely, I turned to the person on the other side of me, which happened to be Andy, and I quickly absorbed myself in another conversation. It was a variant on walking away. I pretended I hardly noticed when Zoey touched my shoulder and said goodbye a few minutes later. But I watched her as she left, and there was a puzzled look on her face.

Stupid, *stupid*, *stupid*, I said under my breath as I let myself into my flat later and flung all the windows open. Of course she didn't know anything. That conversation had not been heading anywhere dangerous. She was just a random woman who happened to come from America. And I had spoiled a lovely evening. For just a moment there I had felt like I was tiptoeing out of my black and white half-world into a Technicolor movie.

Six

I gave her my mobile phone number. That was big. That was huge. I never gave anyone my mobile phone number unless I had to. But before I'd had second thoughts, I had given Zoey my mobile phone number. I woke up suddenly in the middle of the night panicking about it. It was another sticky night, and I knew I wouldn't be able to go back to sleep until I'd dealt with it. I dragged myself out of bed and fumbled around the living room in the dark until I found my courier-style bag with my phone in it. I switched the ringer off. That way, at least I could screen calls. If Zoey rang then I wouldn't have to answer. I put the phone under a cushion on the settee to muffle any vibrations if a call came. Then I got back into bed, feeling stupid and uneasy. I hated the feeling that someone could intrude on my privacy just by ringing a number, especially someone I didn't know very well. I didn't know what had come over me, how I had managed to drop my guard. I'd had too much to drink, I was too relaxed. I had been enjoying myself too much. I was usually so careful with personal information.

I hadn't meant to give her my number. She'd been showing me her phone, because it was one of those BlackBerry-style devices. Except it wasn't a BlackBerry;

it was something else like it. And she'd been showing me how she could access the internet and send emails from it, and how it made reading and writing texts much easier, and she'd said, 'Send me a text and I'll show you.'

So I had. I'd sent her a text, just a stupid message which said, 'Hi. Nice 2 meet u.' And of course that had put my number in her phone. And towards the end of the evening, before I'd started ignoring her, before she had given me that intense look when she'd asked me if I'd ever been to America, when we were still chatting, she'd said, 'We should hang out some time. I'll give you a call this weekend, okay?'

And I had nodded, as if it was totally okay. A strange American woman who could have been related to Rivers Carillo knew my name and my mobile phone number. She was probably going to give me a call. *Stupid, stupid, stupid.*

I spent the day avoiding Zoey's call. I left my phone where it was, under a cushion on my settee, and I went out for the day. I was avoiding Danny as well. I had managed not to see him all week, not since he'd asked me out, but I was afraid that if I stayed at home he might catch me, and talk me into it; and I still wasn't sure if I was ready.

The weather was hot again and I had no particular destination in mind. I walked south, smelling the tarry, slightly rancid scent of London on a hot day. I walked past the Brunswick Centre and Coram's Fields, past Great

Ormond Street Hospital, and then I lost myself in the Dickensian maze of little streets and yards in Holborn.

Sir John Soane's house was my favourite place in London, and the basement was probably the coolest place in the city at that moment. It was dank and dark, and full of white stone and marble plundered from classical buildings in Greece and Rome. It was a fantastic Gothic riot of a place. There was a memorial to Soane's dog, and a memorial to his wife, and a huge stone sarcophagus, like a giant bathtub, dedicated to the Egyptian goddess Nut. It was a basement full of columns and hidden corners, and unexpected shafts of daylight; and because I knew it well I had always felt safe there, half-buried underground. No one could find me there; nothing could reach me. Sometimes I wished I could stay there for ever.

I couldn't, of course. After a while the museum guide started looking at me suspiciously. I left and walked out into Lincoln's Inn Fields, blinking in the sunshine. I crossed Kingsway, walked past the Freemasons' Hall in Great Queen Street, and tried to lose myself in the summer crowds in Covent Garden. I perched for a while on a concrete bollard, eating an ice cream and watching the buskers: there was a unicyclist, and a man who made balloon animals. It was just my usual Saturday afternoon time-killing. I often did it. But that day I had to admit that I felt more than usually tense. Trying to relax – trying not to be scared, trying to lead a normal life – was making me tense. I felt as if I had dropped too many barriers too quickly and by doing so had put myself at risk. I felt naked. I kept hearing American accents around me. I was convinced that I would turn around and suddenly Zoey would be standing there, arm-in-arm with Rivers Carillo, pointing at me.

Enough. This was ridiculous. I had decided to stop all this nonsense. Friends were a good thing. Everybody knew that. I'd been happy last night. Zoey was good fun. There was no reason to be scared. There was no reason to be suspicious of her. America was a huge country. There was virtually no chance that she knew Rivers Carillo, or knew of my connection with him. And she had already promised that she wouldn't ask me about my past, about what she assumed was my 'secret heartbreak'. We had a pact. We'd shaken hands on it. What harm could it do, making friends with Zoey Spiegelman?

I wandered home, hot and footsore. I had a long shower, washed my hair and got changed into some fresh, cool clothes. I went down to the newsagent's on the corner and bought a paper and an ice-cold can of Diet Coke. I lay around in the flat with all the windows open and I read the paper from cover to cover. I was putting off the moment when I'd have to check my phone for missed calls. I sorted out some marking that I needed to do before Monday, and I put it in a neat pile on my desk. I planned what I was going to wear for the next week at school and I ironed a couple of blouses. Then I ran out of things to fill my time. Finally, I walked over to the sofa. I dug out my mobile phone and I nervously checked it for messages. Sure enough, Zoey had called.

I was expecting a friendly, breathless, full-on kind of message, the way she had sounded last night. Instead, when I listened back to my voicemail, what I got was this: 'Beth, call me. We need to talk.'

She sounded brisk, offish, abrupt, peremptory. Rude, maybe. I thought about those words: 'We need to talk.' They sounded ominous to me. What about? I barely knew the woman. What did she need to talk to me about? What could she possibly want to say to me? I wanted to know. I didn't want to know.

I sat there for a while, rubbing the palms of my hands up and down my thighs, paralysed by the pros and cons of a simple phone call. Eventually the part of me that was intrigued overpowered the part that wanted to run away. I picked up my mobile phone, checked the list of received calls and dialled her number with trembling hands. She was there. She seemed pleased to hear from me. She sounded friendly. We agreed to meet the next day, for coffee and shopping and maybe some lunch. Sunday in Camden with a friend: what could have been more normal? It all seemed perfectly pleasant. Maybe I had misread her tone of voice on the voicemail. Maybe she wasn't good at leaving messages. But still I had a nagging fear: why did she want to see me again? Why did she want to spend time with me? Did she have a secret agenda?

Seven

Most people – most casual, unobservant acquaintances – would probably have described me as 'nice' or 'pleasant'. I was always neat and tidy and inoffensive to look at, and the same was true of my conversation. I was good at polite, conventional responses. I was known as a good listener. Of course I was, because usually that was pretty much all I did – listen. 'Goodness.' 'Really.' 'How interesting.' 'Tell me more.' 'I don't know. What do you think?' Those were the kinds of remarks I made to punctuate conversations, carefully steering away from any chance of being asked questions. Acquaintances who were a little more observant, or who spent more time with me, sometimes seemed puzzled at my persistent refusal to talk about myself, the way I deflected questions about anything from relationships to reminiscences. My polite but consistent rejection of most social invitations was also cause for comment. But only those who tried to get really close – Danny with his kiss and his dance moves; Zoey with her shoulder-touching – got to experience the full Beth Stephens brush-off. I hadn't mastered the polite way to do that. There probably was no polite way to do that. And, as it turned out, that was what Zoey wanted to talk to me about.

'Here's what I was afraid of,' she said. 'I was afraid that you thought I was coming on to you, and that's what freaked you. And I thought I should clear the air and make sure you realised that I wasn't. Coming on to you. Because I'm not gay. Not that there's anything wrong with being gay. God knows, it's virtually the default setting amongst female stand-ups. Not that that's a bad thing. Anyway, I get it a lot, the lesbian thing. It's the vibe I give off, I guess. I sit too close to people, apparently. I look too engaged and interested. It's all part of this American-in-London thing. I haven't learned the correct body-space dimensions yet. And you're shaking your head at me, which means I'm wrong. So therefore I'm forced to consider something else entirely, and I'm not too happy about it.'

'What?'

'Well, the only other explanation for your boorish behaviour on Friday night is that you are extremely, offensively rude.'

It was nearly midday and it was already mercilessly hot. We were drinking overpriced bottles of water and we were sitting by the canal at Camden Lock, people-watching. The smell of dope and falafels hung in the air. Zoey, bold and bright in a turquoise vest top, was waiting for an answer.

'Sorry,' I said eventually, limply. 'I'm really sorry. You're right, it was rude of me.'

'So, was there a reason for your rudeness?' She pulled her hair back into a ponytail and I noticed a faint fuzz of unshaved hair in her armpits. She seemed to be the kind of woman who wore her imperfections with pride. I wouldn't have dreamed of leaving the house with armpits like that.

I could have told her to piss off. I could have walked away and never seen her again. Or I could say something, and risk it, and possibly make a friend. And that's when Danny's words came back to me: 'Friends are a good thing.'

'I get scared.' The words came out suddenly, and I wasn't sure that I meant to say them.

'Scared of what?'

'I don't know.' I paused, and then retreated into a white lie. 'Maybe that you'll realise that I'm just not that interesting?'

She took a long slurp from her bottle of water and frowned at me. 'That is not even close to being true.'

I was about to protest, or to say something else to change the subject, but Zoey held her hand up to stop me. She looked over her shoulder, a sharp frown creasing her forehead. She was looking at something – someone? – in the distance and I followed her gaze, half-expecting to see Rivers Carillo sitting there grinning at me.

'What is it?' I asked.

'Oh, nothing. Thought I saw someone I knew, that's all. But I didn't. Hey, let's walk.'

And she got up briskly, with the assumption that I was going to follow her, and I did. We were browsing through racks of tie-dyed T-shirts and vintage jeans when she resumed the conversation. 'Now, where were we?'

'You told me I was incredibly rude, and then that I was lying.' I said it flippantly, a smile on my face.

'Oh yeah! And now I've just been every bit as rude as you were, walking off like that while you were talking. So I guess I'd better forgive you.'

'Actually, the real reason was that I thought I had a migraine coming on.' Migraines and marking: my favourite excuses. Both of them did occur in my life, just not as frequently as I told people.

'And my grating, loud American voice suddenly became too much.'

I laughed. 'Something like that.'

'Okay, you're still lying to me. But that's okay. It's intriguing.' Zoey stroked her chin theatrically, like a psychiatrist in a comedy sketch. 'Tell me what migraines are like. I've always wondered. Is it just a fancy word for a really bad headache?'

I was relieved at her sudden change of subject. Here was something I could talk about without any difficulty. 'A migraine is like the absolute worst hangover that you have ever had: the headache, the sickness, the loss of balance, the visual disturbances and the feeling that you really would be happier if you were dead. Except, unlike hangovers, you have none of the fun stuff first.'

She laughed, suddenly and loudly. 'Oh, that's good,' she said. 'That's good. I could probably use that sometime. Would you mind?'

'Use it? What do you mean?'

'Material. You know, on stage. Jokes. Comedy. Gags.'

'Sure.' I was flattered. 'That's me: Beth Stephens, purveyor of fine material to the comedy trade.'

I looked at her, and she was looking at me and we were

both smiling and suddenly everything was okay. We were friends. I could do this. This was easy. It was like riding a bike or falling off a log.

We found seats in a little café for lunch, and I asked Zoey a question I'd wanted to ask the night before. 'How did you get into doing comedy?'

She put her head on one side, as if she had heard the question a million times before.

'Sorry,' I said. 'You must get fed up of answering that one.'

'Well, at least you haven't said what most people say.'

'Which is what?'

'You haven't said, "Oh my God, you're so brave. It must be so scary. I could never do it."'

That appalling English accent again. I laughed.

'No, really,' she said. 'That's what almost everyone says. Everyone who asks me about comedy. That's the first thing they always say. I'm quite hurt that you haven't told me how brave I was.' She was smiling.

'Oh my God, you're so brave. It must be so scary. I could never do it.'

Zoey laughed. 'Too late.'

'I didn't say it because you didn't seem scared. You were obviously nervous beforehand, sure, you know, with the Coke spillage . . .'

'Yeah, sorry about that.'

I waved my hand to show that it didn't matter. 'But being nervous isn't the same thing as being scared, is it? On stage, you looked completely at home. You didn't look scared at all, so I figured you weren't. I guess different things scare different people. I don't think there's anything brave about doing something that doesn't scare you.'

'That,' she said, 'is almost profound. And it leads me back to the question I asked earlier. What scares you? What scared you off last night?'

I had walked right into that one. She put her elbows on the table, rested her chin on her hands and turned those intense, searching eyes on me. Immediately I was, of course, scared. I could feel myself physically shrinking away from her. What scares me? Why did people keep asking me that? Zoey had me pinned in place with her stare; she wasn't going to be happy until I answered her with something at least close to the truth. I was supposed to be changing my life. I was supposed to be taking risks, making friends, living like a normal person. I took a risk then. I breathed deeply, leaned forward and twisted my hands between my knees. 'This,' I said, gesturing at her and me. 'This scares me. This whole making-friends business.'

'Oh my,' she said, clearly believing me. 'That *is* interesting.'

Eight

The velvet jacket was hanging on the back of my bedroom door. I fingered it to feel the soft, luxurious fabric. It was a deep, dark green. The colour was redolent of a pine forest. Zoey had made me buy it. 'Try it on,' she'd said. 'It'll look beautiful on you.'

All that Sunday afternoon she had tried to get me to buy something that wasn't black, grey or white. She'd dragged me all around the markets at Camden, grabbing armfuls full of brightly coloured blouses and tops and skirts and holding them up against me. I had to be firm several times with her, to avoid being thrust into something flouncy in salmon pink or lime green. Then she steered me into a vintage shop under one of the railway arches, as if she'd just had a brainwave, and that was where she'd found the jacket hanging on one of the rails.

Now, back home in my flat, I fingered the jacket again. The pile on the velvet was wearing through in places, but it was still thick enough to stroke. The jacket had beautiful silver buttons, embossed with a pattern of flowers. I ran my thumb over the buttons, feeling the pattern with my thumb's fleshy tip. I put it on again, enjoying the way it fitted me perfectly. Not only that, it looked right. The colour did something to me. It lifted my complexion and made my greyish eyes look clear blue. And yet it was dark enough to be unobtrusive, to blend with my wardrobe full of blacks and greys. It was beautiful and it was theatrical and yet it was totally wearable. It was a luscious jacket, the kind of item I would never usually have allowed myself to buy. I hadn't been able to resist it.

It was far too hot to be wearing velvet, but nonetheless I left the jacket on for a while, admiring myself in the mirror. I shook my hair and ran my fingers through it, plumping it up so that it looked big and wild. I pulled out a lip-gloss and smeared some on, and then smiled at myself in the mirror. I looked very different. I wondered if this was the me that I would have been, the person I would have grown up to be, if only things had been different. I made up my mind. Still wearing the jacket, I knocked on Danny's front door. When he answered I said, 'Do you still want to take me to that gig?'

His smile lit up his whole face. 'Yes, please,' he said. 'You look beautiful, by the way. Sort of . . . glowy. Around your eyes. Really . . . nice.'

A guitar and a drum kit. That was all they had, those two scruffy young American guys in T-shirts and jeans. I couldn't work out how they could make so much noise. It thumped and vibrated and I could feel it in my ribcage and deeper, somewhere deep inside me. They were playing some kind of electric blues. Danny had tried to explain them to me: 'The Black Keys. They're from

Ohio. Dirty, scuzzy blues. Kind of like the White Stripes but without all that fancy dress shit.'

I'd humoured him, pretended that I knew what he meant. I was still asking myself why I'd accepted his ticket, why I had agreed to go out with Danny. Was it because spending the day with Zoey had been such good fun that I didn't want to lose the feeling? Or was it because I didn't want to stay in the flat by myself? It felt colder and whiter and bleaker than it had before. I wanted to be somewhere dark and noisy and safe, and full of people.

The fiction was that Danny had had a spare ticket, but really he'd bought it especially for me. I knew that, and he probably knew that I knew that. But neither of us said anything, because that would have forced definition on the night out together, and neither of us wanted to do that. And besides, the Scala was just around the corner so it wasn't exactly a date or anything. That's what I kept telling myself, anyway.

The venue was packed: heaving with people, swaying and pushing and shoving, all in time to the music. There was something primeval and swampy about the beat. Each song began slowly and then built to a climax, but all in a rhythm that somehow seemed to match the beat of my heart or my brain, or maybe the way I was breathing. Danny was on my right-hand side, standing so close to me in the tightly packed mosh pit that I could feel the hairs on his forearm against my bare arm. I was watching the stage through a small gap between two heads in front of me, my nose almost buried in someone's sweaty shoulder. Every so often the momentum in the crowd built into a surge of moshing, or jumping, or pushing; like the wave in a wave pool spreading across the auditorium. Danny looped his arm around my waist so that we couldn't get separated. He hugged me closer to him and it felt nice. Who would have thought that I could have felt so safe and secure in a hot, sweaty cauldron like that?

The band went off stage. We called for an encore. That was what you did at gigs, apparently. You had to make a noise and keep it going until the band came back on again. That was the rule. We cheered and we clapped, and then I just stood there stamping my feet because it was easier and because my throat was hoarse. The Black Keys came back out and played a few more songs, and there was more moshing and jumping and pushing, and then it was all over. But I could still feel my heart thumping madly against my ribcage.

It took ages to get out of the theatre. The lights came up, and I could see that the place was swarming with guys in jeans and T-shirts, inching their way towards the exits. I could see just a few women, mostly younger than me, with sweaty faces and smudged black mascara and eye-liner, clinging on to the guy with them, picking gingerly over the beer cans on the floor. Danny took hold of my hand. He didn't say anything, just grabbed my hand in his as if it was the most normal thing in the world, and guided me through the crowds and out of the theatre. His fingers were long and strong, and it felt secure. I clung on to Danny. I could barely stand. I was both exhilarated and exhausted. All my joints hurt. I wondered if I was too old to mosh. My ears were buzzing and I could hardly hear a thing. All I knew was that I felt as if I'd just been in a really tough, satisfying fight that I had won, or as if I had just had really good sex. And that might have explained what happened next.

As we walked down the side street off Euston Road towards our block of flats I stumbled on a kerb. Danny caught me by the arm, and then wrapped his arm around my waist again. I let him. He pulled me closer to him. I reached my arm around his waist and hugged him to me. As we waited for the lift he looked at me, a look full of meaning and questions. I nodded, to tell him 'yes' to all of them. In the lift he stood facing me and put his hands on my hips. He leaned forward and kissed me gently on the lips. I responded, closed-mouth to start with, teasing him a little. I put my hands on top of his hands, and kissed him back harder. The lift arrived at the fifth floor. We ran along the balcony holding hands, and by unspoken agreement we went to his flat.

You learn interesting things very quickly when you have sex with someone you already know. Danny had very clean teeth and very soft lips. I ran my tongue across his front teeth and enjoyed the smoothness of them. I loved the feeling of rubbing my thumb over the stubble on his head. As I pulled his T-shirt over his head I noticed that he had a tattoo high up on his left shoulder, some kind of Celtic-knot symbol. It was very pretty and delicately drawn, the kind of tattoo I would have chosen myself, if I had chosen to have a tattoo, which was unlikely. He had a line of dark chest hair starting midway down his stomach. He had the merest hint of a beer belly, a tiny soft little paunch that he tried to suck in. He had freckles on the backs of his shoulders. He liked to bite and knew where to make it hurt in a good way: deep into the dip between my neck and my shoulder.

The sex was nice. It was friendly and comfortable and warm, and soft in the right ways. Afterwards we snuggled together on the sofa and listened to music. Danny gave me one of his shirts to wear, and he pulled on his T-shirt and boxers and played DJ. As he'd done so often before, he played songs that he thought I'd like, or that he thought I ought to like, from CDs and LPs and even some vinyl singles. He made instant coffee in chipped, stained mugs and as usual I pretended to like it. He found some slightly soft chocolate Hobnobs and we finished the packet. We talked about the music he was playing, and then he stood up and beckoned me over. He wanted to dance. I looked at him standing there, tall and dark and much better-looking than I usually gave him credit for. Such a lovely man. Such a good friend. The sex had been so nice. I wanted him. I wanted to dance with him. I wanted to be with him. I pulled the shirt around me, shook my head and burst into tears.

'Hey, what's up?'

His voice was so gentle that it made me cry even more. I shrugged my shoulders.

'What did I do?'

'Nothing. It's just me. I'm a bit emotional at the moment.'

Danny frowned, deep in thought. I figured he was probably about to ask me if I was premenstrual. I thought that was probably what was going through his mind. But instead, 'Is this because you "don't do relationships"?' He did the inverted commas with his voice. He twisted his face as he asked the question, looking like he was afraid what the answer would be.

'Oh God, Danny, I don't know. Stop quoting me. I don't know what I'm doing, all right?'

He stroked my arm.

'And stop being so bloody nice.'

He looked at me again as a sudden thought appeared to cross his mind. 'Are you worried this might spoil our friendship?'

I nodded. It was all I could manage to do. *Don't let go. Don't let go. Mustn't let go. Keep these emotions in check. Don't let him see how scared you are.*

'I like you. You like me. We get on really well. This has been fun. It would be nice to do it again some time. This doesn't have to be a big deal.' Danny was talking to me very quietly and simply, all the while stroking my arm. 'Look, we're both a bit shit at relationship stuff. I know there's something about you, Beth. I'm guessing there's something that's made you scared. Maybe you'll tell me about it one day. But I don't really need to know, okay?'

I was shaking. He was being so sweet that I thought maybe I was on the verge of telling him the whole story. I was very tempted. How easy it would have been. I wondered what he would say. But I knew I couldn't tell him. I couldn't tell him the truth. Why the hell did he have to be so nice? I pressed my lips together tightly to stop any more words coming out. I set my chin firmly, reached out my arms and hugged Danny hard.

'Stay the night?' he asked, gently, quietly; as if he didn't want me to hear the question in case the answer wasn't what he wanted.

Half of me thought it was a mistake, a dreadful mistake. There was no way I should drag him into the awful mess that was my life. But the other half of me thought that that had already happened. I had already had sex with him so maybe it was too late. All I could think about was how much I hated my flat, and how white and empty it was, and how much I didn't want to go back there; and how lovely this hug felt, so I nodded. 'Yes,' I whispered. I figured that I could deal with the fallout later.

Nine

This was weird. I felt good. I felt fine. I felt happy. A couple of days after sleeping with Danny I checked myself in the mirror and I looked great. I had been sleeping well. I had been eating well. I hadn't checked my list in days. What had come over me? Maybe it was the weather. It was still dry and sunny, every day, and we were starting to get used to it. I was enjoying the sense of waking up and knowing it was going to be warm. I enjoyed taking the summer weather for granted. I thought that it must be what it would be like to live in a Mediterranean country and not have to worry about clouds on the horizon. There were just a few more days of school left before the holidays, and I was due to have lunch with my exciting new friend Zoey Spiegelman.

She met me outside the school gates and I took her to a nearby café. I steered her to a dark booth inside at the back, making some excuse about wanting to stay out of the sun. Of course, that wasn't it at all. It was force of habit that made me always choose the least conspicuous table in any café. We sat down and looked at the menus, and I was suddenly overcome by awkwardness. I literally did not know how to do this – this friendship thing. I fidgeted with my menu and made some half-hearted remark about the weather.

Zoey picked up her own menu. 'So, what's good here?'

It struck me as an absurdly American thing to ask. 'It's a café. It's baked potatoes and paninis and sandwiches and stuff. Nothing's particularly *good*. They don't have a special or anything like that. It's just food.'

Luckily she laughed. I went across to the fridge to get us some cold drinks, and she said, 'Hey, neat jeans.'

They were Marks and Spencer *Per Una* jeans, bootleg with a bit of Lycra for fit; they were the most conservative, ordinary, untrendy jeans it was possible to buy. They were jeans for the woman in her middle youth, I told her.

Zoey laughed again. 'It's cool that you can wear jeans to work. Teachers never wore jeans when I was at high school.'

'It's a fine line,' I said. 'You can wear jeans, as long as they're new and smart and dark indigo. But there comes a point when the jeans get older and more faded, and suddenly they're verboten. It's quite a difficult decision. Sometimes when I'm getting dressed in the morning I have to hold my jeans up to the light to check if they're still dark enough to wear. I think they should make a colour chart, just so you can check easily.'

She was listening to me; looking hard at me with those green eyes. She was smiling at me. 'Tell me more,' she said. 'This is good stuff. I could use this. Great material. Do you mind?'

'So that's why you want to be friends with me,' I said. 'Because you like my material.'

Zoey looked serious all of a sudden. 'Do you mean

that? Do you really want to know why I want to be friends with you?'

I nodded.

'Because you're cool. You're funny. You're different. And also, I like you. This will sound weird, but it's kinda like I've known you for years.'

I frowned at her. I felt uneasy. I wasn't sure what she meant by that. Part of me felt uncomfortable, in case she really thought that we had met before and she wanted to know where. Part of me suspected it was a line straight from some American self-help book called *How to Make Friends*. But another part of me was flattered; seduced, even.

'And also,' she said, changing her tone to one of offhand rudeness, 'frankly, I'm lonely. I lost all my friends in the break-up. He got custody of them all. Here I am, stuck in London, waiting for the divorce to go through, trying to make a living as a stand-up comic, and I'm lonely. I need a friend. Anyone will do. And you were there. You looked desperate. So I took pity on you.'

'Thanks,' I said, keeping a straight face. 'I appreciate your candour.'

She smiled at me and that was the awkwardness over. I relaxed. It was lunchtime. It was nearly the end of term. This was what normal people did – they had lunch with friends. We chatted about stuff – safe stuff. We talked about our favourite films. Zoey told me about her life as a comic. She related funny stories about all the grotty clubs she'd played. Every time I spoke she leaned towards me, green eyes wide open, seemingly fascinated by my lame stories about my family and my job, and my weird kid sister, and what it was like being a vicar's daughter. We steered clear of her divorce and my 'secret heartbreak', as she had dubbed it on Friday night. And I made sure I asked her nothing about America. Just in case; on the remote off-chance that, out of all the millions of people in that vast country, she might at some point have met Rivers Carillo.

An hour passed quickly. We left the café, and there was a bunch of girls from Year Ten sitting outside with ice creams. They grinned and nudged each other. I thought they were probably still giggling about that stupid joke I had made the previous week. Zoey and I walked back to the school, said goodbye with a quick cheek kiss outside, and agreed that she would ring me in a couple of days and we'd go shopping or to the cinema together. She waved goodbye and I watched her bounce off down the street. I had had a good time. I was still smiling to myself as I walked upstairs to the staffroom, which was empty after the lunchtime rush. I had time for a quick cup of tea before my next lesson. I put the kettle on, stuffed a tea bag in my mug, and went to check my pigeon-hole.

There were a couple of memos from the head, an overdue essay from the most procrastinating of my pupils and a copy of the English department's newsletter. I picked up the pile of A4 paper and carried it over to the kitchen area to read as I waited for the kettle to boil. As I shuffled the papers in my hands something fell onto the floor. I knelt down and picked it up. It was a white envelope. A plain white envelope, quite good quality. A standard-size envelope, the sort that took a piece of A4 paper folded in three. There was nothing written on it but it was sealed and there was obviously something inside.

I made the tea and sat down. I was puzzled and a little apprehensive. I had the envelope in my hand and I ran my finger along the top to open it. I pulled out a single sheet of plain white paper and unfolded it. There was writing on it. Handwriting. Neat, small handwriting with compact capitals, just a couple of sentences in black ballpoint pen. I could hear my heart thumping and my fingers were trembling. As I read it, I felt the blood drain from my cheeks. This is what it said: *Remember, I'm watching you. I know everywhere you go.*

There's an expression people use about having your heart in your mouth. And that was what it felt like. It felt like having an actual lump lodged in my mouth, right back towards my throat. The lump tasted metallic. One of my worst nightmares had come true. He had found me. He – someone who knew my secret. I was sitting there in that friendly, untidy staffroom at school with that letter in my hand, and I felt like I'd been staring at it for hours.

'Are you okay, Beth? You look dreadful.'

It was Lesley, standing there with an armful of files. I hadn't seen her come in. She sank heavily into one of the squeaky vinyl armchairs. 'Seriously, Beth, you look terrible.'

I folded the letter and stuffed it quickly into my bag. 'I don't think I'm very well.' My voice sounded as if I was being strangled. 'I think I have a migraine coming on. I think I should probably go home.'

*

Remember, I'm watching you. I know everywhere you go.

It had happened. The thing I had been dreading for years. My carefully constructed life had been torn apart.

Ten

Rivers Carillo. Back then, before I killed him, when I was in love with him, when I still thought I was in love with him, the 'S' on the end of his first name enchanted and concerned me in equal measure. I was enchanted by the fact that his name was plural. He told me it was just an old family name, but I preferred to believe that he had been named after not one river but all rivers, everywhere: the very concept of river-hood, of river-ness. I was concerned because I wasn't sure how I would introduce myself when we were eventually, inevitably, married. 'I'm Rivers' wife.' 'I'm Rivers's wife.' I tried both, saying them out loud in the privacy of my attic bedroom. In fact, the question was academic because he already had a wife. But I didn't know that then.

The first time I saw Rivers Carillo he was sitting at the big wooden kitchen table in Joanna's house in San Francisco. Joanna, my sister's godmother, was with him. It was about ten in the morning and she was still wearing her silk wrap. Her long greying fair hair was caught up in an untidy knot on the back of her neck and her mascara was smudged into the crêpey skin under her blue eyes. Her left hand held a roll-up; her right hand was wrapped around one of her chunky earthenware coffee mugs. A stocky dark-haired man stared across the table at her, a slight smile playing on his lips. He had curly hair and vivid dark eyes that were fixed on Joanna. He had broad shoulders and he sat with a kind of hunched, pent-up energy. Such was their absorption in each other that I had to clear my throat to let them know I was in the room.

When you see two people having breakfast together and one of them is dressed in a bathrobe, chances are that they've just slept together. Sure, I know that now. Then, at eighteen, I didn't read the signs. For one thing, Joanna was way too old for sex: forty-five at least. For another thing, the smile that Rivers Carillo gave me as he turned to look at me was so full of surprised wide-eyed lasciviousness that I knew at once he was interested in me. I looked back at him, with equal interest. He was, I reckoned, about thirty. He had a pugnacious jaw and sexy creases in the corners of his eyes. He was not quite handsome but he was certainly the most attractive man who'd ever paid me any attention.

He smiled at me. I blushed. Joanna frowned. 'Who's this?' he asked.

Perhaps that should have been another clue. She didn't introduce us straight away. She stubbed out her cigarette before she answered. 'A young friend of mine from England who's staying here for a while. Lizzie Stephens.'

'Lizzie,' he repeated. He seemed to savour my name, all the while smiling at me. I felt myself starting to sweat where my too-tight T-shirt rubbed under my arms. I pushed my hair behind my ears and then pulled it back again, afraid he might notice that my ears stuck out. I was wearing a Lycra miniskirt and strappy sandals, big hoop earrings and too much eyeliner. I looked like a cheap tart or a backing singer in a pop video. He looked at Joanna quizzically and then back at me. 'Well, since our hostess isn't going to introduce me, I'll have to do it myself. My name is Rivers Carillo and I'm a poet.'

He winked at me and that was it. A wink and I was gone. I was under his spell. I was so young. So young and stupid and naive. I was a kid, just a kid. How could I have guessed what I was getting into?

Lizzie Stephens, the girl I used to be, seemed like another person to me. I struggled to remember what it felt like to be her. She was waiting for her place in the sun, her time in the spotlight, pretty sure it was going to happen any time soon. But already she was a little jaded (a play that didn't go well; a sticky end to a teen romance; the anxiety that she might not turn out to be as bright and brilliant as she'd hoped and dreamed).

I was pretty. Yes, definitely I was pretty once. I spent time on making myself look prettier. I used mousse to scrunch my hair into wavy tendrils; trained one curl to dangle into an eye, Gloria Estefan or Amy Grant style. I was a little heavier then and my breasts were bigger. I wore Lycra, lots of Lycra, and button-through tops, and I seemed always to be on the verge of bursting out of my clothes. I had great skin that didn't need foundation. My skin glowed. My eyes glowed. People told me that when I smiled, the smile lit up my face.

Lizzie Stephens was so full of promise. She was beautiful and silly and she thought that life was a banquet laid on especially for her. She was both knowing and naive, and I wished I could reach out into the past, shake her by the shoulders, slap her across the face and tell her – what? Be careful? Keep a close watch on your heart? Don't fall in love too soon? Beware of married men? Don't give yourself away too cheaply? But she'd already been given all those warnings – mother, teachers, books, friends – and she hadn't listened properly to any of them.

Don't lose yourself. Don't let go. Don't let yourself fall. Perhaps that was what I would have said, if it had been possible. Sometimes that was what I wanted to say to my pupils at school. I wished I could protect them too. I had to watch them growing up too fast. I would see them out at weekends, in their miniskirts and those skimpy tops, and I wanted to warn them. But they wouldn't have listened to me. At eighteen I wouldn't have listened to me. I listened to no one. And as a result I fell. I fell early. And I fell hard.

Looking back at the awful events of that summer, as I did almost every day, I wondered whether any of it would have happened had it not been for a foul dress, a hot day and a bad review.

It all started with my sister's wedding in late June. I was eighteen. I had just finished my A levels, I was about to leave school, I was a grown-up at last – and yet there I was dressed in the bridesmaid's dress from hell. Some evil spirit had made my sister choose lilac satin for her bridesmaids, the cheap kind of satin that was so stiff you could have sent the dresses up the aisle by themselves. The dress had puff sleeves that did nothing for my skinny arms, and the bodice was tight across my chest. I'd been a late developer and it seemed that my breasts were still growing. The colour of the fabric meant that every tiny drop of perspiration was instantly visible.

By the end of the reception I was tired and fed up, and my whole head ached from the smile I'd kept clamped to my face throughout the afternoon. People I barely knew kept coming up to me, pinching my cheek and saying, 'You'll be next.'

It sounded like a threat.

I was sitting on a dustbin outside the back of the restaurant smoking a cigarette that I'd cadged off the best man when my sister's godmother found me. She'd arrived in a flurry of suitcases and air kisses the day before, and had spent less than half an hour in our house before heading off for the best hotel in town. Now she perched on the dustbin next to me, brushed the hair from her eyes, took the cigarette from my hand and smoked it herself.

Joanna was my mother's oldest friend. They'd grown up together and had gone to the same schools, both junior and senior. But while my mother had followed the traditional path of husband and children, Joanna had made a career for herself as a childless bohemian divorcee. She'd gone to art school, and then managed to marry and divorce two rich Americans, leaving her with what was rumoured to be a huge house in San Francisco. None of us had seen her in years but once in a while she'd deign to remember my sister's birthday, sending her expensive presents that were either much too young or too old for her. When she was twelve it was a bottle of Chanel No. 5 that broke in transit, the perfume seeping into the padded envelope. At fifteen it was a Sasha doll. I was eleven at the time, and I desperately hoped my sister would give the doll to me. She didn't.

'Who chose your dress?' She spoke in a husky drawl that owed a lot to cigarettes and Honor Blackman.

'Sarah did.'

Joanna shuddered. 'It's ghastly. Simply ghastly.' She stubbed out the cigarette. 'Do you have another fag stuffed up one of those appalling sleeves?'

I shook my head. She made an exasperated noise and rummaged in her handbag. She pulled out a tin of tobacco and some rolling papers, and started to roll. I watched her, fascinated. I'd never seen anyone make their own cigarettes before. She saw me watching, rolled another one and handed it to me. I didn't want it, but there was no way that I could politely refuse it. I'd never smoked a roll-up. It tasted like mud, or what I imagined mud tasted like, but I managed to inhale without coughing too much.

'You're an actress, I hear.'

I grimaced. It was a sensitive subject. I had always acted; always dreamed of becoming an actress. That spring I'd played Juliet in our local am-dram society's annual Shakespeare production. It was my big chance. I had fantasised about being talent-spotted; about landing a role opposite Tom Cruise in a big Hollywood movie as a result. And then the local newspaper reviewer described my performance thus: 'Teenager Lizzie Stephens makes a pretty if somewhat wooden Juliet.'

It hurt because I knew that it was true. All through rehearsals I'd been pushing back the nagging suspicion that I really wasn't very good. Good enough, perhaps, with a nice face and a clear voice, and enough intelligence to stress approximately the right word in most of my lines. But I wasn't even the best actress in an amateur performance of *Romeo and Juliet*. To my family, I raged at the spite of the reviewer. Amongst my friends, I laughed it off. But in truth I was deeply upset – not by the bad review but by the frustration of having a dream shattered at eighteen years old. For most of my life I'd been the actress of the family – it was my role, my 'thing', my special talent. What was I supposed to be good at now? How was I supposed to express myself?

So when Joanna asked about my acting, it triggered something – because it was a hot day and my face hurt from smiling and my dress was hideous and uncomfortable and I wanted to scream. I took another puff on the disgusting cigarette, kicked my heels against the dustbin that I was sitting on and poured out my heart to her: the dreams, the build-up, the frustration, the self-doubt, the sense that I was about to explode out of my skin unless I could express myself in some way. The way that being an eighteen-year-old girl in a small town could make me want to scream or run through the streets naked or tear off my own skin with my bitten fingernails.

Joanna didn't respond immediately. She calmly

finished smoking her cigarette and then rummaged in her handbag. She pulled out a packet of mints and offered them to me. I accepted one, embarrassed by my outburst. She popped one in her own mouth and sucked it for a while. Then she said, 'And what happens next?'

'Sarah and Chris will go off and get changed into their going-away clothes and then we all have to stand outside the restaurant and wave them off. I think Chris's mate Andy is tying some tin cans to the car and doing something with shaving foam.'

She smiled. 'That's not what I meant. What happens next for you?'

'I'm going to university. London. To do English.'

At one point I'd planned to get a place to study drama, but was now thankful that I'd eventually chosen English. I'd selected my college on the basis that it was said to have an active drama society but I didn't think I'd be bothering with it now, now I knew for sure that I couldn't act.

'Oh.' Joanna didn't seem that interested. 'What are you doing with yourself this summer?'

'I've got a job. I'm going to work for this friend of Dad's. In an office. He's an accountant. I'll be doing filing, I guess.' I had no idea what the job would entail as I only had a shaky grasp of what accountants actually did. Something to do with money and maths, two subjects I knew very little about. But I knew I was lucky to be offered a decent job and that the pay would be useful. A lot of my friends from school were spending the summer travelling, but I couldn't afford to go anywhere.

'Nonsense,' said Joanna. 'You can't work in a dreadful

office. Why don't you come to San Francisco and stay with me?'

I laughed. I thought she was probably joking. She was my sister's godmother, not mine. I hardly knew her. And if she wasn't joking, then she was just taking pity on me after my outburst. I looked at her face, all lean and cheekboney. She seemed serious. 'Really?' I asked.

'Yes, really. Now, we'd better get back to see what ghastly clothes my god-daughter has chosen for her going-away outfit.'

Eleven

Something was off from the moment I arrived in San Francisco. Joanna wasn't there to meet me at the airport. That's odd, isn't it? You tell your mother's oldest friend, your sister's godmother, what time your flight arrives, you expect her to be there to meet you. It's part of the job. I rang her number. She answered, sounding like she barely remembered who I was, and told me to catch the airport bus.

The 'airport bus' was a minibus, driven by an ageing hippie. Six or seven of us – some Japanese students, two men who I assumed were gay, a pair of German tourists and me – gave him addresses and directions and he wove his way around the city, dropping us off in turn. I tried to take up as little room as possible as I stared out of the window and took in the scenery. Restaurants and fast-food places – ugly buildings in the middle of big car parks. Petrol stations. Here and there a small shopping mall. Random outcrops of luxury houses. Then the city began. Slummy streets, homeless men in doorways. Cars, buses. A glimpse up a vertiginous side street. Big Victorian mansions. Up and down hills, unexpected glimpses of the sea. A skyscraper like a skinny pyramid or a needle pointing towards the sky. Pocket-handkerchief parks. Apartment blocks next to tiny wooden houses like something out of a fairy tale. Corner grocery stores – Italian, Indian, Korean. A stretch of main road where suddenly everything was Chinese: the street signs, the names on the shops. Shop windows full of embroidered silk slippers and bright red chicken carcasses. And, everywhere, hills. A switchback ride. The sun low in the sky, glinting off the sea and off windows. A city of beautiful, brief peep-show views.

Joanna's home was a picture-book Victorian wooden house painted blue and white, with steps up from the street, a wooden porch wrapped around one side, a profusion of bay windows and a turret with what I learned was called a widow's walk – a high circular balcony with a wonderful view of the city. Everywhere the house was decorated: intricate lacy woodcarvings edging windows, balconies and the porch. The minibus driver hauled my case out of the back of the bus and set it down on the pavement next to me. I stared up at the house for a few moments, taking it all in. Then I lugged my suitcase up to the big square porch and rang the doorbell.

Joanna stood there, cigarette in hand. She didn't smile, she didn't hug me, she didn't ask me about my journey. She looked at me and her expression said it all: annoyance, disappointment, regret. She didn't want me there. She wished she'd never invited me. She'd invited a passionate actress, a blossom in an appalling frock. And when I arrived at her doorstep she realised she'd got a scared eighteen-year-old small-town girl in cheap tarty clothes from Top Shop.

*

Joanna's house was full of *things*: pottery and paintings, stained-glass hangings, bits of tapestry and embroidery on the walls. My room was in the attic, an airy, sloped-roof room with a double bed that took up almost all the floor space and with my own little bathroom tucked under the eaves. Next to my bed was an elaborate Victorian planter containing a nearly dead dusty ivy.

The heart of the house was the kitchen, a huge room in the basement, four floors down from my room. Joanna held court there, and in the evenings people came round for dinner and there was wine. There was also conversation that flew over my head. Sometimes a young man would appear, some guy in his late teens or early twenties, perhaps; often the son of someone else sitting around the table. 'Elliot's studying at Berkeley,' or 'Jonas is a very talented photographer,' Joanna would tell me; and always she would introduce me in a way that was difficult to live up to. 'Lizzie's a very promising actress,' or 'Lizzie is a budding writer.'

Was I? Had I given her any reason to think these things? Or was she just trying to make herself feel better about having a very ordinary teenage girl as her house guest for the summer? I would have to spend the evening talking to some skinny, intense guy who would later ask me out, as if it were his duty. And the next day I would meet him for lunch or coffee or to tour an art gallery or a museum, and we would stumble through an awkward conversation before saying goodbye, both of us apparently relieved that the ordeal was over.

Joanna was trying to find me a boyfriend (the generous

interpretation) or was trying to find someone to take me off her hands. Having a guest is a chore, I'm sure of it. It's like a ghost in your house who keeps popping up when you least expect it. I tried to be self-sufficient, setting off every morning with my public-transport map and my guidebook, staying out all day sightseeing, or even just sitting in cafés with a book. But every evening there I was, back in her house, back in her kitchen, back in front of her and needing to be fed and talked to and dealt with.

I tell you all this so that you can understand why I assumed that Joanna intended Rivers Carillo for me on that first morning she introduced us. He smiled at me. I blushed. Joanna frowned. He winked, and my heart was his.

'Where are you going today?' Joanna asked me that morning.

'Alcatraz.'

'You'll have such fun,' said Rivers Carillo, winking at me again.

An hour later I was down at the waterfront. My boat trip to Alcatraz didn't leave for another half an hour, so I was killing time watching the sea lions. I wonder if they're still there. I guess they are – one of the most popular free attractions in the city. A colony of sea lions, assembled on wooden pontoons just off the pier. Huge, sleek, dark brown creatures, so fluid in their movements that you'd think they didn't have bones. They would sun themselves and then, bored, restless or hungry, plop down into the water and another sea lion would take their place. Fights would break out – spats over a female, or a prime place on a pontoon – and the fight would end with one of the animals sliding into the water with barely a splash before finding another pontoon to rest on. It was difficult not to anthropomorphise them, to give each one a character and motives. I was riveted. I felt I could have watched them all day.

There was a lot of jostling for position, not just among the sea lions but among the humans watching them. People pushed and shoved to get to the front, to find the best place to take pictures from. So when I felt a hand on my shoulder I didn't think much of it. I assumed it was just someone pushing me out of the way. The blowing in my ear? That was a different matter. I turned, angrily, and came face to face with a pair of dark, laughing eyes. Rivers Carillo.

'I was wondering if I'd find you here,' he said. 'I thought you might want some company on your day out.'

Alcatraz was awesome – literally, awesome. It was forbidding and also beautiful: a cluster of dilapidated buildings on a craggy island in the middle of a glistening blue sea with matchless views of the San Francisco skyline, which seemed almost close enough to touch. Wild flowers grew out of the crannies in the rocks and mortar. It was ruggedly beautiful, and I was there with a ruggedly attractive man.

There was a particular prison cell at Alcatraz in the

corner of the jail building that was nearest the city. They told us that on New Year's Eve prisoners in that cell could hear the parties on the mainland, the fireworks and the horns sounding on all the boats out in the harbour. I shuddered when they told us that. I squinted through the tiny outside window in the cell wall and tried to trace the well-known skyline. I felt a hand in the small of my back and then Rivers Carillo was nestling next to me, trying to peer out of the same small window. I felt his stubble rub against my cheek. His hand stayed on my back, and then it moved – I'm sure it did – to rest on my bottom. It stayed there for a while. I did nothing to stop it. In fact, I may have encouraged him with a flirty wiggle. He grinned at me; I grinned back. We were co-conspirators in jail together.

There was another cell that they allowed you in and then shut the door on you, with a loud clang. The cell was dark and crowded, and I was standing very close to Rivers, so close that I could feel his forearm touching mine. I leaned in a little closer and I think he did too. Perhaps he was standing a little too close to me for propriety, but I didn't care. I felt his hand touch my hip, but maybe it was just for comfort. It was scary, dark and claustrophobic in that cell.

Later, we sat in the sunshine on the wall that overlooks the drop down to the ocean and the skyline of San Francisco. He asked me questions about myself: where I lived, what books I liked, what music I listened to. He asked me about my acting, my family, my plans for the future. I tried to play the part of world-weary, cynical, seen-it-all young adult in my replies, but I probably just came across as a callow teenager.

Whatever. We were definitely flirting. He flirted with me and I flirted back. He recited a poem; I said I liked it and asked him who wrote it. He told me that he had. I knew I should be asking him more questions about himself but I didn't. Instead I let him ask me stuff and I tried to sound as interesting as possible with my responses. I was sure he liked me for my mind.

He took a photo of me, San Francisco in the background. Then one of the other tourists offered to take a picture of the two of us together and we moved apart slightly. I felt Rivers stiffen. 'No. No, thanks. It's okay,' he said. 'We're not together.'

On the ferry on the way back to San Francisco he said, 'That might have taken some explaining to your parents – a photo of you looking cosy with a middle-aged stranger.'

'You're not a stranger,' I said.

He looked at me, shook his head and laughed. 'Wrong response. You were supposed to say, "You're not middle-aged." '

I looked at him. He was grinning.

'How old are you, anyway?' I asked.

'Thirty-eight. Does that seem really old to you?'

I shook my head, firmly. I was surprised, but determined not to show it. He was twenty years older than me. More than twice my age. I smiled to myself. There was something magical about that figure. Twenty years older: he was Mr Rochester or Maxim de Winter. Rivers Carillo was the perfect age for me.

Twelve

An eighteen-year-old girl in charge of her own sexuality is at least as dangerous as an eighteen-year-old boy in charge of his own car. She might even be *more* dangerous, because there's no test that you have to pass, no theory, no practical. One minute you're at school dreaming of pop stars and TV actors and romantic heroes in novels; the next minute you're out there, all tits and legs, tarted up and made up and ready to go.

I knew what love was. I'd read about it in books and seen it in films. I knew it made your heart beat faster and your eyes glow, and it made you feel alive. Love made stuff like eating and sleeping seem mundane and unnecessary. I knew so much about love that I'd ended things with my home-town boyfriend a couple of months earlier because he made me feel none of those things. I'd watched my sister Sarah with her fiancé Chris and I'd shaken my head sadly, full of teenage wisdom and understanding, when I'd decided that they couldn't possibly be in love because Sarah was so calm about her forthcoming wedding.

I was a deep and passionate person, and I was destined to fall in love deeply and passionately with a deep and passionate man.

Or I was an annoying, naive, pretentious teenager destined to have her heart broken into tiny pieces.

I thought that Rivers Carillo was the hero of a romantic novel: the dark, mysterious older man brought back to life by the young innocent girl with hidden depths. He was Rochester, enchanted by the ethereal, pixie-like Jane Eyre. He was Maxim de Winter, all gruff and forbidding, proposing abruptly over breakfast to the poor, plain, nameless heroine.

In fact, as it turned out, Rivers was another character from romantic fiction: the married seducer who preys on innocent girls. I know that now; I didn't then.

I was in love with Rivers Carillo, I'm pretty sure that I was. I counted the days, hours and minutes since I'd seen him, or until I'd see him again. He would turn up for dinner at Joanna's sometimes, and we would pretend that we barely knew each other. His foot would find mine under the table, or he'd wink at me, or he'd grab hold of me in the hallway as he left and whisper instructions on where we should meet the next day. It was always somewhere public: the food court in the basement at Macy's on Union Square, the lobby of the St Francis Hotel, the cable-car turnaround at Powell and Market Streets – places where I might find myself anyway, places where two people might accidentally bump into each other.

He took me sightseeing. One day he showed me around Chinatown, and took me into shops that I would have been too shy to enter on my own. He showed me the strange foodstuffs – the bright red chickens, the birds' nests, the eggs boiled in tea – and he struck up conversations in pidgin Chinese/American with old, toothless men behind the shop counters. I admired the silk slippers and shoes and purses, running my fingers over the gold embroidery of lions and dragons and flowers. There was a pair of green slippers I particularly loved. 'Those would really suit you,' said Rivers, suddenly close to me and talking right into my ear, his stubble against my cheek. I thought he was about to offer to buy them for me but he didn't.

Another day we 'bumped into each other' on the steps of Grace Cathedral, a huge Gothic-style church on top of one of the highest hills in the city. Just outside the cathedral there was what looked like a maze, paved into the stonework on the ground. It wasn't a maze, though, strictly speaking; it was a labyrinth, a path to follow that took you inexorably from the edge to the centre, supposedly to represent one's twisting spiritual path through life. I was enchanted by it. Rivers sat down on a low stone wall nearby, so I left my bag there with him and started walking through the labyrinth. Around and around, doubling back on myself, I twisted my way along the path, feeling the exhilaration of being at the very crest of one of the highest hills in San Francisco. It was a bright, sunny, breezy day and I was very happy. I finished the labyrinth. I reached the centre. I gestured across to Rivers, my fists in the air in triumph. But he wasn't there. My bag was, sitting all alone by that stone wall, but he had gone.

I picked up my bag, checked that my purse was still there, and stood for a while, trying to see where he'd gone. Eventually I spotted him, in the small park opposite the cathedral. I was about to run over but then I noticed he was talking to someone. A woman. The set of his body said he didn't want to be interrupted. I walked across to the park and sat on one of the swings. I kicked it higher and higher, all the while watching Rivers talking to that woman. And when she left, I brought the swing to a stop so suddenly that I scuffed the soles of my sandals. Rivers came and sat on the swing next to me. He smiled at me. He didn't say anything about the woman, and neither did I.

You see, I did know that something was strange, off, about our relationship. I did realise – at least subconsciously – that he didn't want anyone to know about us. I did notice that he never took me into restaurants, or introduced me to people. I was grateful for that later, of course; many times I've thought, 'Thank God no one ever saw us together.' Back then I was annoyed and offended, but I figured it was just one of his funny ways. He didn't want people disapproving of us, or of the age difference between us.

'Joanna doesn't know about us, does she?' he asked me one day. And I was proud of myself for keeping the whole thing a secret. I knew my sister's godmother wouldn't approve of my relationship with a man who was twenty years older. But I hadn't realised why she would be extra disapproving about my relationship with this particular older man.

There was one day that Rivers came back to Joanna's house with me. I forget why, exactly. I think I had bought something heavy, or maybe I had a blister or my shoes had broken. Whatever it was, I remember being a bit whiny, so Rivers hailed a taxi and then got in it with me. 'It's okay, Joanna's out all evening,' I said.

'I know,' he told me. He winked and squeezed my knee.

We got a bottle of wine and a couple of glasses from the kitchen and climbed the four flights of stairs to my little attic bedroom. Rivers put the glasses on the windowsill and poured the wine. I put a tape on, one by Wilson Phillips that I'd bought just a couple of days before. The summery sound of the music suited my mood. I grabbed my wineglass and sat down on the bed, acutely aware that it was the only place to sit.

Rivers looked around the room. He picked up the book lying next to the bed – *Pride and Prejudice* – and flicked through a few pages. He rummaged through the pile of tapes by my stereo. He looked at the ivy in the pot and pulled off a few leaves. 'This is dead,' he said. He stepped into my little bathroom and glanced around, fiddling with the bottles of lotion and the make-up on the shelf under the mirror. Finally he came and sat beside me on the bed. He kissed me on the lips, and his mouth tasted of the white wine we were drinking. I opened my mouth slightly and he kissed me again, this time taking my bottom lip between his lips. We each had a wineglass in one hand,

and we were balancing our glasses as we kissed, trying not to spill the wine. I leaned towards him and tried to make him kiss me harder. But he pulled away from me. 'I know you want more,' he said, 'but that's all you're getting for now.'

I did want more, but also I didn't. My body told me I wanted more. I wanted to go on kissing him, to feel his tongue in my mouth, to feel him bite down on my bottom lip. I wanted to thrust myself at him, to have him fondle my breasts and more. But, at the same time, I didn't want it. I was still a virgin. Not only that, I was a vicar's daughter, a nicely brought up vicar's daughter. My virginity was the one thing I thought I should keep, at least for now; at least until I was sure that he loved me.

Rivers stood up, still with the wineglass in his hand. He unfastened the little French doors that led out onto a tiny, rickety balcony, walked out there and took in the view. 'Shit,' I heard him say.

'What is it?'

'Joanna's back early. Go downstairs, grab her and keep her talking while I make my escape.'

He kissed me quickly again as I left my bedroom to go downstairs. And once again, there was the wink.

I knew barely anything about Rivers Carillo at this point. I knew he was thirty-eight and a poet. I knew, because he told me, that during term-time he taught literature at some university in Indiana. But every summer he came out to what he called his 'spiritual home',

San Francisco, to 'reconnect with his muse'.

Yeah, I know. I should have realised then that he was a shallow, pretentious fraud. But I was a naive eighteen-year-old with a thing for older, artistic men. I was a naive eighteen-year-old who took people at face value. And so I thought he was talented, artistic, deep and passionate – the kind of man I had always been destined to fall in love with. I was a stupid, stupid girl.

Thirteen

R*emember, I'm watching you. I know everywhere you go.*

One sheet of paper and nine words. That's all it was. Nine words – but it felt like the whole world had changed. I'd been living on a fault line for seventeen years and finally the earthquake had struck. All those years of fear, wondering what might happen, if anyone would find out, if I'd really got away with it. All those years of fear, and there it was: a white envelope, a sheet of white paper, nine words, neatly handwritten in black ballpoint pen. A standard sheet of white laser-print paper, no watermark, no smudges. A single sheet of paper, thin and deadly, like an arrow breaching my defences.

I got back to my flat on that Friday afternoon and I locked and bolted the door, as usual. I leaned against the front door, standing in the hallway of my flat, and out of nowhere I started laughing. Suddenly the note seemed hideously funny. I remembered the man at Leicester Forest East, running after me to give me my carrier bag and calling me 'duck', and how scared I'd been then. That was nothing compared to this. I was laughing because – well, I'd been afraid for so long, and now it was finally here. It, the judgement, the avenger – whatever it was.

Whoever it was. It had finally caught up with me. It was almost a relief. And then, in the way that hysterical laughter tends to, it turned into sobs, and I found myself sinking down, still leaning against the front door, until I was sitting on the prickly doormat. And on that sweltering day in London, another day when the temperatures were soaring close to thirty degrees Celsius, I sat there feeling colder than I had ever done in my life.

Eventually I got out my list. What else could I do? I got out my list, and I dug out the manila file from the place where it was hidden on the bookshelf and I reread everything I'd written, every piece of information I'd gathered together. I was trying to control my fear through information, or simply by doing something, anything. I checked the internet. I searched Rivers Carillo's name on it for what felt like the millionth time. There was nothing new, nothing added, from all the other times I'd searched. I didn't know what I was looking for, anyway. Maybe a police report. The kind of thing you'd get in a TV police procedural. Something to say the case had been reopened because new evidence had been found – a 'cold case', they'd call it. Or more far-fetched: a close relative of his who'd had amnesia for seventeen years had suddenly remembered the identity of the girl that Rivers had been seeing the summer that he'd died. Or a report that the body they found wasn't Rivers Carillo at all. But there was nothing. Nothing had changed.

Everything had changed.

Why now? I kept asking myself. Why now, after all these years? As I paced around my flat I caught sight of my green jacket hanging on the back of my door and I realised that something *had* changed – *I* had changed. I'd decided to stop being afraid; I'd decided to start being happy. Had this person – the letter-writer, the stalker, the avenger – had they seen me with Zoey, laughing and joking and acting like a normal, happy person having lunch with a friend? Had they followed me to the Black Keys gig, waited outside and watched me leave arm in arm with Danny? Had they seen me go into Danny's flat? Had they waited outside until I'd emerged the following morning looking happy? Was that the trigger?

And that made everything even worse, because that meant someone had been watching me for years, watching my fear, feeding off it; waiting for their moment to strike – the moment when I'd dropped my guard, the moment when I'd stopped being afraid. And that someone was probably close at hand right now.

Assess the threat level. That sentence came into my head from nowhere. Maybe it was something I'd heard on TV, from a survival programme, or from some American miniseries about disaster threatening the Earth. What was the threat level? More to the point, what was the threat? What was I being threatened *with*? I was being watched. Somebody knew exactly what I was doing and who I spent my time with. Someone was out there. I'd probably seen them at some point – in the street, on the Tube, hanging around outside school. They knew where I worked; no doubt they also knew where I lived. They probably knew everything about me. But what did the note mean, and what were they threatening to do to me? To carry on watching, that much was certain. But what else? Were they going to expose what I had done? If so, to whom? Was I in physical danger? What should I do? Should I leave? Should I run away and hide?

Someone was watching me and I didn't know who. And I didn't know what they planned to do to me. The questions went round and round, round and round, swirling around inside my head. There were no answers. I had no idea what to do. I'd come to a decision, an explanation, a plan of action, and then it would float away again. There was no one I could tell. How could I, without revealing what I had done all those years ago?

Impatient, frustrated and afraid, I turned off my computer. I looked at the note once more, flattened it out, then folded it up again, put it back into the envelope and slipped the envelope into the file. I put the file back where it belonged, hidden between the atlas and the DIY book, weighed down and hidden where no one would find it. I looked at my white walls, at the sparsely furnished rooms, at the small pile of books, the few CDs on the shelves. I looked at what my life had come to, what my life amounted to. I couldn't think of anything else to do. I turned off my phone. I turned the television on, loud. I cooked some pasta and tried to eat it. I watched something on television – I don't know what, maybe it was a sitcom, maybe the news. I ran a bath and lay in it until my skin wrinkled, drinking red wine, as if a hot bath and enough alcohol could somehow persuade me that everything was normal. And, in the end, I made myself go to bed. I curled up in a foetal position, my duvet tightly wrapped around me, and I tried to go to sleep. What else could I possibly do?

Fourteen

There he was again, out of the corner of my eye: Rivers Carillo. I knew it was stupid. He was dead; I killed him. Whoever was stalking me was not Rivers Carillo. How could it be? But still, there he was, the next day, haunting me at another motorway service station; haunting me yet again when I was trying to run away. There he was, serving behind the hot-food counter at Pease Pottage Services, just south of Crawley. He was wearing a white hat and overall, and he was serving all-day breakfasts to frazzled-looking families. From time to time he looked across at me and seemed to grin. I looked away. I moved my seat so that I was sitting at a different angle, so it was difficult to make even the slightest eye contact. I was hiding under the baseball cap I usually wore only on bad hair days, and I pulled the rim further down over my face. I was trying hard to keep myself together, to act as normally as possible. I took a long gulp of Diet Coke and filled in another clue in the *Times* crossword with a shaking hand. The crossword was calming me slightly, letting me focus on working out anagrams and other word puzzles, putting letters into blank squares, feeling a sense of control. It was what I needed.

After a while I made myself look back towards the hot-food counter and – of course – it wasn't Rivers Carillo at all. It was just a kid, a young guy, not much more than twenty, with a cheery face and a frizz of curly dark hair poking out of his hygienic hat. And it occurred to me that all the time I'd been bothering about him, that spectre of Rivers Carillo, someone else had probably been watching me, someone I wouldn't recognise. I looked around me cautiously, as discreetly as possible, feeling as if every hair on my body was standing on end. Just the normal Saturday crowds. Nobody looked suspicious. Everyone looked suspicious.

I was running away. I didn't want to be in London. I couldn't stay in my flat. I'd woken just after seven, the sun already streaming through the gaps in the blinds, the flat already stuffy and airless. I had a headache and my throat was dry. I'd stumbled into the bathroom and splashed water onto my face. I could see in the mirror that the skin around my eyes looked puffy and bruised. I went back to bed, tossed and turned, and eventually fell asleep again, waking frequently in the midst of horrific dreams.

I'd tried to stay in bed. I thought maybe I could stay asleep all day, all weekend; hiding under my duvet, escaping the fear that way, killing time, killing the empty days. But by mid-morning I was wide awake. I felt hot and sweaty, and I couldn't find a cool place on the pillow. I got up again and walked around the flat, counting to myself. Then I stood in front of my bookshelf for a while, my arms tightly folded so that I wouldn't be tempted to fish out the letter from the file and read it again. I opened the big window as wide as it would go, and I stuck my head out and breathed in the sticky London air. There were roofs and windows as far as I could see, each hiding people that I didn't know: hundreds and thousands of them, people and people and people, and one of them wished me harm. In the street below my window someone was kicking a beer can along the street. The sky was white with the threat of humidity and extreme heat. I knew that I had to get away.

So there I was, on the run. I was looking for some air, and a chance to escape for a while. I wanted to lock the door on that sheet of white paper with those nine words on it: to put some miles under my belt; to get away, to hide. And so I was on my way to a place that I guessed would always be a refuge, however old I got. I was going to spend the weekend with my parents. I even had a half-formed idea – a glimmer of a plan – that I might tell them what had happened: tell them everything, and let them sort it out. That's what parents are supposed to do, isn't it? But I knew I would never do it. I knew I would lose my nerve at the last minute.

My parents lived in one of those small Sussex seaside resorts that aren't Brighton, a town full of bed-and-breakfasts and down-at-heel cafés. We'd moved there when I was thirteen, and my parents must have liked it because they stayed. There was a grim concrete shopping centre built in the 1960s that the local council was planning to knock down when they could decide what to build instead. The latest idea was a new leisure centre-cum-civic theatre. The main shopping precinct seemed mainly to specialise in shops selling sports shoes, greetings cards and Chinese medicines. There were at least four charity shops, filling spaces where big-name high-street stores used to be. The beach was mostly shingle, the pier was falling down, and the town's only glories were a few streets of faded Victorian villas, one terrace of attractively restored Georgian houses and the brightly coloured municipal flower beds, always filled with pelargoniums and impatiens in various eye-searing colours. My mother had taught me the Latin names for plants; she was a keen gardener. But I knew that another name for impatiens was Busy Lizzie, because that's what my father used to call me: Busy Lizzie, or sometimes Dizzy Lizzie or Whizzy Lizzie or Fizzy Lizzie. Variants on a theme: I was the child who soaked up attention, who was never still, who was always dancing and acting, and acting up. I threw tantrums if I was ignored for more than five minutes. I was difficult, a pain, a little madam, a show-off. It was no wonder that my parents were so pleasantly surprised when I returned home from my summer in San Francisco as a newly quiet, restrained woman called Beth.

Did I blame my parents for never noticing that something was wrong – badly wrong – with me? I don't think so. Not really. They had so many other things to think about. My dad was a vicar – I suppose he still was; you never stop being a vicar, do you? He still filled in sometimes, covering for other vicars who went on holiday or had nervous breakdowns or affairs with parishioners, taking services at a variety of local churches. Back when I was a teenager, we'd lived in one of those Victorian houses in the old part of town, a huge rambling vicarage with seven bedrooms that had now been sold off and converted into flats. Both my parents took their pastoral roles seriously and kept an open house. You never knew who might be staying under our roof: homeless drug addicts, pregnant teenagers thrown out by their parents, African theology students with archaic Biblical names like Zachariah and Simeon.

There was a lot of love in our home, but the love was swirling and unfocused. It was up to each individual child to grab as much love from my parents as we could, as they passed by on their way from one good work to the next. It was very easy to hide from, if you didn't want to deal with parental love. And then, when I was older, there was a whole thing with my younger sister Jem: hospital appointments and big medical decisions and operations, and suddenly she was the focus of family life as the rest of us left home. All this might explain why I was such a show-off as a child and yet I'd been able to fly under the radar ever since.

I was, ironically, the child who gave my parents the least worry. My older sister Sarah was divorced and bringing up teenage kids on her own, up there in what my parents considered to be the grim North. Jem – the youngest child, the baby, the one who had been ill as a child – was permanently infantilised by the family and my mother didn't seem to realise that she was now a grown woman. Jem was seven years younger than me. She was involved with websites or videos or graphic design, and from time to time I would bump into her in Soho or in

Camden, and we'd make half-hearted promises to each other to have lunch. She had a lot of piercings and tattoos and variably coloured hair, she wore strange footwear and T-shirts with Japanese logos on them, and none of us really knew her at all.

And then there was me: the killer who lived in a state of permanent fear. Or to describe me the way the world saw me: there was Beth, the sensible one, the schoolteacher with a nice little flat in London who visited her parents dutifully every couple of months. My mother did occasionally worry that I was lonely; I think she thought that I might be a lesbian and she wished that I would come out and tell her, because she would have been really supportive. In fact, she probably would have been thrilled. But, mostly, my parents didn't worry much about me. They thought I had my life all sorted out. What would they have said if I had told them?

My parents wished they could still live in a house like the vicarage. They would have liked a sprawling house to fit their image, their dream, of the sprawling extended family. But instead they had a little bungalow on the outskirts of town, with a neat garden that I had to remember to admire every time I visited. It was probably not their fault that our family split apart like curdled milk. Except maybe, because we shared that vicarage with every needy person in the parish, because there was no privacy and no separate family time, Sarah and Jem and I had all built walls around us and between us in our different ways. Mine was the least definable but definitely the most impenetrable.

*

It was very hot, even there on the coast, the kind of heat that hits you like an insult as you get out of an air-conditioned car. But at least there was a whisper of a breeze off the sea. I parked my car on the street that sloped gently down from the Downs and towards the sea, and I breathed in the fresh air. My mother was in the front garden, planting or uprooting something in one of her tubs. She was kneeling, her hands – ungloved – deep in the soil. She saw me, smiled, and stood with difficulty. I noticed that she was starting to get old. She hugged me, careful not to touch me with her dirty hands, and asked me if I liked what she'd done to the garden. I gave her a cautiously general response about how pretty it was looking despite the lack of rain. Then she said, 'You look tired,' and before I could answer she added, 'But never mind, you've got that lovely long holiday ahead of you.'

Inside, the porch was full of supermarket carrier bags stuffed with jumble, presumably on its way to a church fête. My mother put the kettle on and I went through the airless, shabby bungalow and out to the conservatory, where my father was doing the same crossword that I'd been attempting to complete earlier. His new reading glasses made his eyes look enormous as he looked up at me. 'Busy Lizzie,' he said tenderly, ruefully, his dry lips brushing my cheek. He'd taken to calling me that again; I didn't know why. I slumped down into one of the cane chairs and looked around me, at all the familiar ornaments and at the tatty carpet, and the furniture that had seen better days.

For half a moment I considered confessing. I should tell my father what I did, all those years ago. 'Dad, I have something to tell you.' That's how I would have begun. My father would have looked up, vaguely. 'Dad, I killed someone.'

What would he have said? Would he have dealt with the shock? Would he have asked me to tell him everything, all the details? Would he have taken it in his stride, as a vicar should, and offer me forgiveness and absolution in exchange for repentance and penitence? Not that I believed in all that. I had killed any vestigial faith that I might have had on the day that I killed Rivers Carillo. I grew up in a house surrounded by people of deep Christian faith. It was always there for the taking, and somehow I'd taken it for granted. But I had never bothered to develop my own faith. Any belief that I had was probably always destined to die very quickly, like the seeds in the parable that were sown on rocky soil. Forgiveness seemed like a cop-out. I didn't believe that anything could be that easy. And yet I still yearned to confess.

But as my father put the crossword down on the table to talk to me, I could tell at a glance that he had got one of the answers wrong. Suddenly I wanted to cry. I wanted to cry because my parents were getting old. I wanted to cry at the stifling familiarity of it all. I wanted to cry, because I was tired and scared and because there was love there if I wanted it, but I couldn't take it, not properly. I wanted to cry because I was wondering what my father would have said if I *had* told him; whether he could have coped, or whether the truth would have killed him. I wanted to cry because I'd been there for five minutes and already I knew that I wouldn't be able to stay for long. Already I wanted to walk away.

Dinner was early, and it was some kind of bean stew. My mother was convinced I was a vegetarian. I'd told her, countless times, that I ate meat. I'd been eating meat all my life except for about eighteen months in my mid-twenties. But I didn't have the heart to tell her again. Later, we left my father dozing in front of *Who Wants to be a Millionaire?* and my mother drove me the short distance to the seafront.

We walked along the prom in what was, I suppose, friendly silence. It was still very warm, and suddenly I got the urge to paddle. I walked down to the sea, took off my sandals, rolled up my jeans and hobbled over the last few inches of shingle and into the sea.

I don't think I had ever known the sea in Sussex to be that warm. It lapped around my ankles, gently licking and fondling my feet. I found a rare patch of sand to stand on, and the grains dribbled around my toes. There was a yacht with a white sail moving slowly along the horizon. I closed my eyes. I could feel the evening sun on my right shoulder. I could hear the seagulls shrieking to each other. I could feel tears start to form in my eyes. I thought: maybe I can just stand here – in this precise spot – for the rest of my life. I counted to four, to eight, to sixteen, and then I turned around and walked back up the beach.

My mother looked at my face and said, suddenly, sharply, as if she had just discovered something, 'Are you all right?'

I thought for a moment. This was what I wanted to say: 'Mum, I have something to tell you. I did something stupid – bad – wicked. A long time ago. When I was eighteen I killed a man, and I ruined my life. And now it's come back to haunt me.' I wanted her to tell me it was all right. I wanted her to hug me; to kiss me and make it better.

But this was what I actually said: 'Yes, of course I'm all right. I'm just tired, that's all.'

'You work too hard.'

'No, I don't. I work more or less as hard as millions of other people do.'

'Well, it's the holidays soon. Are you going to come and stay with us at all?'

That question. The one she would always ask. 'I don't know. Probably not. I have lots of stuff to do, people to see. I've got paperwork to finish, and I want to get cracking on my lesson plans for next term.'

'You haven't forgotten the party, have you?'

The party: my parents' fortieth wedding-anniversary party, the big party looming a couple of weeks from then, the party that they'd been planning for months. Yes, I'd forgotten it.

'No, of course I haven't. I'll be there. Looking forward to it.'

'Are you seeing anyone?' The other question she always asked.

'Kind of,' I said, remembering my night with Danny. And then I shrugged, wondering if I should continue with him; wondering if the note-writer would let me. 'I don't know. Maybe.'

'Do you want to bring him with you to the party?'

I looked at my mother. I think she already knew what my answer would be. 'Probably not. You know, I wouldn't want to expose him to our family en masse.'

My mother smiled to herself. She knew me well enough, at least, not to push any further.

I always had bad dreams when I slept at my parents' bungalow in the narrow, tightly blanketed single bed in the tiny, flowery, dusty guest bedroom. That night was no exception. I dreamed of being trapped in a lift that was crashing over a cliff. I dreamed of masses of envelopes and parcels being pushed through my door and piling up until they trapped me in the hallway of my flat. I dreamed of being chased into a narrow alleyway by Rivers Carillo who was dressed in the white hat and overall he'd been wearing at the motorway services. But when he caught me, it wasn't Rivers Carillo at all but Danny Fairburn. When I woke up I wondered what, if anything, that was supposed to mean.

Fifteen

I didn't want to hurt Danny. Please believe that. I didn't want to hurt Danny and I didn't want him to get hurt. I didn't want him to be collateral damage in my nightmare. It wasn't fair to let him get involved with a woman who had killed someone, a woman who was being stalked by someone who knew her secret. As I drove back to London from my parents' house I knew what I had to tell him. I would have to let him down, very gently. I would have to tell him it was a mistake, us trying to have a relationship, and that it would spoil our friendship. I needed to nip it in the bud before it developed any further. It would hurt him, but it would be less hurtful in the long run. I knew what I had to do.

Danny Fairburn was unlucky in love. Make that 'unlucky in love', for that was the very phrase he'd used soon after we'd first met. He'd added the inverted commas himself, with a pause and an arch of the eyebrows, knowing that he was using an appalling cliché. On the rare occasions when our conversations had touched on such matters, I'd gleaned that he had married young and divorced early because his wife – his childhood sweetheart – had left him for a friend of his. Since then I'd seen him in action a couple of times, trying to chat up girls in pubs. I'd tried, in a gentle, joshing way, to let him know that a full-on discussion of the oeuvre of Neil Young or the Wachowski Brothers was not a good way to attract most women. We had had one dangerously intimate conversation, a few months earlier, just after he'd split up with a girl he'd been seeing for only a few weeks, a blonde, high-maintenance, utterly unsuitable woman. I'd gently tried to suggest that he should find a woman he liked, a mate; and he'd said, 'But not you, right? Because of the witness-protection thing?'

He was such a sweet and lovely guy. He had his obsessions: his lists of his top ten films, his alphabetised CDs; but what guy doesn't? He was happiest when he was telling me things. He was interestingly boring, a sexy nerd. I liked him very much, and I knew that he liked me a lot too. And so I felt terrible over what I was about to do. But I also knew that it was the only thing I *could* do. I had to break it off with him.

But when I got back to my flat after my drive home to London from the coast I could see Danny on the walkway outside his front door, sitting on a deckchair with his feet up on the railing, reading a book, enjoying the late-afternoon sunshine. He was wearing baggy combat shorts, and his legs were long and wiry. He saw me arrive. He smiled at me and his eyes lit up. Before I even had my key in my door he had come over to me, that huge smile on his face, and he touched my cheek. He looked at me, deeply, and then he kissed me.

And I kissed him back. Blame my lack of sleep, my fear, my vulnerability. I found that I couldn't help myself.

*

We were in a pub in Kentish Town. There was some kind of acoustic open-mike session going on, and it wasn't particularly good. There was a young guy singing, sweltering in an army jacket, trying to look hip or cool or however singer-songwriters were supposed to look. He had a guitar, and paused every so often when he struggled to find a chord. He had a pretty voice and a pretty face, with a little bit of bum fluff under his chin. He was singing a world-weary song about love and hate, even though he was only about twelve. Danny and I were drinking beer and we were getting gently merry. We were applauding like crazy each time the singer finished one of his songs, and I even bought him a drink and took it over to the little stage area.

'You look really pretty,' said Danny, squeezing my hand under the table. I squeezed his hand back. I had lip gloss on, and a whole vat of Touche Eclat hiding the dark circles under my eyes. I knew I was doing the wrong thing. I was pushing away the shadows, shutting the door on my fear, and in the process I was pulling someone else into my nightmare.

There was an embarrassing silence and then we both started talking at once. Danny was telling me something about music, one of the fascinating-yet-dull monologues he liked to take refuge in – something to do with Nick Drake, I think – and I was asking him how his weekend had been. We looked at each other and then we laughed, and then we started kissing again, and I knew I had no resistance any more. Danny kissed my eyebrows, of all things. I shut my eyes and then he kissed my eyelids, very gently. I ran my fingers up and down the firm bones in his neck at the top of his spine. Our lips locked. Our tongues met. I felt desire in every inch of my body. It had been so long since I'd let myself do something like that.

The pub was filling up and a couple of blokes came to sit at the other end of our table. 'Oi, get a room, you two,' one of them said. Danny pulled away from me. 'Shall we?' he said, and I nodded.

I didn't want to give it up, that closeness. Whatever it took, I didn't want to let go of it. I invited him back to my flat. I never did anything like that; I barely let anyone cross the threshold. But I wanted Danny in my flat. Afterwards, we lay on my sofa in a tangle of limbs and bits of clothing. Danny's latest mix CD was on the stereo and we were just lying there, listening to it. Willie Nelson was singing 'Someone to Watch over Me' and, although I knew that the letter, that vicious piece of white paper, was lying in a file just a few feet away, I felt safer than I had in years. My fingers were linked in Danny's and every so often I kissed one of his.

After a while I got pins and needles in my arm. I disentangled myself, and realised that Danny had been asleep. He stretched and groaned, and smiled at me. 'Hello, sleepyhead,' I said. 'Do you want to stay the night?' I said it casually, but inside I was pleading with him to stay.

He shook his head. 'No. Better not. I've got some stuff to sort out for work tomorrow. I'd better go now.'

He picked up his jeans and T-shirt and pulled them on. He picked up his shoes and carried them in his hand. At the door he stopped and turned back to me, enveloping me in a big hug. 'So, is this a relationship?' he asked, making inverted commas with his voice around the word 'relationship'. He grinned, to let me know he was joking, sort of.

'Course it isn't. I don't do relationships, remember?' I was joking too, of course. Except also I wasn't. I wanted a relationship but I didn't want one either. I wanted to be safe, protected, but I didn't want Danny to get hurt. I didn't want to get in so deep that I put him in danger – genuine physical danger, or even just the danger of having his heart broken. I needed to keep this as ambivalent as possible. But Danny just laughed and kissed me on the forehead.

As he kissed me I got a sudden cold feeling – a feeling that maybe I'd just been even more stupid than usual. Suspicion, unease – it was something like that. I'd got the note the day after I'd first slept with Danny. Surely he wasn't involved. It can't have been him. I put my guard up again. I could almost feel the armour clanking into place. Before Danny left I needed to ask him something. I told myself that I was just checking; that I didn't suspect him, of course I didn't. But something told me to rule him out. 'Danny, have you ever been to San Francisco?'

I'm sure that my tone of voice was cold and hard, maybe even accusatory. Danny looked surprised for just a moment and then, because it was him, and because he liked answering questions, and because he didn't think too hard about other people's motives and meanings, or perhaps because he wasn't all that good at reading them, he gave me a considered answer. 'No. No, I haven't. I've been to Austin, as you know. And New York. And also New Orleans. That was amazing. Pre-Katrina, of course. I went with a mate, and we hung out in bars listening to jazz and blues. I'd love to go back there now, to see what's happened to the place, but maybe it would be voyeuristic. I don't know. They say that they're trying to encourage tourists back so maybe it would be okay. But the city I'd like to go to next, if I'm honest, if I get a chance to go back to the States sometime soon, is Chicago. Apparently there's a fantastic live-music scene there.'

Bless him. Such a Danny answer. Not the slightest flicker of interest in why I'd asked, and not the slightest possibility that he had any connection with Rivers Carillo whatsoever. I had just felt I needed to be sure.

I closed the door behind him. I bolted all the bolts. One, two, three, four. I walked around the living room, counting my steps. Four, eight, twelve, sixteen. I pulled some clothes on. I looked out of the window and listened to the night-time sounds of London. I made myself a mug of tea and I turned on the television, flicking from channel to channel to find something to watch. I was feeling fine and then all of a sudden I wasn't. My flat felt very empty again and I was scared, deep in the pit of my stomach.

Sixteen

There were many things in my life that I was afraid of, but I had never thought that going to work would be one of them. I sat on the edge of my bed for quite a while that next morning, the Monday after Danny nearly stayed the night, the first Monday of the last week of term. I wondered if I could – should – call in sick. I could feign another migraine, or perhaps extend the fictional one I'd pretended to have on Friday when the note had arrived. I sat on the edge of my bed in a sweat of indecision until it became too late to call in sick, too late to do anything except leap under the shower, dry my hair, pull on a pair of black trousers and a white shirt and run for the Tube.

I don't think I'd ever noticed before how the school loomed over the narrow street it was in. The three-storey frontage was red-brick and imposing, like that of so many Victorian institutional buildings. It seemed that morning to be impossibly tall and dark. At the top of the building, the chimneys were decorated in elaborate, twisted, patterned brickwork. I stopped and stared at them and was chilled by their dark outline against the weird white humid sky. Someone could be up there, I thought. Someone could be hiding, watching, from an eyrie on the roof of the building.

I was late. Too late to go into the staffroom, too late to check my pigeon-hole; and I was glad about that. I was too scared to look, too scared to see if another white envelope had appeared. I was completely unprepared for lessons. I knew I'd have to busk it. But it was the last week of term; it would be okay. Year Seven, my first class of the day, were fidgety, looking forward to the holidays, so I let them do their favourite thing. We moved the desks into a circle and I let them act the mechanicals' play, 'Pyramus and Thisbe', from that year's Shakespeare, *A Midsummer Night's Dream*. I took one of the seats in the circle, a seat that couldn't be seen from the glass panel in the window of the classroom door, as safe as it was possible to be, and I tried to empty my mind.

I didn't get to the staffroom until the mid-morning break. I cast a quick sideways look at my pigeon-hole. No sign of a white envelope, just the usual memos. I pulled the papers out gingerly and stood there, my back to the staffroom, as I flicked through them, checking for another envelope, almost unable to breathe.

'Did you get the note that I put in your pigeon-hole?'

The deep voice made me jump. I turned, the bunch of memos falling from my hand and onto the floor. Jeff Woodhouse, IT: tall and dark and loud. He'd asked me out once, and I'd said no. 'You?' I could barely believe it.

'What do you mean, "you"?'

'*You* sent me that note?' My mind was racing, trying out different possibilities – why he'd sent it, why he'd written it, what he meant by it, who he really was.

He had picked up the papers from the floor. He handed them to me. He was smiling. 'No, no. It was from one of the girls. She asked me to give it to you.'

'Who?' I knew I was snapping at him. I tried to make my face look neutral.

'Didn't the note say? That's a bit weird.'

I took a deep breath and tried to sound as calm as possible. 'Jeff, who gave you the note?'

'Uh, I think it was Vicky. Vicky – Barron, is it? The ginger girl in Year Ten. With the non-regulation skirt. One of the smokers.'

The smokers. The group of girls who lurked outside the school gates at lunchtime, holding cigarettes behind their backs whenever teachers walked past, as if we didn't know what they were doing. The girl had been there with her cronies when I'd met up with Zoey that Friday.

I found Vicky Barron leaving a French class in the language building with a bunch of her mates. I tried to adopt my best calm, stern teacher's voice. 'Vicky, can you please explain the note that you gave to Mr Woodhouse – the one you asked him to put in my pigeon-hole?'

'Oh, you got it, then. That's good. He made it sound like it was really important.'

'He? What do you mean?' Chills went up my spine and settled on the back of my neck.

'This guy. He came up to me, gave that letter to me, asked me to give it to you.'

'What guy?'

Vicky shrugged. 'Just some guy.'

'Did you know who it was?'

'No. It was just some bloke. He just said would I give it to that lady when she got back from lunch. So there you are.'

I looked at her closely. I could smell cigarette smoke mingled with mint on her breath. I forced some words out of my mouth. 'Vicky, this "bloke", the man who dropped this letter off, what did he look like?'

She looked blank for a moment. Then she furrowed her forehead. 'Um. I don't know. Just a bloke.'

'How old?'

'Quite old. About your age? I dunno.'

'Come on, think. What did he look like? What colour hair? Was it dark?'

'It might have been. Yeah, I think so. I wasn't really concentrating.'

'What did he sound like?' I thought for a moment, and then I asked the question I really wanted the answer to. 'Was he American?'

It surprised her. 'American? I don't think so. Why? Is it important?'

She just stood there, looking at me as if I was mad. One of her mates laughed. I turned to her and realised it was Chloe, Chloe T., from my Year Ten English set. 'Miss Stephens,' she said, 'maybe he was a private detective? Maybe he found out what you did, about chopping up that girl last year?'

And with that, all the girls started laughing – not maliciously, just as if they'd been trying hard not to laugh, and now they had to let it all out; as if they were all sharing a really great joke. I felt myself go cold again, and then hot, and then I realised I was blushing. I felt so stupid. I'd been taken in by a stupid, thoughtless, practical joke. 'Oh, very funny,' I managed to say, before turning and walking away, wondering whether to laugh or cry.

It seemed so obvious all of a sudden. The girls had liked my joke. They knew I had a strange, black sense of humour – that joke had proved it. And so they'd decided to take it further. It was the end of term, the time for playing practical jokes. I was generally thought to be a pretty cool teacher, the sort who wouldn't mind a joke like that. They'd seen me go out for lunch with Zoey; they knew I wouldn't be in the staffroom. They'd taken their chance and written that vaguely threatening note, and they'd knocked on the staffroom door and asked Jeff Woodhouse to put it in my pigeon-hole; and it was all such an obvious, silly prank that I wanted to cry with relief.

There were lots of things I could have done. I could have asked straight out which of the girls had written the note. I could have compared the handwriting with the latest bunch of essays from Year Ten. I could have compared the paper with the stock of white A4 we used at school. There were lots of things I could have done to check it was just a prank; that one of my pupils had sent it to me. But I didn't. Was that because I didn't want anything to unconvince me?

That evening, when I got home, I took the note out of

the file where I'd put it. I made my decision. I tore the letter right down the middle, lengthways, enjoying the straightness and evenness of the tear as it followed the grain of the paper. Then I took those two long pieces of paper, lined up the edges and tore lengthways again. Twice more, until I had nothing but narrow strips. I lined them all up and tore widthways this time. It was a jagged tear – I was going against the grain. More widthways tears – now I was just ripping up the strips into tiny shreds, angrily, destructively, as small as I could possibly get them. And eventually all I had was a lot of little confetti-sized pieces of white paper. I scooped them up in my hands, went across to the open window and tossed them out.

I wanted it to be a grand dramatic gesture, but there was no wind to carry them. The pieces simply fluttered downwards, like dandruff or a half-hearted snow shower, catching in window boxes and on sills, and behind the drainpipe; and the rest of the pieces fell to the ground, onto the pavement outside my flat. I knew that next time I walked outside some of them would still be there. The pieces of paper would be taunting me, saying, 'Are you sure that's all it was? Just a schoolgirl prank? Are you sure that someone isn't watching you?'

Seventeen

'Hey, you look great!'

Zoey sounded, I think, surprised. But she was right. I did look great, or at least as near to great as it was possible for me to look; as near to great as I'd looked in a very long time. It was extraordinary what a few nights of deep, relaxing sleep could do. I was doing something completely out of character for me. I'd taken Zoey up on a last-minute invitation, with barely a second's thought. I was doing something spontaneous. She'd phoned that evening, and I had answered my phone. That in itself was unusual. She'd invited me out to watch what she called her 'Edinburgh preview'. 'I need good unbiased feedback,' she said. 'You seem like someone who will give me an honest opinion. So, how about it? Want to come?'

And I had said yes, because it was the end of term, and because I was being bold and unafraid. I said yes. And with that spontaneous decision I drew Zoey Spiegelman into my nightmare.

I do believe that evening was the happiest night of my adult life to date. What a sad, constrained, tight little life I'd led until then, if a night in the upstairs room of a pub in Kingston-upon-Thames hanging out with a new friend that I barely knew counted as the happiest that I'd ever been. But I felt relaxed and calm, and also I felt needed. Zoey explained what she meant by her Edinburgh preview. 'I'm taking a one-woman show to the Fringe this year. First time ever. It's a dream come true. I'm only going for ten days, second half of the Fringe. I can't afford anything more. I can't take any more time off. But I have a great venue sorted, and all I need now is to get my material together.'

The room was filling with people, mostly groups of friends in their twenties or thirties, taking their places at the tables that were crammed into the little room. In one corner there was a black curtain and a microphone – the stage area. There was an expectant hubbub. People were chatting and reading the flyers that were on the tables, and ordering drinks and generally getting ready to have a good time. Zoey was jittery, full of nervous energy, pulling at her hair, scribbling things on a piece of paper and then onto her hand. 'Forty-five minutes I'm doing. At least. Forty-five to fifty-five minutes it's supposed to last. How the fuck am I supposed to remember that much material?'

'You'll be fine, mate. Just remember, it's a narrative. You're telling a story.' This came from a very tall skinny guy who had manoeuvred his way across the crowded room from the bar carrying two drinks, a pint of lager and a pint of water. He gave the water to Zoey. He had long dark hair and a full beard, and he looked like an elongated

Jesus. 'Just remember the story,' he said. 'One thing after another. Follow the story. And if you forget something, well, fuck it. It's not like the audience knows what's supposed to come next.'

Zoey introduced us. His name was Steve. We looked at each other, neither of us quite sure who the other was or what we were to Zoey.

'You two are on constructive criticism duties, okay? I want notes, feedback, thoughts. What you liked, what you didn't like, what worked, what didn't and why. Steve, you need to check the video camera's working. And also, go get Beth a drink. The poor girl's parched.'

I saw her take a good look around the room, checking all the faces, getting an idea of who was there. Steve bought me a beer and we settled ourselves at the back of the room. He lit a cigarette. The lights went down and the hubbub stopped. The compère took his place in front of the curtain and behind the microphone and started warming up the audience. He asked for names, had some fun with the people at the front table and told some topical jokes. Next to me, Zoey jumped up and down on her toes, and swung her arms around, raising her energy levels or fighting off her nerves. She closed her eyes and took some deep breaths. The compère introduced her: 'Ladies and gentlemen, all the way from America, the fabulous Zoey Spiegelman!'

And with that, she ran to the front of the room and grabbed the microphone out of its stand. With a giant burst of nervous energy and a huge megawatt smile she turned to the audience and shouted, 'Hey, how ya doin'?'

*

Zoey was good. She was very good, even better than she'd been the last time I'd seen her. She had a gift for making people laugh. She had a gift for making people warm to her straight away. She was loud, but on the chirpy, likeable side of loud. Her smile, her hair, the way she bounced up and down, in and out of the tables at the front, interacting with the audience – everything seemed exactly right. She began with some of the material I'd heard before, jokes about being an American in England. She talked about the use of the word 'toilet' where she would normally say 'restroom', and how – even as a blunt American – she felt awkward about asking for the toilet in shops. 'It's too much information. It's like going up to a store clerk and saying, "Listen, I have an urgent need to empty my bladder. Do you have a porcelain receptacle I could use?"'

She talked about other people's personal space, and how she kept accidentally invading it. She mentioned Tube etiquette, and how she freaked people out by sitting next to them and starting up conversations, just to be friendly. She illustrated her point, making one of the audience members in the front row squish up on his seat, so she could sit next to him for a moment. 'It's not just me,' she said. 'It's my whole country. It's the American way. We're just trying to make friends. We invade people's space because we're trying to be friendly. Why do you think we went to Iraq?'

And then Zoey moved on to more personal stuff. She talked about her marriage, how she was seduced by a British accent. 'I thought he was just like Jeremy Irons in

Brideshead Revisited. Turns out he was more like Jeremy Irons in *Reversal of Fortune*.' She paused for a laugh but there wasn't one. 'You know, the movie with Glenn Close as his wife, and she's in a coma because maybe he poisoned her?' She looked around the room, seemingly unfazed by the lack of laughter. 'Too obscure? Just not funny?'

She took an imaginary pencil to an imaginary sheet of paper and crossed out the joke, and moved on to the next thing; and I was really impressed by her verve and confidence, the way she handled a joke that didn't work. Some of the later material about her husband was very bitter, but still funny. She'd been hurt, badly hurt, obviously; and yet somehow she'd managed to turn it into a joke. Perhaps it was her way of dealing with things; her way of facing up to her past and making it safe.

Zoey came off stage all sweaty and buzzy and Steve and I both hugged her. He spoke to her at length. He gave her the feedback she'd asked for, some of it quite detailed. 'The Jeremy Irons thing is never going to work. Too fucking middlebrow, and the rhythm's wrong. I know you were wondering if Ralph Fiennes would work instead – *English Patient* and *Schindler's List* – but I think that would be as bad. Plus it would bring in the whole Holocaust issue. You'd be comparing him to a fucking Nazi, and you probably want to avoid that. I say bin it. Bin that whole bit. You don't need it.'

Zoey nodded. She took in everything he said, a serious look on her face. She wrote some of it down in a little notebook. 'Thanks,' she said. 'This is great.'

They cheek-kissed and he tousled her hair. 'Gotta go,' he said. 'I'm headlining in Soho,' and he left. Zoey turned to me, smiling. I knew she wanted some feedback from me, too, so I gave her some thoughts, I can't remember what, mostly just praise. I couldn't compete with the depth and detail of what Steve had said. And then all at once the evening was almost over and I didn't want it to be.

'Do you want to come back to my place for a drink?' she said, and once again I did something I never normally would have done. I said yes.

'Comedy is truth, exaggerated,' said Zoey, almost the whole way through a bottle of red wine. She was at the precise point of drunkenness where she was hyper-articulate, verging on pretentious, without yet becoming slurry. 'Stand-up comedy at its best is a bit like poetry. The really good comedian finds words to express thoughts and moments that you may not recall ever having thought or experienced, but as soon as you hear them, you know that you have. And so you laugh. It's recognition. It's the joy of hearing that elusive fleeting thought or experience expertly pinned down.'

She poured herself another glass. I had barely touched mine. I always took care not to get drunk; not to suddenly find myself blurting out things that I wished I hadn't said. 'Do you know what every comedian's favourite sound is?' she asked.

I shook my head.

'The anticipatory giggle. Not the full-on laugh: the anticipatory giggle. Because it's the start. It's the promise of great things to come. It means the audience wants to laugh, they're willing you to make them laugh. And then, unless your punchline's really weak or you screw up your timing, there's every chance that the giggles will turn into waves of laughter spreading around the room and, on a good night, with a great gag, an extra line, and then maybe a surprise reversal, a twist in the tail, the waves of laughter can feel like . . .' She took another gulp of wine and smiled. 'It can feel like the warm ripples that go through you when you know you are just seconds away from an orgasm.'

'Stand-up comedy – as good as sex?'

She thought for a moment. 'Better. Sometimes. Well, I suppose it depends on who you're having sex with.' She downed her glass of wine and poured another, finishing off the bottle. 'So, what did you think of Steve? Do you think he likes me?'

And then, before I could answer, Zoey did something I hadn't seen her do before: she blushed. 'Listen to me,' she said. 'Thirty-three years old and I'm sounding like a high-school girl.'

Zoey's flat was in Clapham, at the very top of one of those tall Victorian terraced houses, buried under the eaves. I was surprised that her door only had a Yale lock, no bolts. Despite that her place felt very safe. There was a narrow hallway, painted the dark blue-green of the deepest bits of the ocean, and all along it there was a series of antique mirrors, none of them matching. The distorted glass threw off wobbly reflections that I noticed as I followed Zoey down the hallway. She had looped strings of lights in the shape of chillies, stars and flowers between the mirrors, and it seemed like the entrance to an enchanted grotto.

The main room of the flat was a tiny bed-sitting room, with a daybed covered with a silky quilt in a deep tobacco brown and laden with cushions. The walls of the room were blood-red, and covered with shelves laden with books and DVDs and CDs. There were pictures on the walls and objects crammed onto every surface, and one wall was almost entirely covered with hundreds of post-cards. The womb-like room was unlike mine in almost every way possible, except for this: it seemed to have been designed as a safe place, a haven; a little cave for Zoey to live in, just as much as my flat was for me.

Zoey covered her embarrassment by going into the cupboard-like kitchen. She came back clutching another bottle of wine, some sparkling water and a bag of posh crisps. She opened them, poured them into a bowl and offered them to me. I took a handful, and then found myself asking a personal question. I didn't do this often, because it meant running the risk of getting asked an equally personal question in return. But this seemed like a harmless subject. 'So, tell me about Steve. I thought you were out of the relationship game?'

'Oh, I don't know. He seems like a good guy. He's a comedian, too. We've done some gigs together. He's great. Very intelligent, very interesting. It's probably nothing serious. He's . . . someone, you know? And sometimes you just need someone, to keep you safe.'

I thought about Danny for a moment. I wondered if he was 'someone', and I wondered if I should tell Zoey about him. But instead I asked her another question, a question that I'd been wondering about since the first time I'd seen her. It came close to breaching our pact, but I really wanted to know. I judged that she was drunk enough not to mind, not to notice, not to ask me a question in return. 'If your husband hurt you so much, why don't you just forget about him and go back to America?'

'Because there's more to London than my ex-husband. I like it here. I started my PhD here and I want to finish it. Also, London's a great town for comedy. There's much more chance of getting spotted here.' Another slurp of wine. 'And, to tell you the truth, the divorce isn't final yet. So there are still legal issues to sort out, and even if I wanted to leave it probably wouldn't be a good idea right now. There are still things to fight for.'

'Okay. But if he hurt you so much, why do you keep telling jokes about him?'

'Because it helps. It's as simple as that. I don't mean vengeance, or anything like that. What I mean is, making it all part of my comedy routine makes it smaller in my mind. It makes *him* smaller in my mind. It converts the whole thing from tragedy to comedy, and that's got to be a good thing.' Zoey looked at me, hard. 'You should try it. You should try comedy. You should get up on stage and tell some jokes about whatever this black cloud is that's hanging over you. Better than therapy. A lot cheaper, anyway. Try it. Go on, I dare you.'

'No.' The word came out very sharply, almost as a shout. Zoey looked at me, a puzzled – almost hurt – expression on her face. I stood up. I needed to walk around. I needed to get out of here. I needed to go. I was standing by the wall that was covered with postcards and I found myself looking at them. Hawaii; Blackpool; the Yorkshire Dales; Florida; Paris. And then one caught my eye. Tall red girders, rising from a cloud of fog: San Francisco's Golden Gate Bridge, such a familiar scene from my nightmares. Rivers Carillo's face flashed in front of my eyes, the way he looked at me when I killed him, the expression on his face: confusion, shock, almost indignation. 'Have you ever been to San Francisco?' My voice sounded strangled as I asked Zoey the question without looking at her.

'Yeah,' she said, coming over to stand next to me. 'I lived there for a couple of years. It's a beautiful city. That's where I first started doing comedy.'

She was standing so close to me that I could smell the red wine on her breath. I turned to look at her, at her profile. And then she turned her head to look at me. Was there a question in those searching green eyes?

'Do you know Rivers Carillo?' I blurted out those words without thinking too hard. It had to be asked, but I felt myself shaking as I waited for the answer. What would it be? A sharp intake of breath, maybe. A shocked 'How did you guess?' A resigned, 'Okay, yeah, you got me.' Or an evil laugh, like a villain in a melodrama: 'Yes,

I'm his daughter and now I'm going to take my revenge.'

I turned to face her, wondering what I'd see in her eyes. And all that was there was an interested, enquiring look. 'Riva Scarillo? No, I've never heard of her. Is she good? What kind of material does she do?'

'She's . . . no, it doesn't matter. Forget it.' Relief flooded me like embarrassment. I smiled, looked at my watch. 'Listen, I really should go.' I picked up my bag, and I touched Zoey on the shoulder, and she followed me down the long narrow hallway of mirrors. 'This was fun,' she said.

'Yes, it was.' It had been, until I'd spoiled it by getting scared and suspicious.

'Let's do it again sometime,' she said, and she kissed me on the cheek.

Eighteen

I saw a lot of Zoey after that. I'd always been careful not to let people into my life, but there was something about her that felt familiar, safe. I recognised her, in a way. She seemed to be the me that I could have been. If Lizzie, that annoying, theatrical, attention-grabbing teenager, had been allowed to grow up normally; if she had calmed down and found a focus, had learned how to interact with other human beings; learned some patience and some generosity, learned how to share and make room for other people . . . if all those things had happened, then maybe Zoey was the kind of person she would have grown up to be.

I enjoyed spending time with Zoey. We got into the habit of meeting up late afternoon or early evening. She worked lunchtimes in a bar in the West End, and didn't want to trek all the way home to Clapham on those long, hot afternoons if she had a gig in central London; and because she was preparing for her Edinburgh show she had a gig almost every evening. I kept her company. It was the school holidays, and I wanted to fill the time. We found places to hang out where we could kill time and stay cool. We'd go and see teatime screenings of films in air-conditioned cinemas – we didn't really care what we saw.

Or we'd drink iced coffee or herbal tea in cool, white basement cafés in art galleries and museums. Sometimes we'd go for an early meal, finding cheap deals in ethnic restaurants – dim sum, cut-price Indian buffets, a little Italian restaurant with Chianti bottles on the wall and an early-bird set-price meal, an Ethiopian place where we ate spicy meat stew with flatbread and our fingers. Zoey always enthused over her food. Even in the worst restaurants she would find something she liked. She liked to share her food – holding bits out for me to try, or picking things from my plate. I liked it. It made me feel part of a proper friendship.

Sometimes I'd go to her gigs with her. I became a comedy groupie, you might say. Zoey seemed as reluctant as I was to have an empty diary, although presumably for different reasons. 'I'd rather do an open ten than sit at home doing nothing,' she told me. An 'open ten', I'd learned, was an unpaid ten-minute spot that newer comics did in the middle of a comedy bill, in order to get experience and to showcase what they could do. A 'paid twenty' was what she preferred, but she said, 'It's all stage time. It's all good.'

I became interested in what Zoey called 'the room' – not just what each venue looked like, but how it – or rather the audience in that room – responded. There were fascinating differences. One night there was a gig at a club with an all-woman line-up, a glitzy room in Clerkenwell with chandeliers and exposed pipes sprayed in gold paint. The largely female audience was loudly enthusiastic, particularly at anything remotely filthy. They whooped and stamped their feet when Zoey did her oral-sex material. Then there was a gig down in leafy Richmond in a cramped room above a pub. It was an older audience, a lot of couples in their thirties and forties, and they were polite and supportive but much quieter. Zoey seemed to struggle, the first time I'd ever seen her do less than brilliantly. It was a tiny stage area, hemmed in by tables, giving her less room to roam around than usual. She was doing her tried and tested routine but it was clear to me that she expected a more enthusiastic response. In the middle of one bit of material, a woman sitting in the front suddenly called out, 'I love your trousers. Where did you get them?'

'Weirdest heckle ever,' said Zoey afterwards. 'And you know what? I could have done something with it. I got these pants at Fat Face. There's gotta be a line there. Some kind of veiled insult . . .' She screwed up her face, trying to work it out, and I wondered if next time I saw her live there'd be a new joke about it.

With Zoey, the conversation was often about her material, her jokes. She would try things out on me and get me to respond, and we would free-associate. I liked it. I felt that I was involved in her creative process, and it gave me a buzz to listen to her on stage, making comedy out of something that one of us had seen or mentioned earlier in the week. And also, it was the kind of conversation I could do. In a way, it was similar to listening to Danny talk about music. Zoey didn't want to know anything about me. She didn't want to hear deep stuff: secrets and revelations and what I really thought about things. She just needed to use me as a sounding board. We kept it mostly shallow, and I found that comforting.

One evening, when Zoey didn't have a gig, we spent another evening in her flat, that cosy little space hidden high in the eaves of the big house in Clapham. She cooked for me. She opened all the windows wide and turned on a fan, and tried to get some air into the flat. The smell of garlic, bacon and tomatoes wafted out of the minuscule cupboard of a kitchen as she cooked spaghetti sauce, which she pronounced the American way, with the emphasis on the word 'spaghetti' rather than 'sauce'. I sipped red wine and browsed the books on her shelves.

Her book collection looked like mine would have done, had I not had several purges in my life. She had the whole *Little House* series by Laura Ingalls Wilder, in well-thumbed paperbacks. I'd loved those books when I was a child. I'd left my copies in a box in my parents' attic and when they'd moved to the bungalow where they now lived I'd told them to get rid of all my childhood stuff. They sold all my books to a dealer for the grand sum of thirty pounds. Zoey had a whole row of Dorothy L. Sayers and Arthur Conan Doyle; she had Jane Austen, the Brontë sisters, a few Dickens. She had books by P.G. Wodehouse and Nancy Mitford. She had *Rebecca* and *The Catcher in the Rye* and *To Kill a Mockingbird*; she had Donna Tartt's *The Secret History* and *Scruples* by Judith Krantz. I'd owned all of these at some point in my life, and I'd jettisoned them all along the way. I had left many of my books behind in a flat in Finsbury Park that I had shared with three other people including a guy called Julian. I walked away when things got uncomfortably serious between Julian and me, and I hadn't had the time or inclination to work out which books were mine. And besides, they wouldn't have fitted in the boot of my car.

I pulled the copy of *Scruples* from Zoey's shelf and flicked through it fondly. It was the book that taught me everything I thought I needed to know about sex. Something was scrawled inside the cover. 'Who's Judith Spiegelman?' I asked as I deciphered the handwriting.

Zoey laughed from the kitchen. She came back into the main room, drying her hands on a towel. 'Me, until the big split. Zoey's my middle name. I figured it suited the new me better.'

I looked at her, standing there, laughing, the light catching the tips of her frizzy hair and making them glow golden. Her green eyes held mine, unblinkingly, and I came very close to telling her – not the whole story, but about Lizzie, and about changing my name when I was eighteen. It was something else we had in common. But instead I turned away and pretended to be incredibly interested in the postcards on the wall. I should have told her. I wish I had. Things might have been so different if we had shared our secrets.

Nineteen

I saw a lot of Danny, too. I'd spend the early part of the evening with Zoey, and then, if I wasn't going to her gig, I would go out later with Danny. I'd get home and instead of my usual long nights with a book or the television, I'd go round to Danny's flat and we'd do something – anything – together. Two or three times a week we went out or stayed in together. I'd never been so busy, so in demand, in my life.

Danny took me to see some kind of folky American band at the Barbican: lots of banjos and fiddles. I didn't like it much. There was no atmosphere in that big auditorium, and the audience seemed to be made up of deeply serious people stroking their chins appreciatively. Afterwards we went for a curry and Danny explained the music to me. I loved it when he did that. His voice was very soft and I could pick up the gist without having to listen to every single word. But for as long as he talked, that was a whole part of the conversation where I knew I was safe from questions or from having to talk about myself.

Then, another night, we went to see a friend of his who played in a band. I enjoyed that a lot more. It was noisy, dark, smoky and very hot, and I snuggled up to Danny and got lost in the music. We stayed in together some nights as well, round at his flat. He would cook me pasta or we'd order a takeaway, and we watched DVD boxed sets of intense American TV crime dramas, or listened to some of his favourite music. And we talked. Not about ourselves, but about things: films and TV and music and books.

Neither Danny nor I were that good at normal conversation. We exchanged facts and opinions and talked about things – actual tangible things, not feelings – because that felt safe. With Zoey, all I had to do was listen to her talk. She made no conversational demands of me beyond the occasional laugh or comment, or the odd interjection to keep her on the subject in hand. With Danny, it was different. We were both awkward, and it struck me that I had no idea how to talk normally to a boyfriend. I had no idea how to make normal conversation. I was so starved of usual social intercourse that I found it easier to substitute facts for social niceties. It was a form of shyness, I guess, or maybe self-defence. Facts were good. Facts were safe. They were a useful currency. I could tell Danny something that he might not know and he could tell me something in return. And it could almost pass for a conversation, if we kept it up long enough.

It was amazing to me how good the sex could be between two such awkward, inexpressive people. Or maybe it was good because it was something else to do that stopped us having to talk properly to each other; something that filled the time when normal lovers would be swapping endearments or discussing their feelings for each other. Sex with Danny was tender and gentle, full of kisses and stroking, and hair being pushed away from my face. It was full of his mumblings – 'Is this okay? And this?' There was usually music playing while we made love. Afterwards, if we were at Danny's place (and we usually were), he would get up and walk across the room to change the CD, and then he'd get back into bed and hold me, and stroke me some more, and he would tell me something about the music on the stereo in his soft, gentle, almost monotonous voice. And I wanted to cry, every time, because I felt guilty about sleeping with such a sweet and lovely man. I felt guilty about letting him stay in my life. I felt guilty about taking advantage of him. I felt guilty about not warning him about me.

We went for a picnic one Sunday. Danny had surprised me mid-morning by knocking on my door with a rolled blanket under his arm and a plastic carrier bag in his hand. We lay on his itchy blanket in Regent's Park, surrounded by hundreds of other people doing the same thing. We ate slightly soft pork pies and bags of crisps, washed down with lukewarm beer and cans of Coke. 'Sorry, this is a bit of a shit picnic,' he said.

'No, it's nice.'

'I should have brought some salad. Maybe some tomatoes or a tub of coleslaw. Or maybe some of those leaves in a bag. All that posh stuff, like rocket.'

'Rocket. When did we all start eating rocket?'

'Or frisée.'

'Endive.'

'Radicchio.'

'Lollo rosso.'

'You win,' Danny said, turning to me and kissing me on the forehead. 'Also, maybe some fancy sandwiches, like brie and grape.'

'Stilton and banana.'

'Mozzarella and melon.'

'Camembert and castor oil.'

He laughed. We kissed again. We held hands and lay there, side by side, in the sun, in companionable silence. It was nice. And then it almost imperceptibly faded from nice to not-so-nice. The silence went on. It went on too long. It stopped being companionable and started being awkward. My hand started to sweat in his, and my fingers started to go numb. The silence hung over us. One of us would have to say something soon, or else I could imagine us lying there for the rest of our lives, neither of us ever talking again. Danny squeezed my hand. I squeezed back. He disentangled his fingers and shifted slightly onto his side. He looked at me, and stroked the hair away from my face. He leaned over me. He took a deep breath. I thought he was about to say something dramatic about the state of our relationship. But instead he asked me if I wanted an ice cream.

I lay there on that blanket waiting for Danny to come back, squinting at the hot summer sky, looking at the other picnickers out of the corners of my eyes. It wasn't even August yet and already we were taking it for granted, that hot summer weather. Already we had the Mediterranean mindset. Already the whole of Britain woke up every day knowing it was going to be hot. We were taking no precautions – taking no jumpers or waterproofs or umbrellas with us when we set off for the day. The whole country was making plans as if every day for the foreseeable future was going to be hot and dry and sunny.

No precautions. We'd been lulled into an unusual sense of security about the weather. How quickly it had happened. And then I thought about me, and the sense of security I'd allowed myself to indulge in. I was doing things I'd never done before. I was dating someone, I had a friend. I was enjoying myself, doing what normal people did. I had stopped taking precautions. That note had scared me more than anything else had ever done, in my whole life. And then I'd just thrown it away. I'd said that it didn't matter; I'd allowed myself to assume it was a practical joke. And somehow, because that note didn't matter, because that one fear was false, I'd allowed myself to relax, to drop my guard, as if I wasn't a killer but just a normal person.

The sky was high and big and so pale it was almost white. It was a huge hot blank space above me. It was a huge blank sheet of paper. And that was when I realised what I was doing, all the time I was with Zoey and Danny, all that uncharacteristic social activity. Summer was looming above me and ahead of me like a big blank sheet of paper – hot and white and empty. I was trying to fill it.

I was trying to scribble all over its pages, like the pages in a diary. I was trying to fill the space with people and things. I was trying to keep my fear at bay.

Summer was the most dangerous season. It was big and it was empty and it could seem endless, and it made me do stupid, evil things. There was too much time and too much light, and it had to be filled. That was what had gone so horribly wrong in San Francisco. The summer had stretched out ahead of me. The possibilities were endless and overwhelming. I had felt tiny in that big city, like a little ant scurrying around trying to impose order and purpose on my life. Maybe that was why I clung to Rivers Carillo like that. Knowing that I was going to see him again helped me draw lines and margins on my blank sheet of paper. It helped me fill my diary.

Hot summers like this summer were the worst. Not only were they endless and empty but they were relentless as well. The sun beat down every day on a mission to burn and expose. It dried up ponds and puddles and killed grass, leaving behind dust and faded litter and hard, caked, cracked earth – soil burned and purified down to its very essence. Day by day London was drying out, getting dirtier, becoming more intense, revealing the cracks at the heart. The days of intense heat were piling up behind us and ahead of us. Travelling by Tube, it felt as if all the days of progressively hotter weather were being stored down there, in those tunnels, waiting to explode. The hot sun had cracked and shrivelled the paintwork on my windowsills, uncovering the rotten wood underneath. Even the little bits of paper, the torn-up note that I threw out of my window, were still there, in the gutter outside my block of flats, drying out and fading but still winking at me, mocking me, every time I left the building.

Danny and Zoey – all they were to me were frantic scribbles in my diary. I lay there in Regent's Park under the sun, surrounded by people and people and people, as far as I could see, and I shivered with fear. Nothing had changed. Nothing would ever change. This would never get better. How could it? I would never stop being a killer.

Twenty

Maybe you've had one of those mornings when you wake up and, no matter how early you went to bed, no matter how long you've been there, you feel as if you've been dragged kicking and screaming from the depths of sleep. Daylight is simply too bright for your eyes to bear. So you sit on your bed or at the kitchen table and eventually – with some combination of rubbing the sleep from your eyes, splashing your face with water and drinking some strong coffee – you begin to feel like a human being. Now imagine that you're sitting there feeling like shit, blinking in the brightness, and you realise that nothing you can do – rubbing your eyes, splashing water, drinking coffee – will make any difference at all. And in fact the way you feel now, as your skin starts pricking and dots start dancing in front of your eyes, and you feel as if your eyelids have been forced open by someone with gluey fingers – that is the best that you're going to feel all day.

I'd told Zoey that a migraine was like a hangover, but the truth is that while they both start out feeling similar, hangovers get better while migraines get worse. With a hangover, there are things you can do, or take: a banana, some aspirin, a can of ice-cold sugary full-fat Coke, a pint or two of sparkling water, a fry-up. With a migraine, there are drugs that you can take, but they don't often work; and also taking drugs involves putting things into your stomach, and sometimes that's something that's impossible to face. It can make things much, much worse.

Before I'd ever had a migraine I'd dismissed them as glorified headaches, in the same way that someone who's never had a proper bout of flu assumes that it's synonymous with a bad cold. Sure, a migraine's main course is a headache – a hard, heavy, metal headache with sharp edges, like a tarnished anvil being forced into your skull and sitting, weighty and immovable, on top of one eye socket. But that's just the main dish of a seven- or eight-course menu that starts with lethargy and nausea, moves through disorientation and dizziness, visual disturbances and aphasia, sometimes facial paralysis, and ends eventually on a lingering quiet note of absolute exhaustion.

And since I had feigned migraines to escape family commitments on a number of occasions, perhaps it served me right that on the one occasion I really couldn't miss – the day I was taking my new boyfriend to meet my family to celebrate my parents' fortieth wedding anniversary – I had the beginnings of the migraine from hell.

Why had I even invited Danny? I guess it had been a spur-of-the-moment thing as we walked back home from the picnic. I needed to do something, to say something, to bring things close to normal, to show some indication of whether I wanted to continue with him or not. I felt bad about being distant from him for much of the picnic. I felt bad for not being a good enough girlfriend. Danny was talking about what we could do during the week, and making plans for the following weekend, and I said, suddenly, out of nowhere, 'I have this . . . thing. A family thing. Next weekend. It's my parents' anniversary. They're having a party, down in Sussex. I have to go to that.'

Danny looked at me, and I think he was wondering if I was about to invite him. So I did. He seemed pleased. He seemed happy. He seemed excited. He squeezed my hand. 'So remind me,' he said, laughing at me. 'Is this a relationship or not?'

I reckoned I had two or three hours before the full force of the migraine hit. I reckoned I could manage the drive down to the coast. I figured I would be able to introduce Danny to my family and then just sit quietly in a corner for a few hours until it was time to go home. No one would expect anything else from me. I could introduce Danny to my nephew Josh and they could talk about music. Josh had seen the Arctic Monkeys recently. I was pretty sure Danny would be interested in hearing about that. Or maybe he could talk to Jem, and she could explain what it was she did for a living, and they could discuss computer games and Japanese comics. My mother and Sarah would be far too busy preparing food and rushing around to talk to anyone – they always took on all the responsibility when there was an event to be catered; they enjoyed it, they wouldn't want me butting in. My father would be his usual benign, vague self. He probably wouldn't even realise who Danny was. It would be all right, I told myself. It would be fine.

But the weather was heavier than I'd ever known it, and my migraine was developing faster. Halfway down the M23 I realised that my eyes and my brain weren't communicating any more. I saw a sign that told me there were roadworks and lane closures, a sign announcing a speed limit of fifty miles an hour, and I knew theoretically what the signs meant but I didn't know how to act on them. I couldn't translate that number on the circular sign with the red ring around it into the speed that I was supposed to go. Danny grabbed my arm as I suddenly steered out of my lane just before it was coned off, and nearly swerved into the path of another car. I couldn't keep my distance from the other cars in the contraflow. My right eye didn't appear to be working and everything was two-dimensional. Cars kept looming in front of me, closer than I'd thought, and I kept having to brake sharply. Danny was getting nervous – tetchy, even. As soon as I was out of the contraflow I pulled over onto the hard shoulder and stopped the car. 'You drive,' I said.

'Don't be like that.' He thought I was annoyed by his nervousness and arm-grabbing.

'I'm not being "like that". I can't drive. I can't see properly. My head hurts. I'm going to be sick.'

I got out of the car and stepped over the low fence onto the grass bank at the side of the motorway. I sat down, my head between my knees. Danny came over, a bottle of water in his hand, and sat next to me. 'Hangover?' he said, gently.

'Migraine.'

He handed me the bottle of water and stroked the back of my neck. I popped an extra-strength ibuprofen from the pack that I had in my pocket, and I gulped it down. I passed Danny the car keys. He jingled them in his hand and then, I guess remembering that I had a headache, suddenly stopped. 'I'm worried now,' he said.

'What about?'

'About meeting your family. If this is what it does to you . . .'

I thought he was joking but I wasn't sure. 'You'll be fine,' I said. 'It'll all be fine.'

But it wasn't. I guess I hadn't listened properly when my mother had told me about the party. I'd been imagining a small family affair. I hadn't expected the whole parish to be there, filling my parents' driveway and all nearby streets with parked cars. By the time we found a parking space and got to the house, the anvil had settled itself over my left eye, and the right side of my face was starting to go numb. Sarah opened the door to us, glass of wine in hand, and the first thing she said was, 'My God, Lizzie, Mum and Dad have hired caterers. They won't let me in the kitchen.' Then, noticing Danny, she said, 'And you must be . . . nope, sorry. No idea.'

I guess I must have introduced them to each other. I know that Sarah led us straight out to the garden. There on the patio my father was sitting on a garden chair, surrounded by a whole bunch of what we used to call the 'old dears', the elderly spinsters from church who did the flowers and fussed around the vicar. I said something, I know I must have done. Danny shook my father's hand. One of the old dears said, 'Goodness, it's little Jemima. Hasn't she grown?' Her voice was so loud it hurt.

And my father said, 'Oh no, this is Lizzie,' and I think Danny repeated 'Lizzie' under his breath and smiled to himself.

The garden was full of people that I half-recognised. Some of them waved or smiled at me. They were all talking too loudly and I couldn't make out what anyone was saying. The sun was blindingly white. There were teenage girls in white shirts and short black skirts handing out things on trays. My mother did a flustered kiss-and-run at some point, and then she saw Danny and stopped, and spoke to him. I found myself sitting on a bench with a plate of uneaten food on my lap. I closed my eyes behind my sunglasses and tried to slip away. I'd lost track of where Danny was. And then he was standing next to me, and Jem was there. I noticed her white legs in chunky black rubber sandals that looked like car tyres. I was trying to introduce them to each other but I couldn't make the words come out right. Something wasn't working: my face, my mouth, my brain. There was a connection missing. *This is what it must feel like to have a stroke*, I thought. And the next thing I knew, Jem was holding my hand and leading me back into the house, into the cool dark lounge, and settling me down in an armchair.

Danny brought me a glass of water, and my mother came in to check up on me, and I could hear her stage-whispering to my father, 'She's having one of her heads.' Sarah put her head round the door and gave me a sympathetic grimace, and then everyone left me alone.

A blacksmith was hard at work inside my head. I curled into a foetal position and put my fingers to my temples, to the pulse points on my head. I was trying to make sense of the throbbing pain, trying to work out the rhythm. When I was a kid I read an article in the *Readers' Digest* about a man who survived three days and three nights on a freezing prairie by giving in to the cold, not fighting it, allowing the shivering and shaking to become part of him. When I had a migraine I always tried to do the same thing with the pain, drifting into it, embracing it, trying to become one with it; trying to discover how it worked, when each wave would come next. Counting, counting, always counting.

Eventually I felt well enough to open my eyes. From where I was sitting I could see out through the conservatory and into the garden. Through half-opened eyes and through two sets of windows, I watched knots of people milling around the garden. Through two sheets of glass I watched my family being normal, doing what normal people do. I saw Sarah's well-mannered daughter Katie circulating, talking politely to older people who she couldn't possibly have known. I saw Danny talking to my nephew Josh, who was all gangly and intense with his body language. I watched Sarah and my mother admiring the garden. That was my job, normally: to walk around the garden with my mother, exchanging Latin names of plants in lieu of having actual conversations about how we really felt about things. And then Danny was talking to Jem, and Sarah joined them, and the three of them stood there laughing together, and from time to time Danny cast curious glances in my direction.

I knew what they were talking about. Jem and Sarah were telling him stories from my childhood. The time I was four and I decided to dance in the park, performing to all the old ladies in their deckchairs. The infamous school concert, when I'd been sent to stand in a corner because I'd punched a boy for singing my solo line by mistake. The nativity play, when I played the angel Gabriel and ad libbed for five minutes when one of the shepherds got stage fright. They were no doubt telling him the same old stories that got told year after year; the stories about Lizzie Stephens, the show-off, the performer, the attention-grabber. No wonder Danny looked puzzled.

Later the thunder finally came, the thunderstorm that had been threatening all day and that had no doubt contributed to my migraine. The thunder boomed and the lightning crackled and sparked. The rain fell from the sky in sheets and bounced off the patio. The girls in the white shirts and the short black skirts ran around covering up food and bringing trays through into the house. The guests started to leave, and my migraine started to lift, and my family gathered in the lounge. My father hugged me and told me that they'd missed me. Sarah patted my hand and came and sat next to me. My mother fussed around in the kitchen, with the catering girls and the ruined leftover food. Danny and Jem had both taken photos on their digital cameras, and the cameras were passed around so that everyone could admire the pictures. It was all so utterly, heartbreakingly normal that I wanted to cry. I wished I could belong properly to my own family. Danny was already more a part of it than I was.

'Lizzie. Lizzie Stephens. You know, I like that name.' Danny was driving me home in his cautious way, sticking exactly to the speed limit, keeping his distance from the car ahead. I was feeling a little better. I was in the lingering exhaustion stage, the washed-out, wrung-out but pain-free bit that follows a migraine. I was annoyed with myself for being ill, for somehow copping out of a potentially tense family occasion; but also for leaving Danny out there, talking to anyone he wanted to, asking questions about me and no doubt finding out stuff. I wasn't in the mood for talking. But Danny was, albeit in a soft, slightly patronising voice that I found particularly annoying.

'I really like your family. They're good fun. It must be great to have siblings. I wish I did. I thought Jem was great. You never told me that one of your sisters lives in London. Anyway, we got on really well. We were saying that we should all meet up some time.'

I made some sort of non-committal noise. Danny didn't get the hint. He just kept on talking. 'So, I guess Lizzie is what your family calls you. Do I get to call you that? Do we know each other well enough yet? Do I pass the Lizzie test?'

'Danny, shut up.' I couldn't stand it any longer.

He opened his mouth and then closed it again. He looked at me. He looked hurt.

'I'm sorry, Danny, but I can't do this.'

'Do what?'

'This. This whole thing.'

He was quiet for a while. I guess he was trying to work out what I meant. After a while he said, 'Sorry. You're ill. Your head hurts. I should just shut up.'

He did for a while. I closed my eyes and tried to sleep. But Danny couldn't let it go. 'What did you mean, "this whole thing"? Did you mean talking to me? Is that what you can't do, right now?'

'I mean this. You and me.'

'You mean our . . . relationship?' His voice cracked slightly. I looked at him, driving. His chin was set in a determined manner. He was looking resolutely straight ahead. 'What do you mean, you can't do it?'

'I just can't. I just can't do it. Relationships.'

'Sure you can.' Danny sounded relieved. Maybe he was relieved because I was generalising. If it was 'relationships' that I couldn't do, then it wasn't him in particular. And if it wasn't him in particular then perhaps I didn't mean what I was saying. I didn't know. I didn't know what he thought. I was trying to end our relationship and he wouldn't let me, that was all I knew. He reached over and took my hand. 'Of course you can do it. I'm not letting you get out of it that easily.'

Twenty-one

The next time I saw Rivers Carillo, I was standing in front of a black curtain and behind a microphone in a tiny, hot, smoky room in the basement of a pub just off Tottenham Court Road. I was about to take the microphone out of the stand. I was about to open my mouth, to try to make people laugh for five minutes. I was about to do my first – and maybe my last – performance as a stand-up comedian. I hadn't seen Rivers for quite a while, except in the bad dreams that were a routine part of my life. But suddenly there he was again, grinning at me. 'Go on, then,' his grin seemed to say. 'Show me how funny you are.'

It was Zoey's idea. It was all her doing. She'd nagged me. The first time that she'd told me I should turn my 'black cloud' into comedy I'd snapped at her. Of course I couldn't do it, although I couldn't tell her why. But then she mentioned it again, several times. I guessed she'd noticed how much I enjoyed spending time at comedy clubs. Maybe she'd noticed the way it made me feel, the way I enjoyed our conversations about jokes and material. Maybe she was one of the few people observant enough to notice Lizzie lurking behind Beth.

Most people would run a mile rather than stand on any

sort of stage. Most people get nervous – more than nervous – at doing any kind of public speaking. Their palms sweat, their throats constrict. I think most people would sooner undergo root-canal work without anaesthetic than do anything in front of an audience. But there are a few of us, a small handful of show-offs, who thrive on audience attention – who love it, crave it, need it. At the age of five I'd demanded ballet lessons. I spent most of my teens planning to be an actress. I had acted in every school play and every youth-group drama production that I could. I had always loved that moment when the lights went down and the curtain rose, and there was an audience sitting there, hanging on my every word. I had always loved that kind of attention. Perhaps it was because I was the middle child, the one who got overlooked at home, the one who had to shout to be heard? It was probably why I was a pretty good teacher – I had no fear about standing in front of a class and talking to a bunch of teenagers, making them laugh with stupid jokes. I was, by nature, a show-off and an attention-grabber. And for the last seventeen years I had forced myself to keep a low profile. I had forced myself to be something that I wasn't. Maybe that was why I agreed to do it.

I'd told myself I didn't have much choice. Zoey had organised it. She'd presented it as a *fait accompli*. She'd rung up and told me she'd organised me a five-minute open spot at a little comedy club, and she gave me two days' notice to prepare my material. I could have told her that I wasn't going to do it. I did make a few protestations – I didn't have enough time to prepare; I'd be rubbish –

but she told me that it didn't matter; that it was a fun, no-pressure club with a low quality threshold. 'It's called Pear Shaped,' she said. 'It describes itself as the second-worst comedy club in London. It's a fun place, usually. It's a great place to try out new material. Some of the acts will be really shitty. But you, on the other hand, will be good. You're genuinely funny. You have a really crisp, dry manner. You have no fear about standing in front of people and talking. Teachers generally make great stand-ups. Trust me, you'll be good. And wear that green jacket. That way, if the worst happens and you die, then at least you'll look good dying.'

Die. Weird, the way comedians used that verb to describe the act – the non-act – of not making people laugh. As if not making people laugh was the worst thing that could happen to anyone.

I agreed to do it. I agreed, because I wanted to do it. I could see a little chink, the possibility of enjoying myself for a few minutes. It had been many years since I had stood on any kind of stage. Here was my chance: a chance to engage with an audience, a tiny audience, in a dark room in a basement. Comparatively safe, as far as audiences went. Who would possibly know it was Lizzie Stephens, teen killer, up there behind the microphone?

I thought about some of the things that Zoey had said about stand-up, some of the advice she'd given. Comedy is truth, exaggerated. Talk about the worst thing that's ever happened to you, but make it funny. Turn off your social editor. When I asked her what she meant by that she said it was something that she'd got from the tutor on a stand-up comedy course she'd taken. 'Your social editor's the thing in your brain – the off switch – that stops you being completely offensive and inappropriate in normal conversation. It's the thing that stops you blurting out things you're itching to say. Call it – oh, I don't know – tact, something like that. The idea is that in stand-up comedy, anything goes. Anything you've always wanted to say but couldn't, wouldn't, for whatever reason – now's the time to say it.'

Turn off your social editor. I thought about that as I stood in front of the mirror in my flat, sweltering in my green velvet jacket, and tried to put together a five-minute routine. Something that I'd always wanted to say, but couldn't. Something that I was itching to blurt out. 'When I was eighteen I killed a man and got away with it.'

I didn't say it out loud. I couldn't; I never had, I thought I probably never would. But I stood in front of the mirror and I said it to myself, and I watched my face. It looked hard and determined, and slightly aloof, with just a ghost of a smile on my lips. I felt a shiver go down my spine, and it was almost pleasurable. Suppose I started my routine like that? Suppose I stood behind the microphone and couldn't help myself? Suppose I turned off my social editor so completely that I just blurted it out? What would I do?

'When I was eighteen I killed a man and got away with it.' I'd say it in my usual slightly posh deadpan voice. This time I almost said it out loud. I mouthed the words, articulating each syllable. I watched my face again, watching the mirror, imagining the audience becoming uneasy. Unease can sometimes make people laugh – I knew that by now. I imagined that maybe there'd be a few titters from the audience. But most of them would be staring at me, wondering if what I'd said was true. So how would I follow that opening line? Reassurance might work: something to break the tension, to key the audience in to the fact that it was okay to laugh. I could go the insult route. 'It's all right, though, he deserved it. He was a bastard.' Or a tosser. A wanker, maybe: that was a good Anglo-Saxon word that I could really sink my teeth into, a nice contrast to my crisp received pronunciation.

Zoey had told me that the K or hard-C sound worked well in comedy because it made your lips automatically go into a smile, and that could have an effect on the audience's reaction. I'd heard a few comedians use the C-word. Maybe that would work. 'It's all right, though, he deserved it. He was a c—' No, I wouldn't say that. I didn't want to say that word out loud, in that context. The vicar's daughter in me was too strong. Ironic: I could kill a man but I could not bring myself to use certain words.

Wanker, I thought. That would be the best choice. That would generate some laughs – some nervous laughs, anyway. Some of those anticipatory giggles that Zoey had mentioned. The men would be shifting uneasily in their seats. Zoey had told me that men were always on tenterhooks when there was a female comic on stage, in case she suddenly did a joke about periods or tampons. The women would have their faces tilted up towards me, already predisposed to like me because I was a woman, and there were so few female stand-ups. That was how I'd felt about Zoey when I saw her first.

I knew by now that comedians didn't just make it up on the spur of the moment. Every line you hear a stand-up deliver has probably been analysed, consciously or subconsciously; analysed and worked on and tested out on a regular audience or a friend, or on a fellow comic on the long journey to a gig, or on a bathroom mirror, like I was doing now. But not this line: 'When I was eighteen I killed a man and got away with it.'

No way. No way I could ever say that. Not now, not on stage. Never. Comedy is truth, exaggerated, Zoey had said. But that line – that plain, unvarnished, unexaggerated truth? No. I couldn't use that line because it was *too* true.

I cobbled together some stuff about family life and being the middle child. I thought up some material about having a vicar for a father, and having to behave myself in church when I was a kid. I wrote some lines about being a teacher, and some of the things that the kids had said to me, and I added a few lame jokes about things I'd seen on television. Zoey put me through my paces beforehand. She made me tell her my material as we ate an early meal in a little Greek restaurant near the venue, and that was one of the most nerve-racking things I'd ever had to do. Why was it harder to perform for one person than for a whole roomful? Zoey smiled a few times and frowned a bit. She seemed a little bit disappointed in me. I waited for her verdict with butterflies in my stomach.

'Forget the TV material,' she said. 'That's hack stuff. Everyone's doing jokes about Gillian McKeith. It's not really worthy of you. The vicar material is brilliant, because it's you, you know? No one else could do that. I think you should start with that. It's your strongest material. You'll get them on side. They'll love it. The teacher stuff?' She held out her hand, palm downwards, and waggled it. 'It's okay. It's not especially new. I've heard similar material, but it's . . . okay. Stick that in the middle of your set. Then, link back to your childhood with that line about bad behaviour and tantrums, and end with the material about being the middle child. Ideally I'd like more of that, you know? More of what makes you *you*. Don't be afraid to go for it.'

I scribbled her notes down on the piece of paper I had in the back pocket of my jeans. I crossed out bits, and drew arrows to remind me what went where, and when I went into the loo to put my lipstick on I practised my new routine, looking at my watch to check the act was long enough.

And it was all completely academic, because I never managed to deliver my five minutes of jokes.

Twenty-two

The gig was at a pub in Charlotte Street, just off Tottenham Court Road. The street was full of restaurants, and on that hot evening everyone was sitting at outside tables as if London had suddenly been transported to the Med. The pub was buzzing with arty media types. Conversations were spilling out onto the street. There wasn't a spare inch of bar space in the pub, and I had to elbow my way to the front to get some drinks. Even then, it took a while for the bar staff to notice me.

Zoey led the way downstairs to a tiny dark low-ceilinged room full of wooden benches. There was a noisy air-conditioner going full blast but it was still very hot. The room was about half-full. As always, I scanned the audience, even though it had been a while since I'd seen him – it was an automatic routine; an impulse. I'd noticed that Zoey did the same thing, always, when she first entered a venue. She would run her gaze around the audience, looking at each face in turn, before she could properly relax. But obviously she did it for reasons very different from mine. She was just trying to get the measure of her audience. She did it that evening, peering into every nook and cranny, and then she rubbed her hands as if she was satisfied. 'Okay,' she said. 'It's looking good. Now, let's find a seat. You're not on until the second half.'

Zoey had been right about the quality control. There were a couple of quite funny guys, then two or three who were truly bad. One of them, a scrawny ginger guy who only looked about twenty, told us afterwards that it was his first-ever gig, and that he'd only written his material that afternoon. Like me, I thought. Surely I'd be better than him at least? Suddenly I was feeling competitive. The ginger guy asked Zoey what she thought, and she was as cutting as she could be on stage. 'You look like a funny guy,' she said. 'Well, I mean, you're a funny-looking guy. So you're halfway there. People are always gonna laugh when you get on stage. All you need to do now is to make up some jokes, so that you can keep them laughing until the end.'

The whole shambolic night was held together by a couple of compères, a man and a woman, who sang ribald, very funny songs in between each act. It was hot and sticky down there in that dark room, and the night seemed endlessly long. And yet it wasn't long enough. I wanted time to stop for a while, to give me the chance to pull the piece of paper out of my back pocket and read it through again. People kept leaving, pushing past the stage area and through a drooping curtain; more people kept coming in, drinks in hand. I was talking to Zoey, and looking at my watch, and fidgeting in the uncomfortable wooden seat, and then all of a sudden I knew that I was on next.

I sat on the edge of my seat, shaking. I sent bad vibes towards the comic who was on stage at the time, hoping that he'd be so bad that the audience would laugh like drains at my material, from the simple relief that I was better than him. I looked at the back of my hand. On Zoey's advice I'd scribbled a few words there, to remind myself of the order of my jokes. The words had smudged slightly in the heat. I stood up and shook my feet, which had developed pins and needles. I walked around a bit at the back of the room, and I waved my arms like I'd seen Zoey do. The compères came back on and did another song. Any minute now they'd be calling out my name. Or at least, not my name, but the name that Zoey and I had invented for the occasion.

I'd insisted on using a pseudonym. I'd muttered something about not wanting the school to find out. Zoey had been checking something on her Tube map when we discussed it, and she decided I should use the name of a Tube station. 'Dollis Hill!' she said. 'That would be great. Or how about Arnos Grove? That sounds like a name. Oh no, wait. I've got it. Chancery Lane. That sounds so cool.'

We'd compromised. I'd picked two stations close to each other on the map, and taken something from each name, and now I was – for one night only . . .

'Victoria Green!'

The call came. There was supportive but not ecstatic applause from the audience of about twenty or thirty people. I walked quickly up the narrow aisle between the seats, willing the applause to last at least until I got to the stage area. I turned around to face the audience and made myself smile. I had one hand on the microphone stand. I was getting ready to take the mike out of the stand. I was trying to remember what Zoey had drilled into me: 'Take the microphone out, move the stand to one side, at the back of the stage. Take your time. Look at the audience. Get to know them. Then, remember, when you start your last joke, bring the mike stand back. That's the signal to the compère that you've nearly finished.' All of that was going through my head. I was trying to remember my opening line. I was trying to remember my made-up name. I was trying to remember anything at all. And that was when I saw him.

He was there, in the far corner of that dark room. He was there, grinning at me. He had a pint glass in front of him, and although I couldn't see his face very well I could make out a mop of curly hair and very white teeth. He was looking at me; he was winking at me. He was challenging me.

I had to run. I couldn't carry on. I pushed over the microphone in my haste and it clattered to the floor. I muttered something to the audience – something like 'Sorry,' or 'I have to go.' Three other comedians sitting near the side of the stage area had to stand up to let me past, and then I had to push through a couple of rows of seats to get to the exit. I could feel my face burning and bile rising in my throat. I could hear the voice of one of the compères, making some joke about me. The audience laughed and clapped. I tried to block out the sound. I clawed my way through the thick black curtain that was blocking the exit and then there was a door in front of me. There was no handle on the door. I tried pushing it, but it wouldn't move. There was just a tiny metal loop where the handle should be. I put one finger in the loop and tried to pull it towards me. It wouldn't budge. I had to get out. I was frantic. I couldn't think straight. I could feel his breath on the back of my neck. I clawed at the top of the door, where it wasn't fully closed. I managed to get a purchase on it with my fingers. I was about to pull the door open when someone burst through in the other direction and nearly pinned me against the wall.

Thank God. I was out. I ran up the stairs, pushed through the busy pub and out onto the street. There was no air. There were clusters of people sitting at the wooden picnic tables outside the pub, and they were all looking at me. I looked behind me. I couldn't see him. Of course I couldn't see him. He wasn't there. I knew that, but I couldn't make my brain believe it. I turned along an alleyway, leaned my forehead against the brick wall and I threw up the beer I'd drunk earlier. I turned around and leaned my back against the wall. My knees were shaking and there was a pain right in the bottom of my stomach. Zoey was standing there and she was looking at me. 'Are you okay?'

'Yeah. Sorry.'

'Stage fright?'

That would do. That was the only acceptable explanation for my behaviour that I could give her. 'Yeah. I'm really sorry. I feel so stupid.'

'Don't,' she said, pulling her mouth into a strange,

rueful expression. 'It's my fault. I'm the stupid one. I made you do it.'

'No. My fault for saying that I would. I've never had stage fright before, but I just suddenly got really claustrophobic in there. It's so hot. Sorry for causing such a disturbance.'

'Don't worry about it.' Zoey patted me on the shoulder, and looked at me again, really closely, as if she knew what was really going on. 'Seriously, it doesn't matter. It happens to a lot of people.'

Then she pulled a tissue out of her pocket and gently wiped my mouth with it. 'So? What do you want to do? Do you want to get a drink? Somewhere else, I mean. I guess you don't want to go back in there.'

I shook my head. 'No, I don't think so. I think I'd better go home.'

'Okay. Look, I'll come with you, yeah?'

'No. Please. I need to be on my own.'

'You sure?'

'Yes.' It came out snappily. 'Sorry. Look, you go back. I'll see you later in the week. I'll be fine. Honestly.' I wanted to get away from Zoey and her probing green eyes, the eyes that sometimes seemed to see right through me. I wanted to go home, pour myself a glass of wine and lie in the bath until I could persuade myself that everything was okay.

Twenty-three

I had lived with fear for most of my adult life and I knew its ups and downs, its moods, its variations, the way it manifested itself. I knew about low-lying unease, how it could leach life and energy from me with its little physical symptoms, like nausea and upset stomachs. I knew about apprehension, the next stage on the dial. I knew about dread, how it could flood over me, paralysing me like a poisoned dart would. I knew that fear, in all its forms, was cold and remorseless. But what I still didn't know was this: was fear internal or external? What happened first? What was the trigger? Something that happened outside of me, outside of my control? Or something inside me, making me hyper-alert?

Just before my life fell apart, I stood in a car park outside a pub in Southampton, on a still hot summer's evening, and I felt the cold wash of dread. Every hair on my arms and on the back of my neck stood on end. I could feel the heat of the tarmac through the soles of my sandals and yet I was shivering. Was that a premonition of what was to happen later? Did I know? Did I suspect? Had I seen something – unconsciously, apparently unnoticed – that had made me afraid? Did I see a figure out of the corner of my eye in a dark shadow? A movement, a disturbance, a ghost? Or am I imposing false memories on that moment? Maybe the fear I remember actually came later, when it – the thing I'd been dreading – actually happened. Maybe I had felt fine all evening until then. Or maybe I was just picking up on Zoey's apprehension.

I'd never known her so nervous. Early that Saturday evening the M3 was busy. There were caravans and cars with roof-racks piled high with luggage, the back seats packed full of children wearing headphones and playing video games. We were on our way to Southampton for a gig, and I had offered to drive Zoey down there in exchange for petrol money and a meal. It seemed a better choice than spending another evening with Danny quizzing me about my childhood, his new favourite hobby since my parents' party.

Zoey was sitting in the passenger seat, alternately shredding a paper tissue and rubbing her hands up and down her trouser legs. There was some new material she was planning to try out, more stuff to go into her Edinburgh Fringe show. She'd been pale and subdued when I'd picked her up earlier that afternoon. I had never seen her like that, so apprehensive, so scared. She was often nervous, yes, like when she'd spilled the drink on me that first time, but she was usually full of a jittery energy, bouncing around like a boxer in his corner before a bout. That day she was different, so different that I asked her if she was feeling all right. She looked almost green as she answered. 'I hate doing shows out of town,' she said.

'That's all. I don't know where these places are, what they're like. Southampton – I've never been there. For all I know it could be some tiny remote hamlet where they hate Americans.'

It wasn't often that I was less scared than the person with me. It wasn't often that I found myself reassuring someone else. But that day it was my job to calm Zoey down, to tell her that everything would be all right, that there was nothing to be scared of; which was ironic, in view of everything that happened later.

'It'll be fine,' I said. 'Southampton's just a normal town. Well, a city, I think. Just a normal city where people live. Quite big in the scale of things. It's perfectly civilised. It's not some rural backwater. It'll be fine. Don't worry. You'll be great. You always are.'

Using a map I'd printed off the internet, we found the pub quite easily. But as I pulled into the crowded car park I started to wonder if Zoey's fears would be justified. The pub was in a down-at-heel suburb of the city and looked unpromising: a big, squat, grubby-looking mustard-yellow building, with tiny windows covered with posters advertising two meals for the price of one, karaoke, quizzes and a meat raffle. We got out of the car into the warm evening, and the air was sluggish. I'd been hoping for a sea breeze but there wasn't one. There were tables outside the pub and people turned to look at us – well, to look at Zoey, I guess: the frizzy-haired woman in the orange T-shirt and the weird purple wraparound skirt, her feet in bright green Crocs, followed by the neat, ordinary-looking woman in a white shirt and jeans.

A bunch of young lads, pints of lager and bottles of beer in front of them, their huge legs in tracksuit bottoms crammed under the tiny table, leered at us; there were glints of necklaces and stud earrings and menacing eyes as they summed us up in a glance. Older couples, dressed up to the nines, looked at us, noted Zoey's clothes and looked away again. A bunch of girls in denim minis and ballet pumps paid us no attention whatsoever. Just an ordinary pub on an ordinary hot Saturday night in a town anywhere in England: that was what I told myself. But there was something about the air that seemed to bristle with menace. There was something about the air in that car park, something about the atmosphere, that made me feel cold to my bones. Or maybe I'm just imagining that in hindsight.

I locked the car doors and looked across at Zoey. She'd gone white and she had her mouth closed tightly, her lips in a wavy line. 'Jesus,' she said. 'This is going to be a nightmare.'

Zoey was right. The gig was a nightmare. It was a big, rowdy neighbourhood pub and the drinkers were enjoying their Saturday-night beer. The landlady told us that it was the first time they'd tried to put a comedy night on there. The stage was right in the middle of the pub, not in a separate room, not even in a separate area. I gathered with the comedians in a huddle at the bar. They were a bunch of scruffy blokes, as always. Steve was there, the tall guy with the Jesus beard from the pub in Kingston. He hugged Zoey and greeted me warmly. There was a skinny hyperactive bloke with sticking-out ears and a cigarette seemingly glued to his bottom lip. Stand-up comedy was not a glamorous or attractive business. Good-looking guys formed bands, I guessed. The weird-looking ones had to work at making people laugh.

They were telling each other stories about the worst gigs they'd ever played. They talked about heckling and fights and threats of violence, and people invading the stage. They were psyching themselves up for a bad one. 'Are you up for this?' Steve asked Zoey. 'You don't have to, you know. We could call it off if you want to. They don't seem too excited to see us.'

Zoey looked deep in thought. 'Hold on a second,' she said, and then to me, 'C'mon, let's have a look at who we have here.'

We did our usual recce of the crowd. I was checking that there was no one suspicious or sinister, no one who might suddenly turn into Rivers Carillo; she was getting a feel for her audience. It was a big, rambling pub, with nooks and crannies and lots of big groups of friends and drinkers. It was rowdy and it was full to bursting. A lot of alcohol had already been consumed. I didn't know how Zoey's material was going to work with these people. But at least there was no one unexpected there: every single person I could see looked exactly the kind of person you'd expect to see in a pub like that, on a sweltering summer Saturday night.

The MC, the skinny hyperactive guy, took to the stage first and it was awful. Not him; he was funny. But hardly anyone was listening, and those who were were heckling him, stupid heckles like, 'Wanker!' and 'Get off!' and 'You're crap, mate.'

He cut his material short and introduced Zoey. She looked pale, but managed to wink at me before climbing to the stage. She looked like she was climbing up to the scaffold to be beheaded. She tried her best but it was no good. No one was there to listen to comedy. Most were busy drinking. A few blokes took an interest in the fact that it was a woman on stage – one showed his appreciation by stroking his crotch and leering at her, a couple of others shouted, 'Get your tits out!' When it became clear that she was an American, there were a few shouts of 'Go home!' and 'Piss off back to America!'

After about ten minutes on stage, desperately going through her usual routine and getting barely a single laugh, Zoey shrugged and said, 'Well, Southampton, thank you very much for your support. You've been a great audience,' and she walked off stage with a grim smile plastered on her face.

She was even whiter than she'd been before. Steve bought her a drink and said, 'Fucking hell. That was tough. My turn next. Any tips?'

I put my arm round Zoey and told her she'd done well. What else could you say to someone who had just – figuratively – died on stage in a rowdy pub?

There was a ten-minute interval and a lot more gallows humour from the comics, still gathered in their little huddle. And then Steve went on stage to try his hand. I had to admire him. He had balls. He went out fighting. He slagged off Southampton and the pub, and told the drinkers they were a bunch of 'ignorant fuckers'. He shouted and ranted with exceptional, foul-mouthed eloquence. He told the bitterest, filthiest jokes I'd ever heard, almost poetic in their scatological nature. He told a joke about anal sex that was so outrageous that I had to catch my breath, and some of the crowd actually began to laugh. But then the atmosphere turned. Steve talked to one of the guys in the crowd, just asked him his name, nothing more, and suddenly there was a smashing sound and a broken bottle being brandished just inches from Steve's face. The landlady rushed over and stood between Steve and the broken-bottle guy, arms outstretched, cool as anything, as if it happened every night in her pub. Steve walked off stage looking shaken, and then the landlady came across and started apologising, and bunches of ten-pound notes were being handed to the comics.

We couldn't stop laughing as we made our way outside. It was a kind of release of tension. We – Zoey, Steve, Jim the MC and I – leaned against the wall outside and laughed till there were tears in our eyes. Zoey and Steve were both very 'jingly', the word Zoey always used to describe her post-gig mood. They were repeating lines to each other, analysing the performances they'd just done and congratulating each other on surviving it. I chatted to Jim, a sweet, quiet lad who said he was heading home to Portsmouth now, just down the road, because his girlfriend had just had a baby, and he was glad to be getting home earlier than he'd expected. And then Zoey said, 'Can we give Steve a lift back? He lives just round the corner from my place.'

I agreed. It wasn't out of my way, and it seemed as if Zoey had already made him a firm offer. The three of us walked across the car park. Steve stopped to light a cigarette. He and Zoey tagged behind me, still in full debriefing mode, while I strode ahead towards the car. Everything seemed okay. I'd forgotten my fear, my dread, from earlier. Or maybe the sheer comic awfulness of the experience had lifted it. It had been good to have a night out of London, however terrible the gig. We'd survived. Zoey and Steve were pleased with how they'd coped. They'd been paid and they'd got a great story to tell. Everything was fine. And then it wasn't.

There was something white under the windscreen wiper. I froze, but for a split second I let myself believe it was a flyer or a leaflet, for another comedy night or a car-wash business or a second-hand record fair, or for anything else you would get a flyer for. And then I got to the car and I couldn't pretend any more. I knew it was an envelope. A white envelope, tucked under the wiper blade. The kind of envelope I'd seen before. The same kind of envelope that I'd found pushed into my pigeon-hole in the school staffroom.

I needed to act quickly. Zoey and Steve were still some way away; they'd stopped to talk in the middle of the car park while Steve finished his cigarette. They weren't looking in my direction. I leaned over and pulled the envelope out from under the wiper, hoping they wouldn't notice. Last time the envelope had been blank. This time it wasn't. 'To the murdering bitch,' it said, in that same neat handwriting that I'd earlier tried to convince myself belonged to one of my pupils.

I don't know how I managed to drive back to London as if nothing had happened. I guess it was a good thing that Steve was with us. I didn't have to talk to Zoey. I didn't have to try to make conversation. They sat in the back seat together and talked about comedy all the way back. They talked about people I didn't know and had never heard of. They were using comedian-speak, talking about other comics and other venues and using phrases like 'great room' and 'neat reversal', and 'I think he's finally found a way to make his material work' and 'she's really not connecting with audiences at the moment.' They were talking about Edinburgh, too; about the Fringe, and the venues they were going to be playing.

I tried to tune out. I tried to concentrate on the road. I tried counting cars. I told myself that if I saw five, ten, twenty silver cars before the next motorway junction then everything would be all right. I tried to tell myself that if I kept counting cars all the way back, then the envelope that I had quickly crumpled into the back pocket of my jeans would have disappeared by the time I got back to my flat. But it didn't help. That was all I could think about – that white envelope in the back pocket of my jeans. It felt like it was burning a hole in my skin. I wanted to scream at Zoey and Steve, to open the doors and push them out of the car so that I could read the note. The murdering bitch wanted to know what he had to say about her this time.

Zoey told me to drop Steve off with her at her flat in Clapham. They were laughing as they fell out of the car. I think they were about to sleep together. Maybe they were already a couple. I didn't know. I didn't care. I drove home through Kennington and Lambeth, over Waterloo Bridge and on to the Strand, and through the strange leery atmosphere of late Saturday night in central London; past grey university buildings and Georgian terraces full of cheap hotels, towards King's Cross and home. I found somewhere to park. I pulled the letter out of my jeans pocket, rolled it up and held it firmly in my hand. I got back to my flat, locked and bolted the door behind me. I unrolled the envelope from my now-sweaty hand. I pulled out the piece of paper and straightened it. My hands were trembling. It was the same type of paper as before, the same weight, the same lack of grain or watermark; the same small, neat handwriting, the same black ink. This was what it said:

Remember, I'm watching you. Does your new lover know how evil you are?

Twenty-four

This is real. This is really happening. That was all I could think. That was what I kept repeating to myself. I think I even said it out loud. This was really happening. Someone was out there watching me, stalking me, watching where I worked, where I went at night and who I was sleeping with. They had followed me to work; they were even following my car. Someone was working hard to scare me, to threaten me, to squeeze all the joy out of my life. Someone had followed me all the way to Southampton just to leave that note on my windscreen. This was dedication, this was vengeance; this was serious hatred.

And it had been going on for weeks. That thought suddenly struck me, stopped me dead in my tracks as I paced around my tiny flat that Saturday night, that Sunday morning. Dawn was already pinking the sky and I was exhausted but I knew there was no point in going to bed. There was no chance of sleeping. It had been going on for weeks; of course it had. I had been so stupid, so quick to believe that the first note was from one of my pupils. Or had I believed it? Really, deep down in my heart of hearts, had I known it was for real? Had I just tried to fool myself? Had I just pretended that everything was all right? And I'd blundered on, despite that earlier warning. I'd carried on, enjoying myself, making friends, dragging people I loved – and yes, I did love them, both of them, Danny and Zoey – into my own personal nightmare, getting more and more involved; doing everything I'd always told myself I wouldn't do.

He'd been watching me for weeks, the avenger, the letter-writer: all those times in the last few weeks when I'd sensed myself being watched, when I'd sensed someone out there watching me. Maybe he'd been there at that comedy club, watching me as I stood behind the microphone ready to perform. Maybe that had been him, sitting there and grinning at my discomfiture, that figure I'd mistaken for the ghost of Rivers Carillo.

Who? Who was it? Who on earth was doing this to me? I got out my list, my list of things that I was scared of. I pulled my manila file from its place on the bookshelf. I sat down and read both the list and the file right through. Who the hell was it?

It wasn't Rivers Carillo. I knew for certain that it couldn't be him. He was dead, I knew he was. I'd seen his head split open. I'd watched him as he died. I'd seen the life leave his eyes. They found his body. They identified it as him. So this couldn't be him. He was definitely dead. All those times when I thought I saw him, I knew really that it was just my guilty conscience playing games with my mind. It wasn't him I should be scared of. It was someone else, someone who knew I'd killed him. Rivers Carillo was just a ghost. I could chase him away any time I wanted to. This was something much scarier. This was a real person doing this to me. Someone I didn't know; someone who knew me intimately.

Rivers Carillo had had a wife, a wife who lived somewhere in the Midwest, somewhere in Indiana. A university town somewhere in Indiana; I didn't know which one. His wife never met me. She never saw me, she probably never knew about me. I was almost certain of that. But maybe she suspected. Maybe she suspected that her husband had lovers, that he'd been seeing someone in San Francisco that summer. Maybe she'd found out who.

Who would have told her? Who knew for sure about Rivers Carillo and me? Joanna, my sister's godmother: she knew. She was one of Rivers's lovers, I was sure of it. She knew about us, or she guessed about us. I was pretty sure of that, too. That was why she'd sent me those newspaper clippings about Rivers's body being found. But why would she have told Rivers's wife about me? What would she have had to gain? No, it couldn't have been Joanna. And besides, she was long dead. She'd died of cancer about ten years ago. There was no way she could have had any connection with this.

I had a list of people who'd seen me that day, the day I killed him. There was a bus driver who'd driven me back to the city. There was the woman at the art gallery, the museum, who'd let me use the toilet. There was the guy at the coffee shop in the Marina District, who may or may not have seen me tearing up that book of Rivers's poetry. Maybe they'd suspected something when they'd heard about the missing man, or when they'd heard about his body being found. One of them might have remembered the teenage girl they saw that day. But there was no way they would have known my name, no way they could have found it out. It couldn't be one of them.

Rivers Carillo had friends in San Francisco. One of them owned a bookstore in North Beach. I met Rivers there a couple of times. Maybe his friend had seen us together, seen us exchange a few brief words. Maybe Rivers had told him all about me. And then there was the friend who lent us his houseboat in Sausalito – the houseboat where we made love that first time. Rivers must have told him about me. He must have told him about this cute English girl he was trying to seduce. Maybe that friend had seen me. Maybe Rivers had pointed me out to him. Maybe he knew my name. Maybe the friend knew that Rivers and I were together on that last day, the day he disappeared. And maybe he'd been looking for me all this time and he had just found me. Found me somehow; I didn't know how.

I thought back and tried to remember Vicky Barron's description of the man who'd handed her the note: about my age, nondescript; tall, probably. Dark, maybe. American? She didn't know, didn't think so, wasn't sure. She never answered that question properly. About my age. Rivers Carillo might have had children. I didn't know for sure.

I made myself a cup of tea. I washed my face, combed my hair and pulled it back. I stood and looked out of the window for a while, watching Sunday dawn across the London rooftops.

I tried the puzzle from a different direction. The night

before – who'd known I was going to be there, at that pub? Could someone really have followed my car all the way through London and down the M3 without me noticing? Or did they somehow know I was going to be there? Zoey knew, of course. Could she, would she have had the time to dash out at some point during the evening and put the letter under the windscreen-wiper blade? Had there been a moment when I'd lost sight of her last night? Had she gone to the loo at any point? Could it be her? Could she be Rivers Carillo's daughter? I did some sums in my head. It was a calculation I'd done before, but I wanted to check. Yes, Zoey could be his daughter, just, if he'd fathered her at nineteen or maybe lied about his age. There was a slight resemblance – something pugnacious about the face and jawline. But Vicky Barron had said it was a *man* who gave her the note, that first note. So maybe Zoey had an accomplice? Who? Steve? He was tall and dark, about my age. But Vicky had struggled to describe the man. Surely even an unobservant fifteen-year-old would have mentioned the beard and the long hair. And besides, Zoey had passed my test – my casual mention of Rivers Carillo, just dropped into the conversation. Her response had seemed innocent and unknowing.

Tall, dark, about my age, not distinctive; no American accent. A name kept coming to mind, a name I didn't want to say. Danny Fairburn. Danny. No, no. It couldn't be. Not Danny. I'd tested him. He'd passed the test. I'd mentioned San Francisco, looked for a reaction and had got none. It couldn't be Danny. But he was the right age. Danny was, I knew, thirty-two. We'd joked about him being my toyboy. He could be Rivers Carillo's son. His colouring was right, although he didn't look much like him otherwise. What about his non-reaction when I'd tested him? But he'd have to be a good actor, wouldn't he, to gain my trust, to feign a relationship with me? And if he was that good an actor, he would have trained himself not to react to questions like that. Maybe he was a sleeper, deep cover; a sleeper pretending to be a mild-mannered English music buff and local authority housing officer when he was in fact an American avenging angel. No, no. I shook my head with relief. It couldn't be Danny. Of course it couldn't. He had already been living in his flat when I'd moved here. He'd lived here for months, before I'd even decided to move, before my last flat had even started to feel unsafe. He hadn't known I was coming to live here; he couldn't have planned it. It couldn't be Danny, thank God.

And also, of course it wasn't him. The note, the second note, had mentioned my new lover. There seemed to be some threat to tell him what I'd done. Thank God. It wasn't Danny. I was more relieved at this conclusion than I could say.

Tall, dark, about my age; someone who wished me harm. An ex-boyfriend? One of the grand total of three semi-serious boyfriends, not counting Danny, that I'd had in my adult life so far? But no, that was stupid, a complete dead end. How would they have known about Rivers Carillo? Why would they call me 'murdering bitch'? I thought again, back to San Francisco. I remembered the young guys that Joanna kept introducing me to; those young guys around my age, those guys she made me go out with, the ones who were supposed to take me off her hands. Elliot, Jonas, Jason: I could vaguely remember their names, some of them. One of them might have met Rivers Carillo at some point. Most of them had been to at least one of those late dinners in Joanna's basement kitchen, those dinners where guests sat around talking about poetry and music and art, and I was supposed to chat to my escort for the night. And sometimes Rivers Carillo was there. Had one of them, one of my young escorts, seen something – a touch, a smile, a wink – something that told them that Rivers and I were involved? Had one of them seen us together elsewhere: in the basement food court at Macy's, the cable-car turnaround on Market Street, the bus out to Golden Gate Park on that fateful day?

It was a stretch, a huge stretch, but nothing else seemed to make sense to me. But why would they do this to me? Why would they want to take vengeance? The new note, the second note, had mentioned my 'new lover'. Did the implied threat mean it was from someone who considered themselves to be an old lover of mine? Again, I was stretching, trying to make the pieces fit. And then I remembered something. One of them – Elliot, was it? – had liked me more than I'd liked him. He'd wanted to see me again and I'd said no. I'd turned him down, and I'd done it in my thoughtless eighteen-year-old way. I'd turned him down in an offhand manner. I might even have laughed at him. I remember thinking, *Why would I want to go out with you when I have Rivers Carillo?* Was that it?

Was this some kind of long-delayed vengeance for a thoughtless, callous laugh?

But if so – and I knew I was clutching at straws here; I knew it only made a tiny bit more sense than any other explanation I'd come up with – why now? And how had he found me?

When the first note had arrived, I'd Googled Rivers Carillo's name, trying to see what had changed, what could possibly have sparked that letter. But it suddenly struck me that I'd been doing precisely the wrong thing. If someone was trying to hunt me down, then *I* was the one *they*'d be Googling. Maybe there was something new about me out there. Maybe I'd done something to make myself more visible. Maybe they had only just found Lizzie Stephens.

I had always tried to keep my internet presence to the bare minimum. The kids at school were all using MySpace and Facebook and something called Bebo, and they kept nagging me to get involved, as if I might have a desire to spread my name and picture all over the World Wide Web. There was, as far as I knew, just one picture of me on-line. It was on my school's website. I'd tried to avoid having my picture taken for the site but I ran out of excuses, so instead I put on the glasses that I was supposed to use for reading, and I combed my hair forward over my face so I was as unrecognisable as possible. It said 'Miss B. Stephens' under the picture, and even my mother wouldn't have recognised me.

I had got into the habit of Googling my name regularly, just to check. Or rather, I Googled 'Lizzie Stephens', once a month at least. The last time I'd tried it was before that first note had arrived. All I'd got were a couple of hits from some Victorian murder trial that featured a servant girl with the same name as me and lots of stuff from genealogy sites. I went over to my desk and turned my computer on. I went to make another cup of tea, and then went back to my desk. I clicked on the Internet Explorer icon, and went to Google. Hands shaking, I typed 'Lizzie Stephens' and waited, expecting the same old links to come up. But this time it was different. The third link on the first page took me somewhere that made me feel cold all over. It was a picture of me, right there on the internet for everyone to see. It was me – it was Lizzie – with my hair all scrunched and curly, in my full late-1980s teenage finery. And just below, something that completely demolished my secret identity, such as it was. It was a picture of me now, a relaxed, informal family photograph, my hair off my face, no glasses, with my usual little bit of make-up, almost smiling at the camera. I looked utterly recognisable. All those years, all that careful reinvention, and my kid sister Jem had blown it with just one entry in her blog.

Twenty-five

I was sitting at a table outside the café in Russell Square, trying to gather my thoughts. I had my baseball cap rammed down over my face and a copy of one of the London free papers to hide behind. I probably looked ridiculous but I didn't care. I was taking sensible precautions, something I should have started doing years ago. I'd chosen this open space because it felt safer than somewhere enclosed. There were plenty of escape routes, plenty of places I could run to if I felt threatened. It was the first time I'd ventured out of my flat since getting that second note. I'd spent Sunday indoors with my phone turned off, avoiding calls from my parents and Danny's ring at the door, and his calls through the letter box. I'd watched old black and white films on Channel Four and tried to empty my head. Eventually I went to bed and tried to sleep, but even when I was asleep my dreams were full of faceless men following me.

I left my flat and took a complicated route to Russell Square. On the way, I popped into the supermarket at the Brunswick Centre and wandered around the aisles, checking that I hadn't been followed, trying to lose anyone who might be tailing me. I went into the toilets there and I changed my T-shirt and put the baseball cap on. Even as I did it, I felt ridiculous. It felt as if I was in one of those paranoia thrillers from the 1970s – *Three Days of the Condor* or *The Parallax View*. I felt stupid doing it, but also stupid that I hadn't started taking precautions like this a long time ago.

From my vantage point outside the café I could see everyone who was entering and leaving, and all the other customers at all the other outside tables. There was a middle-aged couple at the neighbouring table, the man slim with thinning grey hair and heavy black glasses, the woman in some kind of ethnic dress, the pair of them absorbed in their conversation and their lattes. There was a yummy mummy of about my age in a Boden skirt that was plastered with brightly coloured appliquéd flowers. She had two kids, one a little boy of about four, the other a pink-clad girl a couple of years older, and they were running in hyperactive circles around the tables and the chairs. The woman caught me looking at her over the top of my newspaper and she smiled a weary smile. It was probably supposed to be a smile of sympathy at the sticky hot weather, or maybe because she thought I understood her.

Then there was a man alone, a man with dark hair. Tallish, from what I could tell by the way he was sitting. He was sitting there in a white shirt and a pair of suit trousers, his jacket flung over one of the other seats. He had loosened his tie and rolled his sleeves up. He had dark glasses on – very dark glasses. It was impossible to see his eyes behind the lenses. He was in his late twenties, perhaps, loose-limbed and arrogant of posture. He was sprawled in his chair. There was something relaxed yet attentive about the way he was sitting. There was a cold drink – Coke, I think – on the table in front of him. He could have been staring right at me; it was impossible to tell because his shades were so dark. He could have been watching me, hiding in plain sight. He could have been Rivers Carillo's son, or the son of an old friend of his, or Elliot or Jason or Jonas, or someone, anyone, who knew what I had done and hated me for it. Someone who knew what I looked like now, because he'd seen me on my sister's blog.

I'd printed off the page and I had it with me now. The blog was called *It's All True – the story of a girl called Jem*. There was a little square picture of her, half her face, one lens of the heavy glasses that she liked to wear. The piece about me was under a heading that said 'Tell us about someone that you used to know.' It seemed to be a question or a challenge set by someone, maybe another blogger, or whoever ran the particular website, network, whatever it was called. Underneath the old photograph of me, Jem had written, 'My sister Lizzie Stephens, when she was seventeen. She was seven years older than me, and was the best sister ever. She was fun and outrageous and she let me try on her clothes and her make-up. We used to dance to songs on the radio and pretend we were pop stars. She was my best friend.'

Then there was the photograph of me now, that snapshot taken last Christmas. I looked like I normally did: neat, pleasant, ordinary. Jem had written, 'Just when I needed her most, Lizzie went away. Beth replaced her.

Beth's a schoolteacher in North London. She's perfectly nice and everything, but I really miss Lizzie.'

At the top of the piece there was a little symbol of a lock, open; next to it, the words 'viewable by anyone'. The whole world could read this touching piece and look at the pictures. It would have been a heartbreaking little story of sisterly love, if only it hadn't scared me so much.

Jem was walking towards me, across Russell Square. I would have known her walk anywhere. She had scoliosis as a kid. Well, I guess she still had it. I don't think you stop having it. She was eight or nine when they diagnosed it, and she had to wear a brace for months on end. She was supposed to, anyway, but she didn't. She ended up having to have surgery. There was some kind of bone graft from her hip. There was a metal rod in her spine now. She always said that it was fine, that it didn't hurt a bit, but it had given her a strangely jaunty walk: uneven, as if she was exaggeratedly swinging her hips.

When I rang Jem, asking her to meet me, she suggested some place in Soho. I insisted that we meet here, on my home ground; somewhere out in the open where I felt comparatively at home, comparatively safe. Somewhere where I wouldn't stick out like a sore thumb. It was Jem who looked like the odd one out. She was wearing those same huge black sandals that looked like car tyres strapped to her feet, cropped trousers and a tiny, torn vest top decorated with some kind of cartoon. I noticed that the tattoos that had long adorned her shoulders were now snaking down towards her elbows. When she saw me she smiled, and despite the three rings through her bottom lip and the thick-framed glasses that dominated her face, her smile made her look about twelve years old.

'What's with the hat?' she said as she sat down. 'Are you in disguise or something?'

I didn't answer. I pulled the cap off. She was right. It was too obvious. 'I found this on the internet,' I said, and showed her the printed page that I'd brought with me. As I did so, I mentally kicked myself. I hadn't even said hello to my own sister. I'd just rudely launched straight in.

Jem didn't seem bothered. 'You found my blog!' She sounded thrilled.

'It really upset me.' I was trying to keep my voice as neutral as possible. This was still my sweet little kid sister, who I didn't want to hurt.

'My blog?' She was peeling an orange that she had dug out of her huge canvas courier bag, and the juice squirted onto the piece of paper.

'This piece. The photos. All that stuff about me.'

'Why?' She frowned at me, not so thrilled now.

'Why what?'

Jem sucked her orange. 'Why did it upset you?'

'Because you can't just put stuff on the internet like that. It's my life. It's private.'

'Is this why you wanted to meet up?' she asked. 'To tick me off? To come the heavy big sister and tell me what I can and can't do?' Her voice had turned chilly.

'Sorry,' I said. 'I didn't mean to sound like that. I didn't mean to jump straight into it like that.'

'Sure you did. It's what you always do. You specialise in being abrupt. Well, when you're not walking out on people or pretending to have migraines, that is.'

'Jem . . .' That really hurt. She'd been so sweet to me when I was ill at my parents' party. This wasn't going how I'd planned.

'Look,' she said. 'I'm sorry this upset you . . .' and she pointed at the printout from her blog. 'But you need to know that it really upset me too.'

'What do you mean?'

'I mean what I said there, in that post. I needed you. I had that operation, and I had to wear that horrid brace, and Mum and Dad were on my back the whole time about it, nagging me. And all I wanted was to hang out with you. With Lizzie. And do all the stuff we used to do. I wanted things to be normal, and they weren't, because you were, like, this whole other person. You suddenly became an alien pod-person.'

Behind her glasses I could just see the start of tears in her eyes. I was stunned. It had never occurred to me that my eleven-year-old kid sister would have noticed the change that strongly. 'Sorry,' I said. 'I didn't realise.'

'I thought it was because of me.'

Despite the tattoos and piercing I could still make out the vulnerable little girl.

'It wasn't. It's . . . complicated.'

Jem stuck her beringed bottom lip out at me. 'That's you all over,' she said. 'Things are always "complicated" with you. Like there's this big mystery that you've invented. "It's complicated." It's probably the thing you say most. Well, after "Sorry, have to go, I have a migraine." Or, "Marking." Lizzie, everyone's life is complicated, not just yours. Haven't you realised that yet?'

I wanted to cry. But instead I squared my shoulders and I steered the conversation back to the subject that mattered most to me. 'When did you put this on there, this piece about me?'

'I don't know.' She seemed relieved that I hadn't reacted to her outburst. 'There should be a date on it somewhere.' She pulled the sheet of paper towards her, pointed at a tiny figure with her index finger. 'There you are. Third of July, at 11.57 p.m. Does that help in some way?'

It helped. At least, it helped me to know that this must have been what had sparked the letters. The timing fitted, perfectly. The first note had arrived just a week later. 'The thing is, Jem, I really need you to take this stuff off the internet. I don't want photos of me out there for everyone to see.' As I said this, I realised that of course it was already too late; that whoever had been looking for me had found me. But still, I didn't want it there any more.

Jem scowled. 'It's my blog.'

'And anyone can read this. It's personal stuff, about our family. How would you feel if I put a picture on the internet of you when you were five, saying "This is my cute little sister Jemima Stephens," and then a picture of you now? You wouldn't like it, would you?'

She thought about this for a while. She ate a couple more segments of her orange. She swayed from side to side in her seat, weighing something up. Then, abruptly, 'Tell me your secret.'

'What?'

'Tell me. Tell me why you changed. I've always wondered. And don't just say, "It's complicated."'

I looked at her, and tried to make out the expression in her eyes behind those glasses. I picked up the printout of her blog and I folded it in half, lengthways, very precisely, scoring the fold with my thumbnail. I folded it in quarters, and then into eighths. I was warding off the temptation to blurt. It would have been so easy. What an easy person to tell. She would have been cool with it. Jem was pretty much unshockable. She wouldn't have told anyone else in the family about it; she wouldn't have reported me. But she wouldn't have been able to keep it a secret. She'd probably have been proud of it. She'd have posted it on her blog. She'd have drawn a manga-style cartoon strip about it. She'd have told a stranger in a bar about her cool, evil sister. She'd have put the information out there, one way or another. And there was another reason I couldn't have told her. She was my kid sister, and she wasn't as tough as she thought she was. I didn't want to sweep her into my nightmare. And so I lied to her.

'When I went to San Francisco, I met this guy.' True, so far. Jem was listening intently. 'We got involved.' Still true. 'It all went wrong. It became abusive. He hurt me.' Almost true, if you looked at it figuratively. 'I was scared of him. And I'm still scared. He threatened me; he said he'd come looking for me.' A total lie, but Jem believed me, as far as I could tell.

'Shit, Beth. That was aeons ago.'

'I know. I can't help it. Please get rid of those photos.'

'Have you ever talked to someone? The police?' She thought for a moment. 'Nah, they'd be no good. Never are, when it comes to this kind of stuff. Maybe you should get, like, counselling.' She ate another bit of orange. 'Have you told Sarah?'

'No. Why?'

She shrugged. 'Because Sarah's a grown-up. She'd know what to do. Shit, Beth, this is huge. This is unbelievable. I don't mean I don't believe you. I do, course I do. I mean, I believe that you're scared. Jesus, it's freaky. After all this time this guy's still scaring you? What can I do to help?'

'Please, Jem. Take those pictures off your website. And don't do anything like that again.'

'But you can't imagine that this guy's out there, just, like, randomly Googling your name, planning to track you down?'

'I think he might be.'

'Shit. That is fucking out of control.'

I thought I had finally got through to her. She put her hand on top of mine and patted it. I clasped her hand in mine, and we held them like that for a while, something we hadn't done in years.

'Please take those pictures off, Jem. And please don't tell anyone what I've told you. *Anyone*.'

'No problem,' she said. 'I'll tell you what I'll do. I'll lock that blog entry, make it friends only, okay? That means it won't turn up on a search engine.'

I guessed that was the best I could hope for.

'And call me – yeah? – if anything weird happens. Shit. This is . . . complicated.' And Jem gave me a half-grimace, half-grin. She started to walk away across the square and then she turned around suddenly and called to me. 'Sorry, Beth, something I meant to say – I really liked Danny. Top bloke. It was great to meet him the other weekend. Sexy nerd boy – my favourite type of man. He's cracked on you, by the way. Really into you, big time. Don't screw this one up, will you?'

Danny.

Does your new lover know how evil you are?

What on Earth was I going to do about Danny?

Twenty-six

The man in the white shirt with the dark glasses had gone, and there was an elderly couple sitting at that café table now. I hadn't even noticed him leave. I hadn't kept my guard up. I'd been completely unobservant. For all my precautions I realised I was useless at being a fugitive. Whoever was watching me was no doubt too assiduous, too professional, too relentless to be fooled by a baseball cap and a change of T-shirt. He knew where I worked and he knew where I went and when, and presumably he knew where I lived. It was useless, pointless trying to escape. I was exhausted, sick to death of the whole thing.

I stood in the paved circle in the centre of Russell Square, surrounded by the fountains, and looked around me. I'd chosen the park because it was an open space with plenty of escape routes. But there were tall buildings all around: the elaborate façade of the hotel at one side of the square; rows of tall Georgian terraces full of offices and university departments on the other sides. Everywhere I looked there were windows glinting down on me, and behind every window there could have been someone watching me, someone who had me in their sights. What was the point of trying to run or hide?

Whatever they had planned for me, I might as well face up to it.

I threw my baseball cap in the nearest bin. I stood there in the centre of the square and I flung my arms out as if to say, 'Here I am. Come and get me,' and I spun round so that every side of the square could see my face. If a sniper had shot me then, I think I would have been relieved. What else could I do? I was thirty-five years old and I was scared of shadows and ghosts. This had gone on too long. I would be brave and stoic and open. But first I had something horrible to do: I had to dump Danny.

Does your new lover know how evil you are?

It was an ambiguous threat. At the very least, my stalker seemed to be threatening to tell Danny what I'd done. Or he was challenging me to tell Danny first before he – my stalker – got to him. And there was a chance that he was threatening something worse; that he was threatening to take revenge by doing something awful to Danny. It reminded me of something you'd hear in a gangster movie. The villain would make a comment about someone's wife or family, a seemingly harmless comment, but it would be accompanied by a creepy smile and you'd know that it was a veiled threat. And although one half of my brain told me that this was absurd, that this couldn't really be happening, the other half told me that the note behind the windscreen wiper was tangible and chilling. Anyone prepared to follow me all the way to Southampton wouldn't stop at writing anonymous notes.

The threat – although ambiguous – was very real. I had two choices. I could tell Danny the whole story, or I could end our relationship for good. That very day. As soon as he got home from work that evening, I would have to go round to his place and try to extricate myself from his life.

I sat in the Great Court of the British Museum to try to work things out. I wasn't sure whether I was hiding in plain sight or playing catch-me-if-you-can. It was either the safest, most comforting place that I could think of to come, or it was dangerously open. One slight, unobtrusive, nondescript brown-haired woman in faded jeans and a grey T-shirt could easily get lost among the crowds of tourists in that light, airy courtyard. On the other hand, if my stalker was following me, keeping close tabs on me, then he'd have no trouble finding me in that big white space. All I know was that I craved openness and busyness. I didn't want to hide away in the shadows any more. I was sitting at one of the long white communal tables in the café area, as close to the corner as I could get. From where I sat I could see people coming and going in two directions, as they strolled around the huge domed curved area in the centre of the court, where the gift shop was, where the Reading Room of the British Library used to be. I was making my cup of coffee last as long as possible, trying to fill the empty day; trying to work out exactly what I should do.

I couldn't tell Danny what I'd done. No way. He was too public-spirited, too good. He'd make me go to the police and tell them everything – not just about the letters, but about how I'd killed Rivers Carillo. He'd hate me for what I'd done. It would be the end of our relationship anyway, so what would be the point? The only answer was to break things off with Danny. I had to do it in such a way that there could be no mistake. It was the third time I'd made this resolution and the second time I'd tried to carry it through. Last time, as we'd driven home from my parents' house, it hadn't taken. He hadn't listened to me properly, and I hadn't explained myself clearly enough. This split would have to be decisive. The watcher, the letter-writer, my secret stalker would have to know that it was all over. I couldn't risk going out with Danny again.

How could I break things off with Danny without hurting him? I knew I should have thought of that before I'd slept with him that very first time. I did think of it later, after the first note arrived, but then I had put it out of my mind. I had let my emotions, my need for comfort and security, overrule my common sense. I had let my heart rule my head. I had let myself drop my guard, had relaxed and enjoyed myself. How had I dared?

What was I going to do? Lie to Danny and tell him that I didn't like him in that way? Use one of the old clichés? Tell him I loved him like a brother? Like a friend? Tell him that I was very fond of him but it just wasn't the right time? Tell him that it wasn't him, it was me? That would actually be true, for once. In spite of myself, I couldn't help smiling. I was thinking of a line in Zoey's routine, where she talked about how she dumped her husband with the line 'It's not me, it's you.' It always got a delayed laugh, as people worked out exactly what she had said. Once I'd managed to break things off with one sort-of boyfriend just by ignoring him, by not answering his calls – or anyone's calls – for a couple of weeks. I couldn't do that with Danny. He lived too close. I had broken things off with Julian by doing a midnight flit, almost literally. I'd left the flat one evening while he was out, with what I could carry in my car, and I didn't leave a forwarding address. But I was getting so tired of this, this constant running and hiding.

People were coming and going, milling around the Great Court. It was getting close to lunchtime and the café tables were filling up. A big, noisy Italian family with several kids had invaded my personal space. One of the staff, who was wiping the café tables, had just given me the glare, the one that says: 'If you've finished with that coffee, can you leave and make room for someone else?'

I noticed a man who seemed to be watching me. A tall man, bearded, fiftyish – a hippie type in a tie-dyed T-shirt and long baggy shorts. Grey hair in a ponytail. He was in the far corner, in the other café area on the other side of the court, and he seemed to be staring in my direction. I didn't know how long he'd been there, and I didn't know why I hadn't noticed him before. He could have been the stalker. He was the right age, the right type, to have been a friend of Rivers's. Jesus, if only I knew who I was supposed to be afraid of.

In the end, it wasn't quite as difficult as I'd imagined. Danny was still in his work clothes when I rang his doorbell. His top button was undone, his tie loosened. He had a bottle of beer in his hand and he smiled when he saw me. He beckoned me in. And then he stopped smiling. He'd seen the ominous look on my face. 'Ah,' he said. 'You're about to break up with me, aren't you? I hate this bit.'

'Sorry.' I raised my hands in a gesture of hopelessness and let them flop down again.

'Oh well. Can't say that I didn't see it coming. I guess you warned me often enough.'

'Sorry.'

'Please stop saying that. If you're sorry, you wouldn't be breaking up with me, would you?' He sat down on his sofa and took a swig of his beer. I just stood there, feeling awful. 'Is there a particular reason?' he asked.

'It's just all getting a bit too intense for me . . .' I made my voice sound shaky and sad, which wasn't difficult. It was exactly how I felt.

Danny gave a sudden, surprised laugh. 'Ha! I wish.'

'What do you mean?'

'Well, honestly, it couldn't have been less intense if we'd tried. We've had – what? – seven, eight dates? I know you hate commitment and all that stuff. I wasn't asking for that. I just wanted to be friends, and go out sometimes, and maybe sleep together if it felt right. What do they call it these days? Friends with benefits: that's the phrase. It wasn't like I was asking you to marry me or anything. I couldn't have put less pressure on you if I'd tried.' He was warming to his theme now; not so much angry as annoyed. 'You know, I'd just like it placed on record that you were the one who invited me to meet the family. You were the one who stepped it up a notch.'

'I know. Sorry.'

'Stop saying that!' He half-laughed again. 'Christ, what is it about me? And if you say, "It's not you, it's me" I shall probably hit you.'

I said nothing. I just stood there looking awkward and ashamed. Danny showed me to the door. 'Still mates?' he said, giving the word 'mates' its full force. I guessed he meant drinking buddies, music buddies, friends. I gave a non-committal nod and mouthed 'sorry' one more time. I hated myself for hurting him. I hated myself for putting myself in a position where I had to hurt him.

Twenty-seven

Zoey was in her frantic edgy mood, the mood she'd been in when I'd driven her to Southampton just a few days before. She was sitting on my settee with a glass of wine in her hand, tilting the glass backwards and forwards so vigorously that I was worried she'd spill it. She was heading for Edinburgh the next day. She was flying up there, ready to start her show the following day. It was her big adventure and I knew she was nervous about it, but this seemed to be something more than nerves.

We were supposed to have gone out for a meal that night. She'd invited me to join her and Steve and a bunch of whichever of her comedy friends hadn't gone off to Edinburgh yet. But she'd called me earlier to cancel. The dinner was off, she'd told me. She'd sounded weird on the phone – more downbeat than I'd ever heard her. 'Listen, can I come to your place instead?'

'To my flat?' People didn't come round to my flat. I didn't really know what to do with guests. There was nothing for them to look at or do. I didn't like having intruders in there. I guess I was afraid they'd start rummaging through my bookshelves or asking me too many questions about my lack of stuff. It always made me feel on edge and made my flat feel less safe, less of a haven. But I couldn't think of a good excuse to give Zoey. She was my friend. I'd been round to her flat, several times. How could I have said no? 'Um, okay. When? Why?'

'In an hour or so? My place is a nightmare. I'm packing. I have clothes strewn everywhere. I don't want to be here at the moment. I need to escape. I need to talk to you.'

'Steve and I have split up,' Zoey said, still swilling her wine around the glass. 'We had a stupid fight and now he says he doesn't want to see me any more, and I'm way more upset than I thought I'd be.'

'So if you've split up, I guess that means you were going out with him, then. Because I wasn't sure.'

That made her smile, for some reason. 'Yeah,' she said. 'I got involved. Hadn't meant to do that. Not at this point.'

It was like listening to myself talking about Danny. 'So why did you split up? What was the fight about?'

Zoey put the wineglass down on the floor. She closed her eyes and opened them again. 'Life. The past. Things we've done. Things we haven't done.' She waved her arms around vaguely. 'You know what it's like.'

I nodded. I watched her. There was something else she wanted to say, something she was finding difficult. She picked up the wine again and took a gulp from her glass. She fiddled with a strand of her hair, stretching the curl out and watching it spring back into shape. 'He got clingy. Overprotective. You'd be surprised. He does all that foul-mouthed routine on stage but really he's a mensch.'

'A mensch?'

'A good guy. A good, decent guy. Too good.' Still carrying the wineglass, she walked across to the window and looked out. 'This is an amazing view.'

'Yeah. I love it.'

'How long have you lived here?'

'About eighteen months.'

'It's a great apartment. Airy. Minimalist. I wish I could get my place looking like this. But I'm no good at throwing things out.'

Zoey walked around, looking at things. I held my breath, willing her to move away from my bookshelf. She picked up one of the CDs that Danny had made me and browsed the song titles. 'Neat,' she said. And then, out of nowhere, 'Come to Edinburgh with me.'

It sounded more like a command than an invitation. 'Me? What, like, for the Fringe?'

'Yeah. Tomorrow. Come with me.'

I didn't know what to say.

'Shit, sorry. There I am assuming that you've got no plans for the summer. That's rude of me. You're probably going away somewhere really cool.'

'No, no. It's just unexpected, that's all.'

'Look, I'm renting an apartment there, what's called a tenement flat, and Steve was going to share the place with me. And, what with all this, he's decided to stay with some friends of his instead, so I'm left on my own. There's a spare bed. Well, some kind of fold-out bed, anyway. And it'd be much more fun with someone to share the place with me. Come up. It'll be so cool. We can hang out and go and see shows together. You'll have fun. Please?'

I wanted to say yes straight away. It seemed so perfect. It was a way I could get out of London. It was a way of avoiding Danny. It was a way of running away. It seemed like the ideal solution. Except that I was fed up with running away. I didn't want to run any more. I was trying to be brave. I was trying to persuade myself that I should stay and face the music.

'I don't know, Zoey. Can I think about it? Can I let you know?'

'Sure. Call me. You can just get the train up some day if you want to. It's easy.'

She sat down again, and she rubbed her thighs nervously. She felt for something in her pocket. 'Look, if you're not coming, can I give you these?' She was holding a ring with a couple of keys.

'What are they for?'

'They're the keys to my flat in Clapham. Just in case . . . you know, maybe something will happen and you'll need to get access.'

Maybe something will happen. That sent a shiver down my spine. I looked at Zoey very closely. She was trying to say something to me. She knew something. And she was trying to tell me that she knew. She knew I was in danger. She was trying to give me a hiding place. The tenement in Edinburgh or the flat in Clapham: either way, she was trying to give me somewhere safe to stay. But how did she know? Had she guessed from my behaviour? Had she seen me take that letter from the windscreen of my car? Had she known what was written in it? How did she know? *What* did she know?

I took the keys from her and jangled them in my hand. I stuck them in my back pocket. 'Thank you,' I said, thinking about the lovely safe womb-like cosiness of Zoey's little room. 'I'll look after them, okay?'

'Cool.' And again, I thought Zoey was about to say something, but there was a sudden noise, like someone at the door. 'What's that?' she said. But I was already half-way up the hallway towards my front door. I was already looking at the white envelope sitting on my mat. I was already reading the words on the envelope, the words that said 'To the murdering bitch' in handwriting that I already knew too well. I was already stuffing the envelope into my jeans pocket as Zoey came to check. 'What was that?' she said again.

'Nothing,' I said. 'Just a kid knocking and running away, I think. It happens all the time.' I opened the door and looked around, searching for a sign of my stalker. Would I finally get to see him, to find out who it was? The grey concrete walkway stretched around the four sides of the courtyard, five storeys below. There were pillars and doorways, and a hallway on each of the four sides leading to the lifts and the stairwells. In the low sun, half of the building was in deep shadow, the other half still in bright sunlight. I stared towards the shadows, wondering if that was a movement I could see. More than anything I wanted to chase after him. But Zoey was standing next to me, staring at me with those green eyes. It seemed as if she could see inside my head. *She knows*, I thought. *She knows*. I was sure of it. She definitely knew something. She was staring at me, her eyes boring into me, and she wanted to ask me and she wanted me to tell her. I cut in quickly, before she could say anything else. 'So, what time are you leaving tomorrow morning?'

And the tension passed. 'Early. You're right, I need to get going.' She kissed me on the cheek. 'Please come,' she said again. 'It'll be fun. Call me.'

My trembling hands opened another white envelope. My trembling hands pulled out another sheet of white paper. It was the same kind of paper and the same small, neat handwriting. This was what it said: *I told you I was watching you*.

Twenty-eight

Rivers Carillo was always writing. He was a poet. If you were to ask him what he did, that's what he'd say. He carried with him a small black hardback notebook, pocket-sized, with a piece of black elastic that kept the book shut. I've seen notebooks like it since, for sale in bookshops. They're called Moleskines. They cost more than a notebook should, but people seem to buy them anyway. Sometimes Rivers would take the book out of his pocket and write in it, using a silver propelling pencil that he held very close to the tip, which made his writing tiny and square and almost illegible. I know: I used to try to read it over his shoulder or upside-down, but he'd hide what he was writing, putting his arm across it like a swotty kid in an exam.

I could picture him writing. There would be a look into the middle distance, a narrowing of the eyes, a half-smile, sometimes a nod, and out would come the notebook – *scribble scribble scribble* – and then he'd put it away again, twist the pencil shut so the lead was hidden, and look at me with a surprised expression, like he'd forgotten I was ever there. Sometimes I'd ask him to read me what he'd written but he never would. He would just shake his head enigmatically and resume whatever conversation we'd been having before the muse struck.

I saw him give a poetry reading once. He hadn't invited me. He didn't know I was going to be there. He hadn't even told me about it. I saw his name, one on a list of several poets, on a leaflet that was lying on Joanna's kitchen table. I picked up the leaflet, was still holding it when Joanna walked in. 'Do you want to come with me?' she asked. 'It'll probably be a tremendous bore, but we could always go for dinner afterwards.'

It *was* a bit of a bore, in fact. We sat on tiny stools in a cramped room at the back of a second-hand bookshop in North Beach. The whole room smelled of dust and mouldy books. There were about twenty of us in the audience, and various people read poems out loud, and I struggled not to fidget while I forced my face into a facsimile of Joanna's ethereal poetry-listening expression. Rivers was on halfway through the proceedings. His poems were short and full of hard consonants. He read out loud quite well, full of fire and anger. He made eye contact with me at one point, looked away, looked back at me briefly and frowned, and then he ignored me for the rest of the reading.

Afterwards there was red wine. I think it was bad red wine, because it hurt my throat when I swallowed it. I bought a pamphlet of some of Rivers's poems for a dollar. He barely acknowledged me but later, when people started to leave, he came up to me and whispered: 'Here. Tomorrow. Midday. I'll make lunch.'

*

I returned to the bookshop the next day, promptly on the dot of twelve. It was closed. The door was locked and shuttered, there were no boxes of books outside, no sign of life. It was on a steep side-street, and I sat on the steps for a while and enjoyed the view. Houses clung to the vertiginous slopes, and there were little patches of green and pink and red from window boxes and roof terraces. Down the hill, at the end of the street, I could see a much bigger green patch – Washington Square, full of people in small groups sitting on the grass and enjoying the sun. It was a warm day with a bright blue sky and a brisk breeze sending fluffy white clouds dancing across the sun from time to time. Had anyone seen me waiting there? Was anyone looking out of their window? Had anyone seen the way I leaped up to kiss Rivers Carillo when he toiled up the hill carrying a brown-paper grocery bag about ten minutes later? Did someone see us together? Had someone been bearing a grudge all that time?

He had a key. The shop belonged to a friend of his. It only opened at eccentric, occasional hours. Rivers had borrowed it for the day, for this assignation. He ushered me inside, into the smelly darkness, and pulled up the dusty blinds.

Thinking back to that day, Rivers had every right to call me a prick-tease. A deserted bookshop in a quiet street on a Wednesday afternoon. A blanket on the floor of the back room, the curtains drawn. A picnic – bread and pâté and cheese and red wine. Joni Mitchell on the stereo. The archetypal seduction scene. It had probably worked for a dozen other women. But I wasn't a woman. I was a girl, a stupid little girl.

Rivers had a hand on my knee, and then the hand was on my bare thigh, and then some of his fingers were touching me through the gusset of my white cotton knickers. I moved his hand, it moved back, I moved it away again. I pressed into his kiss and our tongues got tangled up together. My nose squashed against his. I pressed my tits against his chest, trying to suggest an alternative place for his wandering hands to go. He got the message, ran his hands up my back, unhooked my bra – he'd obviously had practice – and cupped my breasts in his hands, teasing the nipples with his thumbs. He pushed me down onto the blanket, firm hands on my shoulders, but I wriggled away, pulled my skirt down, pulled my blouse down. 'Not here,' I said, hoping to give the impression that all I didn't like was the dust and the dirt and the darkness, and the breadcrumbs all over the blanket.

Maybe he enjoyed delayed gratification. He smiled at me. He didn't get cross. He didn't call me 'Little Miss Fucking Prick-tease', like he did later. He didn't seem in the least bit surprised or annoyed. He smiled at me, as if to say, 'How dare I presume that you'd want to have sex on a blanket on the floor.'

'Sorry,' I said. And again, 'Not here.'

If I'd have said, 'No,' what would have happened? Or, 'Not now, not yet, not until . . .'

Until what? Some kind of declaration of love, or commitment, or intent – or a marriage proposal, I guess. I was an eighteen-year-old vicar's daughter from a small Sussex seaside resort. I wasn't about to lose my virginity without considerable justification.

That pamphlet of poems that I bought – I carried it around with me and tried hard to like the poems. I had, somewhere at home, a slim Faber paperback with poems by Ted Hughes and Thom Gunn. I thought that maybe Rivers's poems would fit somewhere in that book, if only in terms of the terse language and the metaphors. I was good at metaphors. I knew how to explain them and to write about them. I was less good at judging poetic quality. I'm not sure I'd read enough bad poetry to be able to identify it confidently at that stage. Or rather, not bad poetry but mediocre poetry, average poetry. I can't remember even one line of those poems now. I destroyed that pamphlet. A while back I tried to see if any of his poems had survived, had made it to the internet, but they've disappeared as if they never existed in the first place.

I had that pamphlet of poems in my bag on the day that I killed Rivers Carillo. It was with me when I caught the bus home afterwards, from the bus stop at the plaza at the Presidio end of the Golden Gate Bridge. I could feel it burning a hole in my bag. I got off the bus somewhere in the Marina District, an area full of trendy bars and cafés and yuppie shops. I bought a magazine – *People* or *Entertainment Weekly* or something equally brash – and I sat in a coffee shop pretending to read. I sat in the window of the shop, facing outwards, watching the fog descend and the evening get darker, and as I pretended to read that magazine my hands were in my lap, under the table, shredding that pamphlet of poems, tearing and ripping as if my future depended on it. I put all the shreds in between the pages of the magazine, rolled it up tightly and threw it into a street-corner trash can. Then I caught the bus back to Joanna's house. I let myself into that big, empty house, climbed the stairs to my bedroom and got on with my life.

Twenty-nine

My second-to-last day in San Francisco, the day before I killed Rivers Carillo, he took me to Sausalito. Sausalito: a jaunty name. I had a picture in my head of brightly coloured sails snapping in the breeze. Rivers had dangled the name in front of me like a sparkling jewel when he'd whispered to me in the hallway of Joanna's house, making our tryst for the following day.

What was I expecting to happen? I was expecting something, certainly. My second-to-last day. Something needed to be said or done between us. It seemed appropriate, touching, that he'd told me to meet him at the ferry terminal, down near the sea lions, where we'd met that first day when we went to Alcatraz together.

This could be my last day with Rivers Carillo, was all I could think on the ferry on the way over to Sausalito. I knew the script. He'd declare his love for me, tell me how he couldn't live without me, beg me to stay, offer to follow me back to London. He'd propose to me out of the blue, as if he were Maxim de Winter and I was the naive young girl he'd befriended on holiday. I got one aspect of the casting right, at least.

*

Sausalito had a salty tang in the air. A fresh breeze, a bright blue sky, the jangling masts and rigging of sailing boats in the harbour. A picture-postcard park. A street full of cafés and restaurants and shops. People were sitting outside the restaurants eating big plates of food – beautiful, shiny people. I wanted to sit there with Rivers and have lunch, and then go and browse in the shops, which were bound to be full of driftwood sculptures and scented candles and quirky, artistic greetings cards.

Rivers had other plans. He produced a keyring from his pocket and dangled it from his index fingers, so that the two keys on it jangled and glinted in the sunlight. 'I've borrowed a friend's houseboat,' he said, smiling at me.

'What for?' I said in all innocence, but as soon as I finished speaking I realised how stupid I'd sounded.

'What for? Hey, way to make me feel like I'm corrupting the innocent. The other day, in the bookstore, you said, "Not here." So I thought, what could be more romantic than a Sausalito houseboat?'

It's famous for them, apparently. Sausalito. Houseboats. I know that now. I know lots of things now. Then, I didn't. The biggest thing I didn't know was how to get out of this. Somewhere along the line I guess I must have agreed that I'd have sex with him. And this was the time and the place. I felt like a sacrificial lamb.

You need to understand why this was such a big deal for me. I was a vicar's daughter. I'd been a regular churchgoer all my life. And while I didn't have the strong happy-clappy Christian-commitment thing like my parents and my older sister had, you can't escape the principles of your upbringing that easily. Sex was something sacred to marriage. And if not marriage, then at least within a strong, committed, loving relationship. The truth was that I was saving myself – if not for marriage, then at least for 'the one'; for the someone special who loved me as I loved him. As I walked up the street with Rivers Carillo, holding his hand, dragging my feet slightly, I was saying to myself: *It's okay. He's the one, the special one. He loves me. He wouldn't have brought me here if he didn't.* And also? I was too polite to say no after he'd gone to all this trouble.

My spirits rose slightly when I caught sight of the houseboats. They weren't really boats at all, more like a little community of brightly painted houses, some with several storeys, all higgledy-piggledy, piled up on top of one another. The houseboats faced each other across boardwalks that formed streets. The houses were pink and blue and yellow and white, and there were window boxes full of flowers, and little white picket fences with heart shapes cut into the wood. Cute, pretty little gingerbread houseboats. Except for the one near the end of the row – silvery-grey wood with green mould growing on it; cracked varnish on the window frames and doors; no interesting extra storeys or dormer windows or window boxes and picket fences – just a mouldy old houseboat, smaller than the rest, that looked completely uncared-for. And that was the houseboat that Rivers had borrowed.

*

That houseboat, and what happened on it, was awful. Awful, in every way possible. I sat on the edge of the unmade bed that appeared to double as a couch. The atmosphere was cold, damp and clammy. The sheets on the bed were greyish and all tangled up. There was an orange blanket and I tried to arrange it so that it covered the sheets, but then I noticed a big brown stain on the blanket that I didn't want to look at, so I kicked it to the end of the bed.

Rivers was in the kitchen – the galley, I guess – getting drinks. 'Whisky or brandy?' he called.

I'd never had either. Brandy sounded nicer, so that was what I chose. Rivers handed me a glass, a chunky tumbler with white smears around the edges that might have been toothpaste or paint or calcified water. He'd chosen an old cracked teacup for himself. 'Cheers!' he said, in a mock-English accent, and then he looked around. I think he was embarrassed by the state of the place. 'Hey, we're here now. Let's make the most of it.'

I tasted my brandy tentatively, grimaced, then swallowed the rest down in one go. I didn't like the taste but I loved the warm glow that lingered in my throat and chest. Rivers put some music on – Bob Dylan, I think – and then gestured for me to join him. I stood up, he took me in his arms and we began to dance. Round and round, clinging on to each other, in that tiny cabin, bashing our shins on the edge of the bed. It felt safe, though, there in his arms. It felt romantic, like a love scene should do. I leaned towards him and kissed him on the mouth. That was safe, too; that was something that felt good.

What happened then? There was more kissing, and then Rivers pushed me onto the bed and undid my blouse and ran his hands over my body. I kept my hands around his neck or in his hair, places I was familiar with. He undid my bra and began sucking my breasts, each one in turn. That was okay. That felt okay. It felt quite nice. Then his hands were running around the waistband of my pants. He pushed my skirt up so the fabric covered my face, and then there were those fingers on the gusset of my pants again, rubbing and pushing at the fabric. 'No,' I said, and wriggled away.

He laughed.

'No, really, please, no,' I said. It was all suddenly too much.

'Oh, so now you're little Miss Fucking Prick-tease all of a sudden.' Rivers was smiling as he said it. He seemed more amused than angry. He played with my nipples a little bit more, and then his insistent fingers were there again, on the gusset of my pants. This time I let him. It seemed the only thing I could do. I lay there, very still, like a doll, waiting to see what he would do next.

The bed was uncomfortable. I could feel all the creases in the sheets under me. It was a single bed with a wooden surround, sort of in a box, and unless I kept my arms pinned to the side my elbows kept knocking against the wood. I didn't know what I was supposed to do – should I be unbuttoning his shirt? Pulling his jeans down? Doing something to *his* nipples? Instead I just lay there feeling slightly sick.

Now his fingers were inside my knickers, inside me,

poking and probing. I guess I must have moved away, because this time my head banged on the wooden headboard. 'Hey, come back,' he said, and pulled me back towards him, my blouse creasing and rucking up under my back. He pulled my knickers down and tossed them onto the floor. He rubbed me some more with his thumb. I felt something, a little bit like needing to have a wee.

Rivers stood up, kicked off his shoes and pulled his jeans down. He didn't have any underpants on, and his penis took me by surprise. My first sight of a man's erect penis: purple and ugly. I hadn't expected it to point so emphatically upwards. It was thick and solid and – I know now, with more experience – quite short. I wondered if I was supposed to reach out and touch it. He had something in his hand – a condom – and he pulled it on, the little teat at the end flopping comically. He climbed back onto the bed, lay on top of me and asked, 'Ready?'

I murmured 'Yes'. I was too polite to say anything else, after all the trouble he'd been to.

It was uncomfortable and it hurt, and I didn't seem to have room for him. Rivers rocked backwards and forwards on top of me, his face screwed up with the intensity of it all. My head kept bashing the headboard and I felt as if I had been split in half. I was cold and hungry and I felt sick, and I closed my eyes, braced my hands on the sides of the bed, arched my back, lifted my pelvis and tried really hard not to cry.

He panted and panted and then I felt a sudden sharp pain inside, worse than the worst period pain, and then he stopped panting and instead lay his head on my stomach and told me I was beautiful. I reached down and fondled his sweaty head. Somehow, I felt both sore and numb. There was a warm liquid sensation between my legs. Rivers pulled his penis out of me and there was a sloshing sound. I managed to prop myself up on my elbows. I looked down. Blood. There was blood between my legs and smeared down my thighs and all over the dirty grey sheets.

'Christ,' said Rivers as he looked at the mess. 'Jesus fucking Christ. Why the fuck didn't you tell me it was your first time?'

I remember the tiny little shower room on that houseboat, its walls lined with pine that had gone grey with damp. I washed myself as well as I could in the tiny handbasin, and I dried myself with the very edge of the dirty towel that was hanging over the shower rail. I bunched up almost a whole roll of toilet paper and stuck it between my legs, and then I pulled on my knickers and my skirt. I left my blouse untucked to try to hide the padding between my legs. I looked at myself in the mirror. Someone had once told me that when you have sex for the first time, a new line forms under your eyes, right below the lower lid, just a tiny line, but nonetheless a sure sign that you're no longer a virgin. I peered at the soft, fragile skin under my eyes. I thought there was a line there but I couldn't be sure.

Rivers was in the galley, about to stuff the sheets in the washing machine. 'You need to rinse them first,' I said. 'In cold water. Otherwise, the hot water will fix the stain.'

Obediently he pulled the sheets out and started running the cold tap. 'How do you know this stuff?'

I nearly said: Girl Guide Laundress badge. But I didn't want to appear any younger or more callow than I already had. Instead I said nothing. I found a dishcloth, rinsed it off and started dabbing at the mattress. Rivers came in. 'Don't do that. We'll just turn it over. He'll never know.'

So we turned over that smelly, lumpy mattress and as we did, Rivers caught my eye and gently said, 'I'm sorry.'

He was so nice about it. That's what did for him, really. If he hadn't been so nice then I never would have wanted to see him again, and none of the really awful stuff would ever have happened. But Rivers was nice. He held my hand as we walked back to the place where we had to wait for the ferry. He bought me a hot dog from a stand and made me eat it. He brushed my hair off my face. He told me I was a beautiful woman. He tried to make me laugh. From where we sat I could see San Francisco, all its hills and dips intersected by the grid-straight lines of its streets. Above the city sat a thick toupee of fog. It obscured the top of the Transamerica Pyramid. It looked like a dark thundercloud hovering over someone's head in a comic strip. All of a sudden I didn't want this to be how it ended, with Rivers and me.

I took hold of his hand. I started playing with his fingers. I put one of them in my mouth, like I'd seen people do in films, and I sucked it. I smiled at him, the flirtiest smile I could manage. 'So anyway, tomorrow's my last day in San Francisco. Do you want to get together?'

Rivers laughed. Chuckled. Then a huge laugh. He hugged me to him. 'Babe, you're a piece of work,' he said, and I think he meant it in an admiring way.

Thirty

There I was, running away again. I had hardly any luggage. I had crammed a few pairs of knickers and some T-shirts into the courier-style bag I used for school, and I added my toothbrush, my make-up bag and some anti-perspirant. That way, he wouldn't know what I had planned. He – whoever he was – wouldn't realise that I was going away. I slung the bag across my chest and took one last long look around my empty white flat. Then I walked out, locking the door behind me, trying to hide the trembling in my hands.

I had spent the night wondering what to do. I had closed all the windows and made sure the door was locked and bolted, and I had curled up in a little ball under my duvet and I had nearly gone out of my mind. Stay or go? Stay in the flat where he knew I lived, waiting for him to do whatever he was planning? Or run away, and always wonder? Even by the morning I hadn't made up my mind. I checked the doormat as soon as I woke up. I was expecting to see another white envelope but there wasn't one. I made coffee and toast and turned the TV on. The first thing I saw was a news report on the Edinburgh Festival. It seemed as if fate was telling me what to do.

I didn't know if I was coming back home. I didn't know

if I would dare to come back. My home had been invaded. It was no longer safe. I thought that maybe, then and there, I was walking out for ever. Walking away. Leaving it all behind me. Again.

But there was no need to think about that right now. I had to concentrate on looking natural. I took the stairs down from my flat because that way it was easier to tell if I was being followed, from the sound of the footsteps. I didn't think that there was anyone behind me. All I could hear was the sound of my sandals flip-flopping down the stairs. I was escaping in broad daylight, hoping to disappear into the crowd.

All I had to do was walk across the road to King's Cross, carrying my bag, like I did almost every day of my life. I didn't need to think about the future yet. I had a plan for that day, for the next couple of days. I was going to catch a train to Edinburgh and lose myself in the festival, and I was going to try to get my head straight. Zoey had invited me. She had flown up there early that morning. She was probably there already. There was a bed waiting for me in the flat that she was renting. I hadn't told her I was coming; I hadn't officially accepted her invitation yet. No one knew where I was going. I hadn't told Danny, Jem, Sarah, my parents. This was an escape. My task was to get on the train without him – the stalker, the letter-writer, Rivers Carillo back from the dead – noticing what I'd done.

It was still hot. The air felt stagnant. The dust from the building work they were doing to make King's Cross a desirable location hung in the air and stuck to my sweaty skin. I entered the station concourse. As usual at that time of day – coming up to eleven in the morning – King's Cross was heaving with people: plump Yorkshire businessmen arriving for meetings in the city; gaggles of slightly too showily dressed women down from Leeds or Doncaster or York for a day of shopping and a show. I wormed my way through the crowds, feeling as though I had eyes or sensors all over my body – in the back of my head and down my bare arms. I didn't know exactly who I was looking out for – Rivers Carillo, or someone who looked like him, or someone who looked like they might have known him back in the day – but that day I felt hyper-alert, super-sensitive to everything around me.

I deliberately ignored the giant departures board at the mainline station. I headed straight for the stairs down to the Tube station, my head down, looking like my usual preoccupied self. But as I reached the top of the stairs I swerved suddenly and darted into the ticket office as quickly and as unobtrusively as possible. I had my credit card in my hand and I found an available ticket machine. I tapped the screen quickly, selected my destination, hesitated slightly between open return and single, chose single, then thrust my credit card into the slot and tapped my fingers impatiently. The ticket spewed out and I remembered to wait for the receipt. As I did, I thought that maybe I should have paid cash, untraceable cash. But that would have been beyond paranoid.

Finally I allowed myself to look up at the departures board, but casually, as if I was simply looking around me, taking care not to fix my stare on any particular destination. My train was due to leave in fifteen minutes but there was no platform number announced yet. I stood there for a moment to catch my breath but I felt very exposed. I kept getting bumped and jostled. A station employee with a cart walked past, collecting litter. He narrowly avoided rolling the cart over my feet.

I threaded my way back across the concourse towards the branch of W.H. Smith. People were browsing the bookshelves, killing time. I picked up a couple of paperbacks more or less at random from the 'Buy one, get another half-price' display. No one was watching me, as far as I could tell. I added a glossy magazine to my haul, and then a chicken-salad sandwich and a bottle of water from the chiller cabinet. I joined the queue to the till. Everyone around me seemed intent on their own business. I started to breathe more easily. Soon I would be on the train bound for Edinburgh and I was pretty sure I hadn't been followed. I was nearly home and dry. Until suddenly I felt a hand on my shoulder and I jolted so violently that I dropped all my shopping.

It was a man in a suit, standing behind me. Just a man in a suit: a middle-aged businessman, slightly fat, slightly sweaty, nice smile. He got down on his knees to help me to pick up my stuff. 'Sorry, love,' he said. 'I was trying to tell you there was a till free.'

People pushed past us, tutting, as we gathered up my purchases. I wanted to leave them there, to run off, but that would have looked suspicious. I was flustered, nervous. I thanked the man in the suit. As I got up from the floor with my hands full, I thought I could sense someone staring at me. I looked up, across at the book section. There was a young guy there. T-shirt, combats, dark curly hair. He was grinning at me, and when I met his eye he winked at me. I went cold for a moment. The cashier cleared his throat, waiting for me to pay for my goods. Still flustered, I dug in my shoulder bag for my purse. As I left the shop I looked around me, but the young guy was nowhere in sight. As far as I could tell, he hadn't followed me.

The train pulled out of the station. I settled into my corner seat, surrounded by three elderly women, and I told myself off for my stupidity. Why did I go into W.H. Smith? Why did I buy two books and a magazine? I might as well have stuck a Post-It note on my forehead saying 'I am going on a long train journey in just a few minutes.'

Past York the train started to get less crowded. I was trying to lose myself in the books I'd bought but without success. One of them featured three old school friends, all beautiful and successful in their own way, falling in and out of love with various inappropriate men. It annoyed me. The other one seemed to be a period thriller set in a number of European cities. People kept writing letters to each other to tell them things that they should already have known. My head was aching from the strain of working out who all the people were, and my mind kept wandering back to San Francisco. The characters in the book that I was reading kept turning into faces that I vaguely remembered from that summer, and they started jostling me and looming up in front of me and calling to me and trying to get me to acknowledge them . . .

. . . And I woke with a start and the train had stopped at Newcastle. The old women had gone and there was a young man, ginger hair, a rucksack, asking me if the seats were taken.

He wouldn't shut up. He told me he was a student and that he was studying in Newcastle, but he was clearly not from there because his accent was pure Home Counties. He was staying there – Newcastle – for the summer because 'It's a cool town,' but now he was on his way to Edinburgh for the Fringe because some friends of his from Oxford were putting on a play and he was just going to 'hang . . . you know, chill.'

He seemed like a nice enough guy but he had obviously never learned to read body language. He seemed unable to interpret my polite little nods and shrugs and convert them into 'Please go away because I don't want to talk to anyone.'

I needed to ring Zoey, but I didn't want to make a phone call that my ginger friend could hear. I didn't want anyone to hear me make arrangements. I didn't want any stranger to know where I was going or who I would be staying with. I made my way down the aisle with my bag, squeezed into the smelly toilet, locked the door and put the loo seat down. I perched on it and dialled Zoey's number. She answered straight away. 'Beth!' It was almost a scream. She sounded like she was somewhere noisy, with a whole bunch of noisy people. 'Where are you, hon?'

'I'm on a train. I'm on my way to Edinburgh. Short

notice, I know. Sorry. Listen, you said I could kip at your flat. Did you mean it?'

'Oh my God, yes. This is so cool.' There was a pause. I started to say something. Zoey butted in. 'So, when are you arriving?'

I told her.

'Cool. I'll give you the address. Just pick up a cab at the station. Can't wait to see you.'

When I got back to my seat I saw that the ginger kid had picked up my historical thriller and was reading it. 'Keep it,' I said, and curled up into the corner and closed my eyes.

The Edinburgh Fringe hit me like a punch in the stomach the minute I arrived. I walked up to Princes Street from Waverley Station and was immediately accosted by people who wanted to thrust their leaflets into my hands. I had never seen such a mass of people on the street just hanging around. Not moving, not heading anywhere, just standing and watching what was going on. I needed to fight my way through them to get anywhere. There was the obligatory bagpipe player on one corner, a bunch of pan-pipers across the road and a group of youngsters in togas wandering along the street handing out leaflets and bunches of grapes. I pushed through the crowds, clutching my bag and the map I had bought at the station. The queue at the taxi rank had stretched back for hundreds of yards so I'd decided to walk. It didn't look that far on the map.

The crowds started to thin as I trudged uphill eastwards from Waverley Station, across a busy road, past the entrance to a cemetery, past what looked like a ruined Greek temple, and past a colossal 1930s edifice – local government offices, by the look of it, perched high on a hill overlooking the city. I was on a broad crescent with Regency houses to my left, and a long row of empty parked coaches. I stopped for a while to get my breath back. It was much cooler than in London but still, even late afternoon, very humid. The sky was off-white. I leaned on some railings and looked at the view beyond. Grey streets and railway lines, tiny, far below me. Steps winding down the side of the hill. A green expanse of open land over to my left, a rugged, stepped hill emerging from it.

'Arthur's Seat.' It was a man's voice, behind me. I stood where I was and for a split second my heart sank. I hadn't heard any footsteps behind me. Then my mind managed to process the information. The voice was Scottish. I turned and saw one of the coach drivers, cigarette in hand. He stepped closer to me and pointed at the hill. 'It's an extinct volcano. Magnificent, isn't it? This your first time in Edinburgh?'

I nodded. 'What's that?' I pointed at a building crouched near the foot of the hill. From where I stood, the outline looked like a doodle on a phone pad, as if the architect had taken a shape, like the outline of a leaf or a petal or a boat – and crammed as many of them together as the space would allow, all different sizes. 'That is four hundred million pounds of our money,' the coach driver said.

'The Scottish Parliament?'

'Aye.' He stubbed out his cigarette on the pavement. 'You can tell it wasn't built by a Scotsman.'

At the end of the crescent there was a main road and it was bustling with buses and chippies and kebab shops. I checked the map, crossed over, looked behind me to check that the coast was clear, and started counting the streets on the left. The one I wanted was a narrow cul-de-sac crammed with parked cars, blocked at the end to traffic but accessible via a steep flight of stone steps. Either side of the street, tall terraced grey houses and tenements nestled together. But for all that, it was cheery – window frames were painted in bright blues and greens, and every house had a front garden blooming with summer flowers.

I found the house I wanted and I rang the bell. There was no answer from the entryphone system, but I noticed the street door was open. I pushed it and went inside. The hallway was dark, the walls painted a dark glossy institutional green. Up three flights of stairs, round to the right, and there was the right door. Stuck to the door was a white envelope.

All this way, I thought. All this way, for this. How the hell did he find me?

And then I looked again and realised that the envelope was a different size and shape – smaller and squarer than the ones I'd learned to fear. My name was written on it in right-slanting loopy handwriting that had the indefinably foreign look that I associated with letters from childhood penfriends. *Beth*, it said; not *The murdering bitch*. I pulled the envelope from the door and it felt heavy. Inside there was a note and key. 'I had to go check out the venue,' it said. 'Make yourself at home. Zoey XOX.'

The flat was tiny: even smaller than my place in London. There was one bedroom, almost filled with a double bed. Zoey's suitcase sat on the bed, some of the clothes half-unpacked. Just off the hallway I found the world's smallest bathroom – well, shower room – like a cupboard, or the toilet on the Sausalito houseboat. And the only other room was the kitchen-living room. A big sash window filled the room with light. There was a sofa-bed, a small TV, a chair, a table and a tiny kitchen area. I found some pizza in the fridge – what looked like the remains of Zoey's lunch – and I ate it while watching television. I made a mug of herbal tea. And then I found a blanket in the wardrobe in Zoey's room, curled up on the sofa and fell sound asleep.

Thirty-one

'So this is the room,' said Zoey. 'What do you think?'

She was bouncing around on a small wooden stage at one end of a low dark cellar that was seemingly dug out of the foundations of a tall old building. The walls and the low curved ceiling were painted black and there were rows of low benches facing the stage. I figured that forty or fifty people would fit in, as long as they didn't mind bunching up together and losing their personal space.

I touched one finger to the wall to see if it was as damp as it looked. It was. I wiped the finger on my jeans and tried to think of a suitable way to tell Zoey what I thought of the room. It was her venue for the Fringe. She was planning to be standing on that stage at twenty past ten every night until almost the end of August, the end of the Fringe, trying to make people laugh.

Zoey was excited. It was a good venue, she told me; and twenty past ten was a fantastic slot. 'Well, a little earlier would have been better, or maybe lunchtime or early evening. But ten-twenty is great, especially if we can spread the word. Maybe you could help me out with the flyering?'

I nodded, although I had only a dim idea of what she meant by flyering. I was tired and confused. Was it only yesterday that I'd caught the train up here? It felt like a lifetime ago. I wasn't even sure how we'd got to this room. We'd crossed a bridge near Waverley Station, the kind of bridge that in any other European capital city would cross a great river – the Danube, the Seine, the Thames. I had looked down on to a jumble of railway lines far below us. We'd walked up a busy road full of dawdling tourists, and then there was the Royal Mile. It was pretty much a solid mass of people, trying to hand us bits of paper. As we crossed, we nearly got knocked down by a cyclist pedalling a rickshaw. Then there was another street, and then we were on a bridge looking down at yet another street far below us, as if it was another city entirely. I couldn't work out how the two streets could be connected. There was a tall grey institutional-looking building, and noticeboards outside covered with posters for comedy shows – faces smiling or gurning or looking straight at the camera, photos of people holding umbrellas or leaping in the air or pretending to eat bunches of flowers. There were newspaper clippings stapled to the posters, with printouts of reviews and star ratings.

Zoey had steered me through an open door and instantly I could smell damp. We walked along a corridor, down a flight of stairs and another, and another. It felt like we were descending into the bowels of the Earth. Every wall, every ceiling, was covered with posters for comedy shows. There were people on every floor, forming queues outside doors, tickets in hand, even at this early time of the day. Three or four floors down, a bar. No windows. Same musty smell. Zoey had pushed me towards a saggy sofa and I slumped onto it. She went off somewhere, in a huddle with someone. It was midday. Groups of people were eating nachos from paper plates. There were lots of young people in T-shirts and baggy combat trousers. There were boys with feathery 1970s Rod Stewart haircuts. Older people, forties, fifties, reading *The Guardian*'s Fringe supplement. I saw a guy I thought I recognised as one of the team captains on a Channel Four comedy panel show. I didn't see Rivers Carillo or anyone who looked like him. It was crowded and claustrophobic and confusing, but it also felt safe. No one knew who I was.

Zoey had returned with a key and we'd continued downstairs until we eventually emerged onto the pavement of a dark, narrow street where we'd found ourselves surrounded by tall grey buildings. I looked up to where we'd come from. Way up high there was a bridge across the street. I felt dizzy, as if I was in an Escher engraving.

Zoey had led me along the street and up a cobbled alley under a tunnel. To our right, another tall grey building; to our left, another wall completely covered with comedy posters. At the far right-hand end of the alleyway, as it widened out into a kind of tenement courtyard, Zoey unlocked a door. We ducked into the doorway, through a tunnel with dust and dirt and uneven paving stones underfoot – like some kind of archaeological dig in the foundations of a castle. And finally, just as I wondered where on Earth she could possibly be taking me, just as I started to feel scared, the passageway opened out into this dark, dank cave of a room.

Zoey was still waiting for me to say something about the space. It was a dump, I wanted to say; or a dungeon or a prison cell or a crypt. I shivered, feeling the damp coldness go down my spine and raise goose pimples on my arms. 'It's really cool,' I said, meaning it literally; meaning, what a relief after the hot summer we'd had; choosing the one positive I could think of to describe the place. But Zoey assumed I meant 'cool' as in, well, cool, in the figurative sense. Her face cracked into a huge smile. 'It is, isn't it? It's so cool.'

She jumped up and down on the stage like Tigger. 'Oh my God, Beth!' she shouted, in a voice that echoed and bounced off the walls. 'The Edinburgh Fringe. I'm playing the Edinburgh Fringe! This is it. I've made it. I'm here. And no one can stop me.'

She bounced over to where I was standing, grabbed hold of me and we bounced around the room together until we tripped over one of the benches. Her joy was infectious. I loved her at that moment. I felt full of love for Zoey and her enthusiasm and her wild curly hair and her refusal to be afraid of anything. And as we jumped up and down, and hugged each other, and grinned at each other, and I allowed myself a crazy smile, I realised something: I could get lost here. Well and truly lost. I could hide in the crowd and mingle and have fun and be a normal person, and no one would be able to find me. No one knew I was here.

Except . . . there were six missed calls on my mobile. One was from my mum, just her weekly check-up; wanting to know that I was still alive. Two more were from my sisters, both of them 'just checking' that I was okay; I wondered what Jem had told Sarah to make her phone me. The other three missed calls were from Danny. Danny, my only just ex-boyfriend; Danny, the guy I'd said I'd still be friends with; Danny, the sweet, kind person who still wanted to hang out with me. I thought that I at least owed him the courtesy of returning his phone call.

'Where on earth are you?' Danny's voice sounded puzzled, rattled maybe, but not quite cross.

I was sitting at an outside table at a tiny hole-in-the-wall hummus-and-falafel place in a side street just off the Royal Mile. I was with Zoey, and with Laura and Suze, two other comedians who were doing a show together at the same venue. There was some showbizzy talk about sharing publicity, doing 'joint flyering', 'cross-promoting' their shows, which I didn't quite follow. Laura was late twenties, blonde, skinny and very pretty; she was very 'on' – a little shrill and shrieky. I got the sense that she liked to be noticed. Suze was older, calm, a large but rather beautiful woman with creamy skin. She didn't seem like a comedian – not like the ones I'd met so far, anyway. She was very quiet, almost dull; but she had a serenity that was quite peaceful. Neither of them seemed to know Zoey very well, but they were all trying to get along, falling over themselves to offer to pay for lunch. I wondered what it would be like by the time the Fringe was over at the end of August. Would they be best buddies? Would Zoey cast her spell on them?

I stood up and walked away from them to concentrate on my phone call. I perched on a low concrete bollard. 'I'm in Edinburgh,' I said, trying to put a laugh in my voice; to indicate that it was just a quirky, last-minute decision.

'Edinburgh? Why? How come?'

I was watching – being watched by – a silver-painted living statue who seemed to have decided to start a staring match with me. 'For the Festival. You know, the Fringe?' I still hadn't grasped what the difference was, if there was one. There was a Festival and a Fringe, and I didn't know if they were officially part of each other or separate. 'There's all this stuff on. Like comedy and plays and art and stuff.'

'How long are you staying up there?' Danny was still puzzled, verging on annoyed now.

'Just a few days. Probably. I came on a whim.'

'Are you with that Zoey friend of yours?' Danny's voice changed, subtly, to something a little harder and colder.

'Well, yes, but not like that.'

'Not like what?'

'Not like your tone of voice suggests you think it might be like.' The statue was still staring at me. I wanted to tell it to go away, to leave me alone.

'You can read the tone of my voice?'

'Like a book.'

'Then tell me what tone of voice this is. Have you forgotten about my mourning jacket?'

Annoyed, definitely. Perhaps a little hurt. 'What about your jacket?'

'My Morning Jacket. The band. We're supposed to go and see them tomorrow, remember? You said you were really looking forward to it.'

I'd completely forgotten about them. Danny had been playing me their album for the past few months. He had been putting their songs on the mix CDs he made for me. Big, swirly rock music with a bit of a dance beat. Unintelligible lyrics sung in a dramatic high voice. Kind of passionate-sounding but not really my thing. But because I was so adept at pretence Danny had thought that I really loved the band and couldn't wait to see them live. After I'd dumped him, after we'd split up, he'd been quick to say: 'You'll still come to see My Morning Jacket with me, won't you?' And I had said that I would.

'Danny, I'm so sorry. Really. I forgot all about them. Can you find someone else who wants the ticket?'

'I could sell it for about four times its face value outside the venue, no problem. But that's not the point. I wanted to be there with you. I like going to gigs with you. It makes them special.'

'Danny, I'm sorry. But we're not going out any more, okay? I know I'd said I'd come with you. But I can't. Sorry. But, you know, I'm not your girlfriend any more. Please, find someone else to go with you.'

'But we're still friends?'

He sounded so disappointed and betrayed that I felt as if I was about to cry. I needed to end the call there, before he sussed how upset I was and tried to push further.

Breaking and ending my relationship with Danny was one of the hardest things I had ever had to do, and I needed all my strength to follow it through. I made my voice as icy as possible. 'Sorry, Danny. What can I say to make it better? Look, I'll see you when I get back, okay? We'll talk more then.'

That bloody statue was still staring at me. I stuck my tongue out at it, a stupid, childish gesture. I hated this. I hated what I was doing to Danny. But how could I tell him why I'd run away? How could I tell him why I had broken off our relationship? I stomped back to the café table. Zoey flashed me a concerned look as I sat down. I took a big mouthful of falafel and blamed the water pooling in my eyes on the heat of the spices.

Thirty-two

Zoey thought it was funny how much I enjoyed flyering. Apparently most comedians thought it was a chore, and worse. Zoey certainly did. It involved walking the streets with piles of flyers – leaflets advertising comedy shows – and handing them to passers-by. Zoey's flyer was a glossy sheet of A5 paper featuring a photo of her that had been taken as she hung upside down from something, so that her hair stuck straight up in a shock of curls. To flyer properly you needed to strike up conversations with people and try to persuade them to come to the gig or gigs that you were promoting. Comics hated it, it seemed. But it seemed to me that many of them were intrinsically shy and awkward in their dealings with people. Given my quiet persona and my general air of unobtrusiveness it surprised Zoey – and sort of surprised me – how good I was at it.

The pair of us were working the Royal Mile, mostly, with occasional forays into the maze of backstreets in student land, where – if you timed it right – you could catch the punters going in or coming out of other shows. At the Pleasance Courtyard, for example, or a building nearby that I thought was probably the university students' union and for the duration of the Fringe was hosting a whole bunch of comedy shows. We approached appropriate groups of people – bunches of women in their twenties and thirties, for example – or thirty- and forty-something couples. We were mostly promoting Zoey's show, but if the punters proved interested we would also add in flyers for Laura and Suze. They were doing the same thing in return for Zoey's show.

Zoey and I would stage informal competitions to see which of us could hand out the most flyers. I was proud of some of the marketing lines I'd come up with. '*Desperate Housewives* meets *The Vagina Monologues*' seemed to be working well (I had never seen either of them). With slightly older women and couples, I went for 'It's like *Sex and the City* rewritten by an American Victoria Wood.' With the cool kids, I described Suze and Laura as 'a bit like French and Saunders. Only funny.'

Zoey's friend – ex-friend – Steve was around, handing out leaflets for his own show, when he heard me say that. 'You're good,' he said. 'Want to flyer my show?'

I'd been to see Zoey's show a few times, and it seemed to be going well. Zoey's material hadn't really changed much since the first time I had heard her, but her delivery seemed sharper and somehow more savage and biting. She paced around as if she owned the stage: she used every inch of that tiny wooden platform, and seemed to fill the whole room with her personality. I liked to sit at the back, and watch the audience leaning forward, their shoulders hunched in expectation, and to predict when the laughs would come. I was so proud of Zoey. Although I'd only played a very small part in helping her out, I felt that I almost owned part of the show. I felt more fulfilled than I had in ages. It was a good feeling, one that I'd almost forgotten.

I went to lots of other shows, too. I saw Steve's one-man show, and I was impressed. It was very different from the material he'd done at that nightmare gig in Southampton. It was just as dark and foul-mouthed but it was full of bitingly intelligent humour. He was raging about his Catholic childhood, and the state of the nation, and other worthwhile targets, and I thought it was excellent. We had a drink afterwards, and he asked about Zoey. In my new, happy, fulfilled state of mind, I told him to call her. I encouraged him to get back in touch with her. I knew it would make her happy.

The Edinburgh Fringe wasn't cheap but I was putting it on my credit card so it didn't really count. And then, late at night it was Chinese or pizza or curry or kebabs back at the flat with a whole bunch of people: Laura and Suze sometimes, and some other people Zoey knew, some of whom I recognised from the telly. And then Steve started coming round as well, and occasionally he stayed the night. It all seemed to be back on with him and Zoey. It was a great, relaxed atmosphere, and it was the most fun I'd had in ages.

I felt free. I had run away, I'd escaped, and I'd made it to safety. There hadn't been a single menacing note. I hadn't seen . . . him. Whoever he was. I'd had no sense of being followed. No chills up my spine, no sense of being watched, apart from by that silver-painted living statue. I felt awful about Danny, and I missed him. But I knew that

I'd done the right thing and that he was better off without me, even if he didn't know it yet. Occasionally I thought about my flat back in London and all the stuff I had left there. I wondered if I'd ever be able to go back. I thought about the girls I taught, and on the day that the results came out I wondered how they'd done in their exams. I wondered if I would ever be able to go back to that school, if I dared return to my job. And I worried about money, and about my future, and about what was going to happen to me – where I would go, what I would do – once this glorious interlude came to an end. I found myself praying, something I rarely did. The prayer went something like this: *For now, please God, if you exist, just let me be. Let me enjoy this holiday*.

It was two in the morning. Zoey, Steve and I were finishing off the dregs of a bottle of wine. 'To the best flyererererer ever,' slurred Zoey.

I blushed.

'Damn right,' said Steve. 'You're good at this. Who'd have guessed Zoey's mousy friend was a wannabe?'

'What do you mean?'

'I've seen you out there. You're a performer. You love it, don't you? You're a frustrated comedian.'

I shook my head. 'No, not at all.'

'Oh, go on,' said Steve. 'You can't tell me you've never thought of doing this.'

'She tried,' said Zoey. 'She got stage fright.'

I thought back to that night in that claustrophobic

cellar in London; to the sense that someone was watching me. I couldn't stop myself shivering.

'I bet you have done *something* on stage, though, haven't you?' Steve's eyes were boring into me.

I fidgeted uneasily. 'I used to act a bit. A long time ago. When I was at school.'

'Why did you stop?' said Zoey in a curious voice, as if she genuinely wanted to know the answer to the puzzle.

It was too close to home. I said nothing. I left it a few minutes and then I stood up, unsteadily, went over to the kitchen area and put the kettle on. Time to end the evening. Time to end the conversation. This was not the time to talk about Lizzie Stephens. But the truth was that I was starting to feel a bit like Lizzie again. As if I had come back to life, as if I had burst out of my cocoon and sprouted butterfly wings – whatever hackneyed simile fitted the bill.

The next afternoon I was back on the Royal Mile. I was standing in the heart of historic Edinburgh, at the centre of the Fringe. Zoey was taking a break from flyering that day, but I was holding the fort. It was a sunny day and I was wearing one of Zoey's brightly coloured T-shirts, because I had run out of clean ones. I hadn't felt this relaxed and open and human since – well, since San Francisco. There was a stage – a mini-stage – set up in the centre of the Royal Mile. Three men were on the stage dressed in swimming trunks and goggles, pretending to be synchronised swimmers. Cardboard waves were playing the part of the swimming pool. Next to the stage a row of beautiful young oriental girls in embroidered silk robes –

Thai? Japanese? Korean? – were waiting for their turn to perform.

I handed a flyer to a middle-aged American couple. They told me that they were from Indianapolis and that they loved *The Vicar of Dibley*. 'Oh, you'll love this,' I lied. 'She's American, but she's lived in Britain for years so she's got that great British sense of humour, combined with a big dollop of American sass.' Oh, what nonsense I was talking. And oh, how relaxed I was. They'd said 'Indianapolis' and I hadn't even thought of Rivers Carillo and the list I'd made of universities in Indiana.

A tall man, fortyish, slim, with fairish floppy public-schoolboy hair was hovering nearby, looking as if he wanted a leaflet. He waited until I had finished with the Americans. 'I'll take one of those,' he said.

'Not often that people ask for them,' I said, and I think I sounded slightly flirty. He was good-looking, in a diffident and faintly posh English way.

'It looks interesting.'

'It is.'

We stood there for a while looking at each other, and I wondered if he was trying to chat me up. But he seemed to think better of it, or was overcome by shyness, and he mumbled 'Thanks' and turned away. I glanced idly at the crowds. There was a man juggling with fire – with batons that were on fire – surrounded by a crowd of onlookers. There was a unicyclist making animals out of balloons, and children were jostling around him, trying to get their hands on one of the balloon animals. And then I saw him. Him – someone – a dark curly head of hair – Rivers Carillo. Someone like Rivers Carillo but younger: the man in Russell Square; the kid at King's Cross Station. His head was bobbing up and down amidst the crowds, past the Thai girl dancers, past the unicyclist and the fire juggler, moving relentlessly towards me. And I panicked. Suddenly I remembered how afraid I was.

I ran. I ran up the Royal Mile, up Lawnmarket, up Castle Hill, towards the castle. I ran over the cobbles and the uneven pavement, pushing through the heaving mass of people. And as I ran I could hear that he had started to run too, with determined footsteps that echoed mine. I threaded my way through the clumps of people who had gathered to watch the street entertainers. I cannoned into someone. I looked up, caught sight of a white-painted clown's face. I waved an apology but didn't stop. I kept running up that crowded street, past people trying to hand me flyers and leaflets about fringe shows and sightseeing bus tours and cheap restaurants. I pushed through a party of tourists on a guided tour. I could still hear footsteps behind me. Not just any footsteps, but definitely someone running, someone following me, someone keeping pace behind me. I was getting a stitch in my side, and my breath was catching painfully in my throat and in my chest, high up at the top of my ribcage. A centurion in full Roman armour reached out towards me, grabbed my arm as I ran past, offering to help or trying to stop an accident of some sort. I shook him off. I didn't dare look behind me. I dreaded to think what – who – I might see. I didn't want it to be true but I knew it was. All I could hear was the sound of those inexorable running footsteps, following me up the hill.

An alleyway beckoned on my right, a tiny sliver of space between two shops. I darted into it and leaned against the wall, panting. It was quiet and dark. I stood there for a while, listening out for footsteps, watching the people walking past. I didn't see him, the dark-haired man who was chasing me. After a few seconds, when I was almost sure that I hadn't been followed, I tiptoed through the alleyway, away from the Royal Mile, down some uneven stone steps, towards the light at the other end. I reached out a hand to the cold, clammy stone to steady myself. And that was when I heard footsteps again, slower this time but still distinctive. They were behind me; right behind me, echoing on the flagstones underfoot. He had found me. He was coming towards me. I felt his breath on the back of my neck.

There was nothing I could do except stand there like a statue. At the end of the tunnel was a dizzying vista – a clear, cloudless blue sky, a steep hill down to the Princes Street Gardens, brightly dressed people sitting on the bright green grass. People enjoying themselves. People and people and people, so many of them, without a care in the world. So close, so far away. And there I stood with my mystery stalker breathing down my neck. Suddenly his hand was on my shoulder. My shoulders slumped under his touch. I turned to face the inevitable. Rivers Carillo, his son, his friend. Or one of those faceless young guys from San Francisco: Elliot, Jason, Jonas. Whoever my stalker was.

His face wasn't where I expected it to be. He was taller than I expected. I turned and I was facing a chest, a neck. My eyes climbed slowly. Pointed chin. Sharp nose. Blue eyes. Floppy fair hair. 'I'm terribly sorry,' said the polite, shy, posh Englishman. 'Did I scare you? You dropped these when you ran off so suddenly.'

He handed me my pile of flyers. I stammered some words of thanks. I was blushing furiously, feeling shaken. *Stupid, stupid, stupid*, I said to myself.

'It really does look good,' he said. 'I might come and see it tonight. Will you be there?'

I nodded, unable to form coherent words. He gave me a strange, concerned look, and then he turned and walked back to the Royal Mile, clutching a copy of the flyer. I flicked through the pile of leaflets in my hands, tidied them and straightened their edges. I fiddled with them for a while until I felt a little calmer. Then I set my shoulders and headed back out towards the crowds and craziness. I scanned the street before I emerged from the alleyway, taking the kind of precaution I'd somehow forgotten since I'd been in Edinburgh. There was no sign of the dark-haired man. Of course there wasn't: he had never been chasing me. The dark-haired man was no one, nothing; just a spectre in the crowd.

There was a good audience at Zoey's show that night. I sat on my perch against the wall at the back of the dungeon and watched them as they arrived. I recognised some of the people I'd given flyers to. I nodded at the

American couple from Indianapolis, who waved excitedly at me. I was hoping they'd enjoy the show that I'd talked them into seeing. I was sure it was long past their bedtime. Just as Zoey was about to come on stage a familiar figure ducked into the venue. It was the tall polite floppy-haired man from earlier today. I lowered my head, embarrassed. I didn't want him to catch my eye. But he didn't look in my direction anyway. He found a seat with a good view of the stage on the end of one of the rows in the middle of the cave and sat down.

It seemed as if Zoey was angry about something. Instead of fizzing onto the stage like she normally did, that night it was more of a stomp. She was taking no prisoners. Every punchline was delivered to perfection but there was a weird tone to her voice. It was as if she really meant the material. There was almost a note of hate in her voice. The audience was laughing as much as usual, but some of the laughter seemed a little uneasy, particularly amongst the men. It was the laughter of men with crossed legs.

Thirty-three

Sometimes the worst things happen on the best days. The plane crashes on the way to a dream holiday, a child is lost at sea on the perfect summer's day. A black cloud suddenly hides the sun, and you wonder how you had managed to let yourself believe that the sun would shine for ever. Perhaps happiness always carries with it the underlying threat of dread, because sometimes you are flying so high that you know the only way to go is down.

Or perhaps normal people – I mean people other than me, people who don't live with fear hanging around their necks – do know what it's like to be perfectly happy, without any expectation or dread of the sudden chill that can come at any moment. Perhaps I'm the only person in the world who knows that happiness can be frightening; that happiness can be dreadful in its own way. All I know is this: that day, the day it happened, the day the whole world fell apart, had been – up until then, up until the axe fell – the happiest day I had ever known.

I had the whole day to myself. Zoey and I had agreed that I would take a day off from flyering. I decided that I would simply enjoy myself around Edinburgh, doing whatever I wanted to do. I woke with a slight hangover. It wasn't the sort of hangover that bothered me too much, or made me think of migraines; it was merely the sort of hangover that I knew would be over soon. It was just a fond memory of the good time we'd had the night before. I showered, got dressed and made coffee. I could hear headachy groaning coming from Zoey's room, and it could have been either her or Steve. I didn't want to be a third wheel so I got out of the flat quickly.

I was a tourist that day. I had a wonderful time. I wore sunglasses and another of Zoey's brightly coloured T-shirts. I took an open-top-bus tour around the city, getting off from time to time to visit historic buildings. I explored Edinburgh Castle and gasped at the view of the city from the ramparts. I toured Holyrood House, listening to an audio guide that hung around my neck, looking at tapestries and paintings and old gilt furniture. There'd been a security scare at Britain's airports earlier that week, and because of that all visitors were made to leave their bags in the cloakroom at the entrance to the old palace. Most tourists were complaining but I didn't mind. It was a joy to saunter around the house, the old abbey and the gardens without lugging my courier bag strapped across my body as usual.

Later I went window-shopping in the New Town and tried on clothes that I couldn't afford in Harvey Nichols. I visited an exhibition of 1960s black and white photographs at the beautiful National Portrait Gallery, and then I sat in a trendy café with a good book and an excellent cup of coffee and I people-watched. I saw a comedy show at teatime, a girl called Josie Long, who was sweet and oddball and good-natured and so funny that I forgot myself – forgot everything – for a while.

I had an early evening meal in a little Indian vegetarian restaurant that I happened upon in a side street. The food and ambience were so good that it seemed like serendipity. And then I went to see a hysterically stupid show that Steve had recommended: three guys called We Are Klang. 'See them this year,' said Steve, 'because by next year they'll be big TV stars and you won't be able to get a ticket.' I sat scrunched up on the end of a bench in a tiny room packed with comedy fans, and I laughed so hard that I had to wipe away the tears.

I felt a little disorientated as I left the show. It had got very dark all of a sudden. It was getting late. I thought of seeing another show, but then I decided that the perfect end to the evening would be to go home, watch a bit of television and then try to grab at least an hour's nap on the sofa before Zoey came in all buzzed and jingly from her performance.

I wandered down Canongate towards Holyrood House, against the flow of pedestrian traffic. Everyone else seemed to be walking uphill into town at the start of their night out. I passed a bunch of medieval monks and two people in Tudor clothes. I decided that one of them was probably supposed to be Henry the Eighth. The night air was soft, with a hint of welcome rain. The little grey alleyways and closes – wynds, they call them in Edinburgh – offered tantalising glimpses of crooked old buildings and little bits of open land. At the bottom of the hill I ran my finger along some of the peculiar protruding bits and pieces on the walls of the Scottish parliament building. I still couldn't decide if I loved or hated this messy, ambitious, expensive bit of architecture, crammed onto a strangely shaped piece of land next to Holyrood House.

My route took me into the nearly deserted streets east of Holyrood and passed under two grimy railway bridges, where the pavements were coated in pigeon droppings. Then I trudged up a hill to the busy main road. I crossed the road and down the flight of steps that led into the street where our tenement flat was. I checked my watch. It was just after ten o'clock. Still plenty of time to unwind and nap before Zoey got home. I felt light-hearted and relaxed.

The street door to the flats was unlocked, as always. We'd learned that most of the tenants preferred it that way. I walked into the dark hallway and pressed the timer switch for the light. There was a set of metal pigeon-holes attached to the wall, where the postman delivered the mail. I fumbled in the appropriate pigeon-hole, amongst the leaflets for curry houses and kebab shops, searching for the key that Zoey always left there – hidden in an envelope – on the days that we'd decided to go our separate ways. It wasn't there.

I was annoyed. That was all – annoyed, a bit pissed-off that she'd forgotten to leave the key. It took a little of the gloss from my mood. I stood there for a while, trying to decide what to do. Maybe Steve was still in the flat, I thought. Or maybe Laura or Suze or one of our other friends had been catching up on some sleep during the day

– our flat was much closer to the centre of the city than some other people's were; it had become a bit of a hang-out. There'd be someone in the flat to let me in. But that would be irritating – I had wanted to spend a quiet evening by myself. Or maybe, better, Zoey had left the key in an envelope stuck to the door as she had on that first day. I shouldered my bag again and started climbing up those uncarpeted cold stone stairs.

I remembered that I'd turned my phone to silent earlier, just before I went to the Josie Long show. Maybe Zoey had called me with some kind of message. Maybe she had left the key with one of the neighbours. Or maybe I was supposed to meet her somewhere. I was midway up the second flight of stairs. I fumbled in my courier bag for my phone. I was greeted by a flashing message that told me that I had eight missed calls. The flashing seemed particularly insistent. I dialled voicemail and had the phone clamped between my chin and shoulder as I carried on up the stairs towards the flat. I was juggling with my phone and my bag, and trying to concentrate on the messages, and then the light, which was on a timer switch, decided to go out.

I stumbled up the next few steps in the dark, and nearly tripped as I stepped onto the second landing. I felt with my free hand along the cold, shiny painted walls, searching for another light switch, and all the while I was trying to make sense of the messages that had been left on my phone. The light made me blink when it finally came on.

The first message was from Laura, but it was a bit garbled. Then there was someone else from Zoey's venue, one of the front-of-house people, I think. They were apologising for calling me, telling me that Zoey had given them my number for emergencies; and as I started to climb the last flight of stairs up to our flat I was trying to work out what the emergency was. Had she been taken ill? Had there been an accident of some sort? Up more steps, and I was hearing more of the messages. It was Suze next, and then Laura again, their voices growing increasingly frantic. Zoey wasn't there. She wasn't at the venue. She hadn't turned up. Her mobile phone was on, they were saying. They'd left messages but she hadn't called back. My stomach started to churn and I felt my steps get slower. I reached the third landing. Voicemail was about to launch into yet another panicked message, but I just stuffed the phone into my pocket as I stared at the front door of our flat and realised that it was ajar.

I touched the door with my right index finger. The door moved slightly. I pushed it open. I stepped inside, tentatively. The hallway light was on. That was odd. Almost instinctively, I checked the doormat for an envelope, an anonymous letter. I put my hand on the wall to support myself as I felt my knees start to shake. I swallowed hard. I tried to regulate my breathing. There was no envelope on the doormat, no envelope underneath it. Nothing. I wanted to shout, 'Zoey! Are you there?' But as I opened my mouth I realised my voice wouldn't let me. I walked further into the flat. Gingerly I pushed open the bedroom door and tried to see if Zoey was in bed. Maybe she was ill. Maybe she wasn't answering her phone because she was ill, she was asleep, she was buried under the duvet. Maybe she was still in bed with Steve. Perhaps I had accidentally left the door ajar when I'd left that morning; left it ajar in my bid to creep out quietly without waking them. 'Zoey . . .' I whispered. The bedroom curtains were open; I could tell that by the way the moonlight cast a silver path on the floor. The bed was empty, the duvet thrown carelessly to one side, the sheets wrinkled – just as she would have left it when she got up.

There was a smell. Not from the bedroom but from somewhere else in the flat. I could feel it hitting the back of my throat. It smelled familiar, but it was a familiarity that I had never experienced this strongly. I could taste something metallic in my mouth. The smell hit harder as I walked towards the kitchen-living room. I trailed my right hand along the wall as I walked, feeling the need of some support, some security. There was something sticky on the floor in the hallway. I could hear the sucky sound as I lifted my shoes with each step. I looked down. It was dark, the sticky stuff. Dark reddish-brown.

Zoey had fallen asleep on the settee. Of course. That was all. That was why she hadn't turned up for her show. She had fallen asleep. Look: there was her hair cascading over the back of the settee. There was nothing to worry about.

My feet stuck to the floor again. I looked down. I touched the reddish-brown stuff with my finger. I looked at my finger. I smelled it. Oh God, oh Jesus. It was blood. That was blood on the floor. Lots of it. Where had it come from? Why had someone bled all over the floor?

Zoey had fallen asleep in a really awkward position, her

neck twisted uncomfortably against the back of the settee. She would be so stiff when she finally woke up, and so annoyed with herself for missing her show. I walked further into the living room, across the sticky floor. I walked around the end of the sofa, to face Zoey, to wake her up.

Her eyes were already open. That was odd.

Her legs were splayed awkwardly.

She was clutching her stomach with her hands.

Her hands were red.

Her stomach was bleeding. That was where the blood was coming from.

'Zoey . . .'

I knelt down at her feet. My knees stuck in the blood.

I pulled her hands away from her stomach.

Her hands were holding something in.

Bits of her. Bits of her insides.

She had been cut open.

Someone had cut her open.

I put my hands on her stomach to try to hold her together; trying, somehow, to push the pieces back in, as if that would have helped her.

I couldn't. I couldn't do it. It was too much. There was too much blood, too much of her.

I rocked back on my heels, then forwards again. Backwards and forwards, rhythmically, my bloody hands clutched to my face, my mouth open in a silent scream.

There was a piece of paper resting on Zoey's chest. Eventually I made myself stand up. I leaned over her – over her body. I picked up the note and I read it.

You murdering bitch. Now you know what it feels like.

Thirty-four

What was I supposed to do? What the hell was I supposed to do? I tried to think. It felt like I was paralysed. I didn't know how long I'd been there. I couldn't move. I was standing there, with that note in my hand, and I couldn't move. I couldn't take my eyes off Zoey. I wanted to look away but I couldn't. Her mobile funny face was all twisted and frozen, and it was all because of me. I killed her. He killed her because of me. He killed her to teach me a lesson, to show me what it felt like to lose someone I cared about.

What was I supposed to do? I knew I should call the police. What would I tell them? How could I explain the note? I looked at it again; read it through one more time. With shaking hands I folded it up and slipped it into the back pocket of my jeans. They didn't need to see it. Not yet; not until I'd got it all straight in my head. Not until I'd worked out what I would say.

I staggered across to the kitchen area to get myself a glass of water. I picked a glass from the draining board and I was about to turn on the tap, but then I realised there was blood all over the sink. He must have washed his hands here. He had stood there, washing his hands in the very place where I was standing now.

Now you know what it feels like. How what feels like? To have someone I cared about snatched away from me? Why Zoey? Why had he picked Zoey? Because she was there, in the flat where I was living? Or because . . . oh Christ, the thought came to me with a flood of ice through my veins: maybe he'd meant to kill *me*.

The blood on the floor was still sticky. Did that mean he was still here, in this tenement building? How long had Zoey been dead? Was he still here, waiting for me? Had he been lurking in the shadows when I'd arrived? Had he been watching me, waiting for the scream when I found her body? Had I screamed? Had I actually screamed? I couldn't remember.

I could feel myself struggling for breath. I was about to have a panic attack. It felt as if someone's hands were around my neck. I turned on the tap, watched the blood swirl around the plughole. I filled my glass and tried to drink; tried to calm myself down. And then I heard something, and I froze. Footsteps. Outside, downstairs, somewhere in the hallway. Footsteps, very deliberate footsteps, were climbing steadily, quietly, purposefully up the echoey staircase. I put the glass down. I walked out into the hallway. Still those footsteps kept coming. I darted into the bedroom. I pushed the sash window up, my hands leaving blood all over the white-painted window frame. The moon stared at me, placid and uncaring. Two storeys below, the garden was nothing but a scrappy lawn and a gravel path. Could I jump? No. No, it would kill me. I knew about falls. I knew that a fall from that height could be fatal.

The footsteps were coming closer. My heart was in my mouth. I went to the front door of the flat. I stood there, and put my eye to the spyhole. I was holding my breath. I was ready to fight. I was desperate to know who he was. I was more scared than I had ever been, but despite that I was ready for him.

The footsteps were there. And then they weren't. They moved away. They moved away down the landing and then I could hear them turn and climb the next flight of stairs. I heard a door open and a muffled sound of greeting. The people upstairs were going on with their normal life as I stood there convinced that I was about to be killed.

I had no choice. I couldn't stay there. He could still be lying in wait for me. I had no choice. I had to run. I crept out of the door and then I hurtled down the stairs. I dashed out of the door and onto the street. I looked around me: no one. I pulled my bag against me, making sure the strap was safe around my body. I ran up the stone steps and out onto the main road. I pushed through the swarms of people who were out on the street; the people who were standing outside the pub smoking, as if nothing had happened; the drunks queuing outside the chippie; the couples waiting at the taxi rank. I took a deep breath and then I crossed the busy road and I started to run for my life.

My chest hurt. It was tight and burning and I couldn't catch my breath. I was running faster than I'd ever run. Down the hill, down, down to where the railway bridges crossed the road. I was retracing my steps. Stop – there – breathe. I leaned against the wall and left a red palm-print on the bricks. I leaned forward, hands on my thighs, legs apart. Pigeon shit all over the pavement. I wanted to throw up but it caught in my throat and I coughed, nearly choked. Footsteps coming round the corner. Not him, not him following me; wrong direction. Ambling footsteps, voices. I stepped backwards and made myself as small as possible, leaning my back against the wall. Kids. Students. A big group, five or six of them. Shaggy-haired guys, a couple of girls. They jumped when they saw me. One of them asked for directions. Posh, Oxbridge-type voice. He named a street. I didn't know it. Maybe I did. I don't know what I said. He apologised, reached out a hand to steady me, and I ran. Hurtled. Fast as I could.

My ankles hurt. My knees hurt. I was clutching my side as I ran. He was behind me, somewhere; him, the man who was following me; the man who'd killed Zoey. I knew he was there, somewhere in the darkness. I ran across the road; a car screeched and stopped just inches from me. I didn't even look back, just kept on running. Holyrood Park was dark and empty. The Scottish Parliament building loomed, grey and spiky in the night sky. I stopped again, leaned against it, felt the protruding stones with my hands. I had my back against the wall and I looked around me. Shadows of buildings, narrow alleyways. No sign of him but I knew he could be anywhere.

Walking now, but fast. Alleyways off to my right and left; I darted past them quickly, not even daring to look into the shadows. Up the hill, up Canongate, up the Royal Mile. I checked my watch: just gone eleven. I had thought it was much later. Time was doing odd things. It wasn't running how it should. Too many things had happened in just one hour. Things were happening too fast. Every breath I took was burning in my throat and in my chest.

I needed to find somewhere to stop, to hide, to gather my thoughts. I looked up the street and I could see Henry the Eighth and his group of monks standing on the pavement smoking outside a pub. *They'll keep me safe*, I thought. I thought of them as old friends. It looked as though they were standing guard outside the pub. I sidled in amongst them. Then, when I was sure no one could see me, I dashed into the pub and I was immediately in the middle of a rowdy crowd of people. I pushed through the crowd. Some people looked at me oddly. I didn't stop. I didn't make eye contact. Down a flight of stairs to the ladies'; just one toilet cubicle with a basin, and it was empty, thank God. I bolted the door, but the bolt didn't seem very secure. I pushed the sanitary-disposal bin against the door as an extra precaution. I finally looked at myself in the mirror. I looked like a ghost. A ghost with bloody fingerprints all over my white cheeks.

I splashed my face. No towels. I grabbed a bunch of toilet paper and I wiped myself with it. Better. But there was still blood on my hands, all around my fingernails and under the nails. I tried to scrape it off but it had embedded itself deep and had dried there. Someone was trying the door of the toilet. Someone was trying to get in. I looked at myself again. My face was now hectic, white and red patches. I ran my fingers through my hair. It was wild and wavy. I took a deep breath and another and another. I was telling myself how to breathe.

Out of the door. The girl who was waiting to use the loo gave me a concerned look. I thought that she was going to ask me if I was all right but she didn't. I was about to go back upstairs into the pub but there was a noise from a room along the corridor. Laughs. Shouts. A bunch of people were standing at the door, about to go in. I tagged along, as inconspicuously as possible. A comedy night, free to enter. It was a dark room, tatty old sofas and armchairs arranged in rows facing the stage. I found a spare seat in a corner where almost no one could see me. I curled up in the chair, hugged my knees to myself and started to rock.

'This is safe', I told myself, like a mantra. 'This place is safe.' No one was looking at me. I was secure and hidden in my deep, dark corner. There was a guy on stage: a kid, no more than twenty-five. He was talking into the microphone, telling jokes. He had just split up with his girlfriend, he said. The audience – ten, fifteen people – said 'Ah!'

Zoey said that was always a lie. The biggest cliché with male stand-ups, she said. 'They've always just split up with their girlfriends. Like, they even had one to start with.' That was what she said. That was what she used to say. I could hear her voice saying it. Her voice, with its confident sharp, zingy tones. The voice that was always so sure of itself. Zoey's voice. Zoey, who was lying dead on a sofa in a tenement flat a mile from here. Zoey, whose insides had spilled out onto the floor.

Careful. Don't cry. Don't do anything stupid. Someone might notice me. I pressed my fist against my mouth and my head against my knees, trying to block everything out. Zoey was bleeding. Zoey was lying in a pool of blood. Zoey was dead. Zoey, my friend. He killed her. He killed her to teach me a lesson. People around me were laughing. I couldn't believe they were laughing. Zoey was dead and they were laughing. I looked up. He was still on stage, that young comedian. He was still on stage, skinny and awkward and full of fake woe and Zoey was fucking dead. I wanted to leap up on stage and tell everyone. How the fuck could you keep on telling jokes? How could everyone keep on doing this, this fucking pointless charade?

A noise came out of my mouth. Someone looked round from a sofa in the row in front of me, shushed me. Suddenly everyone was looking at me. Concerned faces. Was I crying? Could they tell there was something wrong? I pushed my way out of that room. An arm reached out for me and I dodged it. I can hear the comedian's voice as I ran up the corridor and back up the stairs. 'Well, my jokes have never had that effect before . . .'

Midnight. Too many people still on the streets. Faces looming out of the darkness. People reaching out to me as I ran past. Questions: 'Are you all right, love?' 'Hey, stop, what's wrong?' Other people laughing in big groups, outside pubs, cigarettes in hand; stopping to turn and stare at me. Gangs of drunks, four or five abreast, pushing me into the gutter as they went past. It was too crowded; too scary. He could be anywhere. He could be one of these smokers, masquerading as part of a group. He could be reaching out to help me, tempting me away down an alleyway. He could be anywhere. He could be anyone.

I saw a church. The word 'sanctuary' came into my head. I had a half-remembered piece of information stuck in my brain, something my father had told me once, or that I'd read somewhere: you could take sanctuary behind the altar of a church, whatever you'd done. They would have to protect you in a church, even if you were a killer. I needed to get in. A church would be safe. There'd be pews to sleep on, and kneelers, and maybe a sympathetic priest, someone like my dad. I tried the door. I lifted the big brass ring in my hand, feeling its cold weight, and I turned it, hoping against hope that the door would open. It didn't. I tried turning the handle in the other direction but that didn't work either. The door was locked, of course. But I rattled it, anyway, as if it would suddenly spring open. Round the back of the church there was a small bit of open space – a square, concreted over. There was another doorway, hidden from the main road. By now it was becoming a matter of life or death to get into the church. I was desperate. I just wanted somewhere to sit down; to lie down, in safety. I wanted to make the world stop for a while. All I had to do was to get into that church and I would be safe, and everything would be okay, at least for a while.

But the side door was locked too. I rattled the handle

frantically. I knocked on that wooden door until I scraped my knuckles and they started bleeding. I pushed it as hard as I could. I rammed it with my shoulder; I kicked and punched at it. But it was locked, and there was no answer and there was no way I could get in. All I was doing was hurting myself. Sucking the blood from my grazed knuckles, I sank down on the ground, onto the cold flagstones, and I started crying with huge heaving sobs that could probably be heard from the street. I needed to rest. I needed to gather my thoughts. I leaned my back against the door and tried to stop crying, tried to count, tried to breathe normally.

I must have closed my eyes. I must have gone to sleep, because suddenly a huge hand gripped my shoulder and wrenched me from some kind of dark, amorphous nightmare. An undefined face loomed over me. I was terrified. I probably cried out – screamed – something like, 'No! Leave me alone!' This is it, I thought; he's found me. The huge hand shook me fully awake. There were Scotch-whisky fumes in my face. I opened my eyes fully and saw a big grey beard covering a red face. A homeless man: that was all. He wanted me to move. The doorway I was slumped in, the doorway that I'd been trying to get through: that was his bed for the night.

Thirty-five

The light from the kebab shop seemed preternaturally bright. The pink neon sign outside was winking at me from across the street. The fluorescent lights seemed to beckon me in. If the church wouldn't give me sanctuary then this place would. It was one in the morning and the bright lights seemed like a gift. I'd been trying to hide in dark corners but perhaps this was the safest place for me now. How could I come to any harm under the glare of a dozen fluorescent tubes?

There were gaudy photographs of the menu, backlit above the food counter. I stood there, confused and indecisive. I pointed at one of the photos almost at random, and then said yes to everything that the man behind the counter offered me: extra salad, onions, cheese, yogurt sauce – everything. I grabbed a can of Diet Coke, fumbled in my bag for my purse and then I took my yellow polystyrene tray of food across to a white Formica-covered table in the corner of the café, from where I could see everyone who walked past, and everyone who came in.

I picked at the food aimlessly. The lettuce was limp and warm from touching the lamb kebab. The flatbread ripped when I tried to pick it up. The meat was chewy and the salad was tasteless, and I was eating for the sake of eating; eating for the sake of doing something with my hands. My mind wandered. I thought about Zoey again. The last time I'd eaten a kebab I'd been with Zoey, here in Edinburgh. We'd walked into the café and she'd asked the guy behind the counter, 'What's good here?' It was a joke, of course; she often said it, ever since I'd picked her up on it that first time. 'What's good here?' But in a way it wasn't a joke; it was just Zoey being Zoey. Zoey loved food. She loved to eat. She loved tastes and flavours. She loved kebabs and curries and chips, and finding new places to eat, and she always had the expectation or the hope that maybe the food would indeed be good. She always had an idea that something on even the most unpromising menu would be good, would be fun to eat.

I ate for fuel, pretty much. I rarely noticed much about what I was eating. But Zoey would nudge me: 'Hey, what's yours like?' Or she'd lean over and steal some of my food – she'd dip her bread in my sauce or scoop up a spoonful of whatever I was eating and she'd try it. 'Yum', she'd say, not always facetiously. 'Here, try mine,' she would offer. 'Isn't that great?' 'Zesty' – that was a word she used often to describe flavours. It seemed such a Zoey word, so full of life and zing and enthusiasm. What would she have thought of the kebab I was eating? But she wouldn't have ordered this kebab. She would have tried the house special, or maybe the plate of food that she'd never come across before. Right now she would have been tucking into something spicy and unusual. And I could have watched her face and I would have known almost instantly from her expression whether it was disgusting or delicious.

Friendship is like electricity. Zoey was all exposed copper wires, fizzing with energy. I was insulated, with heavy plastic tape wrapped around my nerve endings. And Zoey had started to unwrap the tape. She'd started to show me how to fizz and spark against other people, how much fun it could be. *Oh shit. Don't start. Not now.* More tears were crowding into the corners of my eyes, and I had to press my hand hard against my mouth. Even then a few whimpers escaped. *Can't let go*, I told myself. *Can't start crying or I'll never stop.*

I looked around. No one seemed to have noticed. There was an older guy eating his way through a huge mound of meat and salad. There were a few young couples holding hands and giggling. A bunch of young men who might have been Turkish were gathered around the counter, laughing and joking with the guy who was serving. I wondered how long this place would stay open, whether it was an all-night place or whether it would be closing for the night soon. I wondered how long I would be safe here. I wondered what I should do next.

I fingered the note in the back pocket of my jeans. Since I'd found Zoey's body I had been all panic and grief and unfocused terror. Now it was time to put those to one side. I would grieve again later. I'd be scared again later, I was sure of it. But for now it was time to think. I made myself eat my kebab, methodically chewing each piece of food eight, twelve, sixteen times. And I made myself think methodically, too. I tried to make a mental list of what had happened and why it had happened. And I tried to work out what to do next.

Zoey was dead. She'd been killed by my faceless, implacable stalker. He had suddenly upped the stakes. Why? Had there been any real warning that he might kill? I thought back to the notes I'd received. He was watching me, the notes had said. He knew where I was; he knew where I went. There had been a veiled threat that he would tell Danny what I'd done. There had been nothing about this. Nothing about killing someone. No warning that this would happen. But he had called me 'the murdering bitch'. Perhaps it was inevitable. Perhaps I'd been stupid not to see that his vengeance would be murder.

Why now? Why this sudden escalation? The reason suddenly seemed very clear: the same reason he'd started writing the notes in the first place. I was happy. I'd escaped my fear. I was taking baby steps out into the world of normal people. Despite the notes, I'd been happy in Edinburgh. I had been out there on the streets, amid the bustle of the Festival, flaunting my happiness. No wonder he couldn't stand it.

Why Zoey? The question made me shudder. Why the hell did he kill Zoey? It was my fault. It was me who had dragged her into my nightmare. I'd been so careful about Danny. I'd thought that he could be in danger in some way. I hadn't even thought that Zoey was at risk. It was my fault. Zoey was dead and it was my fault. He killed her because he knew she meant something to me. He killed her because of what I'd done all those years ago. She did mean something to me. She meant a lot to me. I knew that now. She had meant more to me than I'd realised. I loved her. I sat there in that brightly lit kebab shop and I realised that I had loved Zoey. She was the best friend I'd had in years. And that was why he killed her.

I thought about that second note. *Does your new lover know how evil you are?* I'd assumed he meant Danny. But the stalker – the avenging angel – had left the note on my car on the evening that I had driven Zoey all the way down to Southampton. He killed her in the flat that we were sharing. Oh Christ, he thought we were lovers. He thought we were lovers and that was why he killed her. I had tried to escape him. I had fled to Edinburgh and I'd thought I had escaped him, but all I had done was sign Zoey's death warrant.

What next? What was he planning to do next? *Now you know what it feels like.* You murdering bitch – now you know what it feels like to lose someone you love. Now you know what it feels like to be truly afraid. He'd had no qualms about killing Zoey. It was supposed to serve as a warning to me. Don't try to escape again, don't try to be happy, because I know where you are and I will kill you. I was sure that he would be coming for me next. He was out there somewhere in the dark – and at that I quickly looked up from my food and gazed around the café. Most of the young couples had gone. The Turkish lads were tucking into food now. The older guy must have left. I hadn't noticed him go. I looked out of the window, trying to see into the dark night, but all I could see was my reflection on the window. I looked pale and haunted, with huge dark circles etched into the skin around my eyes. He was out there somewhere, enjoying my fear. He would string it out for a while, but eventually he would strike.

I wondered if anyone had found Zoey's body yet. I wondered if Suze or Laura had a key to the flat. Maybe Steve did. Maybe one of the girls would have called Steve when they'd got no answer from their repeated phone calls to me. Or, if he didn't have a key, maybe he would have hammered down the door, calling Zoey's name. He would hammer frantically, like I had done on the church door, and he would run at it with his shoulder and the door would break. Or maybe one of them would have got hold of the landlord, somehow, and he would have let them in with his spare key. And then they'd find Zoey. I thought about her body and I couldn't eat another mouthful. I didn't want to eat, ever again.

I should have gone to the police. I should have phoned them and reported what had happened, and I should have stayed there with Zoey's body until they turned up. It would have been safer than being out here, at his mercy. I knew that now. But then there'd be questions, and probing, and somehow I would have ended up telling them the whole awful story about Rivers Carillo. And that would be a disaster. I just couldn't do it.

And now it was too late, anyway. Another awful thought had struck me. The police would find footprints in the blood in the hallway and all around Zoey's body. The footprints were of a woman's size six shoe. There were bloody fingerprints on the sink, and on the white-painted window frame, and on the front door: bloody fingerprints that showed I had been all over the flat after Zoey's death. There was only one conclusion that could be drawn from the evidence there: I killed Zoey Spiegelman. I was responsible for her death, and the police would believe I had done it. There was no escape. All I could do was to keep on running.

Thirty-six

I thought I knew what fear was. I had lived with it for half my lifetime. I knew what it tasted like, I knew the hollowed-out feeling it gave me under my ribs and in my stomach. I knew how it could make every hair on my body stand to attention, like a sensor or an early-warning system. I knew the varying degrees of cold that fear could make me feel. But nothing I had ever experienced before could have compared to how I felt when I woke the next morning.

When people in films are in dire straits – chased, cornered, fleeing for their lives – someone always says to the heroine, 'Get some sleep,' or 'Get some rest.' Someone did a survey once, and found that the sentence was the most used in films – of any sentence. More even than 'I love you.' As if whatever monster is chasing you, whatever disaster is around the corner, sleep will somehow make it better. As if the next day you will wake up and everything will be brighter.

In fact you wake up the next day and things are worse, because nothing just gets better by itself. And now time has gone by and your fate is closer, and you're still unprepared. The day dawns with its harsh light that peers into all the shadows, and all it does is make the terror even more relentless and real.

The sky was grey, with a bright white band low down in the sky over to the east. The air felt big and empty. No one else was around. I felt as if I had stepped outside the known world and now it was just me and him, a fight to the death. He was waiting for me somewhere; I didn't know where. But somewhere, out there, he was waiting with a knife or a gun to kill me, or a fast car to run me over. There was no one to protect me now. I had to face this on my own.

It was cold: damp, shivery dawn-cold. I pulled my green velvet jacket closer around me and I felt a shudder go through my whole body. I was in a doorway in a little alleyway at the top of the Royal Mile near the castle. I had spent the night there, half-dozing, half-wakeful, just counting the hours until Edinburgh woke up and I could try to get lost in the bustle again.

There was a tall, dour-looking house across the street from where I was sitting. I recognised it: Deacon Brodie's house. We had stopped there on the bus tour. Had that really been only twelve hours ago? I had sat upstairs in that green open-top bus, in the middle of the festival throng, and they'd told us the story of Deacon Brodie, the man who lived a double life: respectable cabinetmaker by day; ruthless thief by night. His story inspired Robert Louis Stevenson to create Jekyll and Hyde. I wasn't sure how much of what the bus driver told us was true. It all got mixed up in my head with the stories of Burke and Hare, the body-snatchers. So many stories of crime and gruesomeness round here. I was telling myself this stuff in my head to stop myself thinking about Zoey, lying like a rag doll in that pool of blood.

The streets around me seemed post-apocalyptically empty: just a couple of homeless men asleep in doorways, on bits of cardboard and old blankets. The nearby shops were all boarded up with metal grilles across their windows and doors. I was tired and I was empty, and I could not stop shaking. Somewhere out here, in this city, was someone who wanted to kill me; someone who had already killed my friend; someone who was prepared to slash open the stomach of a woman he didn't know and didn't care about, just to teach me a lesson. And I didn't know who he was. I didn't know what he looked like. I didn't know who it was that I was supposed to be afraid of.

I stood up and staggered away from my doorway. My legs would barely carry me. I was walking – staggering – looking behind me with almost every step. Could I hear footsteps, or just echoes? I needed somewhere else to shelter; somewhere to sit while I worked out what I should do next. I found a café in a little side street, the kind of café that stayed open all night. I went in and took a seat in the far corner, so that I could see everyone who came and went. I ordered food that I didn't want. I tried to eat my full Scottish breakfast, but the yolk on my half-eaten fried egg unsettled me with its shiny viscosity. It reminded me of the blood.

I left some money on the table and found the tiny toilet at the back of the café. I thought I was going to be sick, but when I leaned over the toilet bowl and started to heave, nothing happened. I looked at myself in the mirror, and tried to wipe off the worst of the smudged mascara with a piece of damp loo roll. There was still a little bit of dried blood on my face, and I rubbed at that too.

And then, as I went back into the café, as I walked towards the door, I noticed a man sitting at a table right by the door. Had he been there earlier? Had he followed me here? He was watching me, intently. He was watching every step I took towards him. He had straggly long grey hair and piercing eyes. He was wearing an old corduroy jacket that was frayed and worn around the collar and sleeves. I could feel my legs start to shake but I forced myself to carry on. He hissed at me, beckoned me towards him. I stopped where I was. I stared at him. Was this him? Again, he beckoned me closer. I stepped towards him. He stood, suddenly, and put his face close to mine. His breath smelled of alcohol. 'Have you finished wi' your breakfast?' he said, in a Scottish accent. 'Mind if I finish it?'

I walked downhill, heading towards the big green area of Princes Street Gardens. I found a wooden bench near the National Gallery. I looked around, peered into the bushes of the park behind me. I listened, hard. I heard nothing. I let myself sit down. I curled my legs up under me and pulled my jacket tighter around me. I took out my keys and I jabbed them into the palm of my hand so that I didn't fall asleep. I sat there, poised, primed to spring up and run away; or primed to spring up and stab my keys into someone's face: whatever it took. I wasn't safe, but I would never be safe. It was somewhere else to sit for a while.

I didn't know whether my life was worth anything any more. I wasn't sure it had been worth anything for years. It was just a bunch of bits and pieces: fake name, fake friends, fake smile, fake pleasantness. My life was a tatty plastic bag, tied up with string, full of stuff that I had accumulated along the way, stuff that I thought was important to me. But at that moment, on that morning, sitting on that bench in the centre of Edinburgh, I realised that it meant nothing at all. I was nothing; I was worth nothing and no one would miss me because no one really knew me at all. Except him: the watcher, the killer. He and I, we were players in a particularly violent computer game. I was nothing but his target. I could run, I could hide, or I could come straight out and surrender. Or I could finish the job myself.

I was cold. I was in shock. I'd had almost no sleep. I was sitting there on a bench wondering if I should kill myself: really obviously, really publicly – so he would know that I was dead; so he would leave all my loved ones alone.

Loved ones. What loved ones? My own family didn't even know me. It was like they just gave up on Lizzie seventeen years ago and accepted Beth instead because she was so much simpler to handle. They loved me – if they loved me at all – because they had to, because I was a member of their family and custom dictated that they should love me. Loved ones. Maybe Zoey had loved me, a bit. But Zoey was dead. Who was there left who loved me for me, for who they thought I was? And then I thought about Danny. And for just a second it was like the sun coming out.

Danny. My friend Danny. Those dark eyes; that steady quiet voice; those strong hands. Danny, so calm, so reassuringly dull. Danny the grown-up with the proper job. Danny would know what to do. Danny would sort it out. Thank God for Danny. 'I'll call Danny; that's what I'll do.' It seemed so simple when I said it to myself. I would call Danny and tell him everything. But not yet, not yet. Too early. Far too early. I wasn't ready yet.

Time passed. I heard cars drive past along Princes Street. A man painted all silver – silver clothes, silver face – sat on the next bench along and smoked a cigarette: an off-duty living statue preparing for the day ahead. I wondered if it was the same one who had tried to outstare me the other day. A woman strolled along the path, a little terrier on the other end of the lead she held. The dog tried to sniff me; the dog-walker pulled it away. She frowned at me and walked on. I was aware that I was rocking to and fro like a madwoman. I was thinking about Zoey and how her hands were holding her insides in. I remembered how I touched her there, how I tried to put everything back in. The blood, everywhere. Her head, lolled back awkwardly like that. Her eyes open and staring. And only the day before, there she'd been on stage, funny and caustic and totally in control. 'Now you know what it feels like,' the note said. And I could feel it; I could feel the pain deep inside my own stomach.

I'd have to tell Danny the full story. It was as simple as that. I had to tell someone; I couldn't go on like this. I'd have to tell Danny what I did all those years ago. It wouldn't matter what he thought of me; he hated me anyway for the way I'd treated him. Danny would know what was best to do. He would tell me that I'd have to talk to the police. I knew that. I would have to tell them how I found Zoey's body. I would have to tell them about the note, the one I found on her body. And all the other notes, too. I'd have to explain it all; how I killed Rivers Carillo all those years ago. I'd have to tell Danny, and then the police. What would happen then? Was there some kind of statute of limitations? Could they charge me with a killing in another country seventeen years ago? Would people have to know about it? Would my parents have to know about what I did? What was going to happen to me?

Thirty-seven

When I was eighteen I killed a man and got away with it.

I had never said those words out loud. I had hoped I would never have to. But now the time had come. The axe had finally fallen.

Edinburgh's old town loomed above me like an illustration from an old-fashioned book of fairy tales, from an era when it was acceptable to terrify children. Tall, crooked, pointed grey buildings huddled around the giant's castle. It was a city from a nightmare: a city of ghosts and goblins and witches, of dark alleys and whispers and hauntings. Looking up at it made me dizzy. I felt that I might fly away on a broomstick or on the wings of a bat.

Help me. I need a friend. That was how I would begin the call. I held the phone in my hand and searched the contacts list for Danny's number. He'd be up by now, just drinking his first cup of coffee, listening to the *Today* programme on Radio 4, maybe checking his emails: ordinary, mundane stuff. He wouldn't be expecting to hear from me. *Help me, Danny; I need a friend.* And he would listen to me and say the right things and maybe he'd make everything okay. But in my heart I knew that nothing could ever be okay again because today – in just a few minutes – I would have to say those words out loud for the first time.

When I was eighteen I killed a man and got away with it.

Just before I made the phone call, just before I dialled Danny's number, just before I told him my awful secret, while I was still sitting there in the stasis of that pre-confession moment, I reached into the deep back pocket of my jeans. I pulled out the piece of paper. My hand trembled as I straightened out the creases. There was blood on the paper, blood from my fingers. I read it over again to myself.

You murdering bitch. Now you know what it feels like.

His voice sounded tired and detached. He didn't want to speak to me; he made that clear with his tone of voice. My first words didn't help much. 'Danny, I need you. I need a friend.' I tried not to cry as I spoke.

'Beth, this is not the time. I'm in a hurry. I need to be at work early. Let's talk later, okay?'

'Danny, no. Stop . . .' I thought he was about to put the phone down and I was desperate. He must have heard something in my voice, because he gave a resigned sigh.

'OK, I'm listening. What is it? What's so important?'

I opened my mouth and nothing came out.

'Come on, tell me.' His voice was gentler now.

'Danny, something awful has happened. Zoey's dead. He killed her. And it's all my fault.'

'What? What are you on about? Is this a joke?'

From nowhere I could feel a hideously inappropriate laugh start to bubble up in my chest. I opened my mouth to let it out and it turned into a sob. Before I knew it I was weeping loudly, hysterically. I didn't care if the silver statue heard me. I just didn't care. And on the other end of the phone there was Danny, all sensible and kind, saying, 'Shhh. Beth, shhh. Calm down. Calm down. Please. Just tell me all about it.'

So I did. In a tiny, shaky voice I told him about Zoey, and about how I found the body. I told him what it looked like, how she'd been sprawled on the sofa, and how much blood there'd been. I told him about how scared I'd been, and how I had run for my life, and he interrupted me. 'Why didn't you call the police?'

'I was scared, Danny. He was after me. He wants to kill me. I know he does. I know, I know, I should have called them. But I had to run. There was a note, you see. He left me a note.'

As I reached into my back pocket and pulled out the letter again, I was going to read it to him, but he interrupted me again. 'Beth, you're not making sense. Who was after you? What note? What on earth are you talking about?'

'The man who killed Zoey. He left a note on her body. A note for me. I've got it here, with me. I can read it to you.' I wasn't telling the story very clearly. I knew that. It wasn't coming out properly. I wasn't explaining myself.

'Beth, if the killer left a note on the body, why have you got it? Why didn't you leave it there for the police to find?' Danny's voice was sharp, as if he was trying to trip me up. I realised that he didn't believe me.

'The note was left for me. It's for me. It's written to me. He killed Zoey to get back at me. He wanted me to know that.'

'Beth, what the hell are you talking about? I'm sorry, I really don't know what you're saying. I don't think you know what you're saying. Are you okay? I mean, of course you're not. That's obvious. Are you ill? Are you in shock? Because you're making no sense at all.'

I tried to pull myself together, to make my voice stop shaking. I tried to make sense: one final effort to get him to believe me. 'Danny, I've been getting notes. Anonymous letters. All summer. Someone's been watching me and threatening me. And the man who killed Zoey is the man who's been writing those notes to me. It's the same handwriting, the same paper, the same man.'

'Christ, Beth, why didn't you say so? Please tell me the police know about this. Please tell me you've reported it.'

'No. I haven't told anyone any of this. Until today. I've been so scared and I didn't know what to do. And now this has happened.'

'One more time, Beth: why not?'

'I couldn't. I couldn't tell the police, I couldn't tell anyone, because . . . God, Danny, there's all this stuff I need to tell you, and I've wanted to for so long, and . . .' I put my hand over my face and I started to hyperventilate.

'Beth, what is it? Why is someone sending you anonymous notes? Why did he kill Zoey?'

'To get back at me for something terrible I did.'

'Okay, I'm listening.' Danny sounded grim. He sounded like he was bracing himself for the worst that I could tell him. I wasn't sure if the worst he was imagining went far enough.

I sat there on that bench in Princes Square Gardens and looked up at the narrow grey skyline of the Old Town that loomed above me. The living statue had moved. Now he was standing on a podium on an open paved area by the National Gallery, and a small group of people had gathered to watch him. It was the start of another day in the life of the festival city, and here I was about to tell Danny everything. Danny Fairburn, serious, caring and kind. This was it; this was the end. I needed to do it. I needed to tell Danny all about Rivers Carillo, and about my summer in San Francisco. I needed to tell him about Alcatraz and Sausalito, and how Rivers and I slept together, and how he was an itch I couldn't scratch, and then everything – almost everything – that happened after that. Nothing in my life would ever be the same again. I took a deep breath and started to tell my story.

'Danny, when I was eighteen I killed a man and got away with it. At least, I thought I'd got away with it. I've been looking over my shoulder ever since and now someone's found out. He's stalking me. He's trying to punish me. And he did it by killing Zoey.'

Thirty-eight

I killed Rivers Carillo on my last day in San Francisco. I hadn't planned to kill him. I didn't go out that morning saying: 'Today's the day I'm going to kill a man.' But the opportunity presented itself, like a little demon sitting on my shoulder, whispering in my ear. I did it, and I've been paying the price ever since.

My last day in San Francisco, I woke up feeling sore but excited. I'd changed, I'd grown up, I'd become a woman. I felt myself 'down there', fondling my tender skin. My breasts felt tender, too: bigger and fuller than before, the nipples harder and more distinct. I'd forgotten all the squalor and the discomfort of the previous day, of that wretched houseboat in Sausalito. All I could think about was the huge thing that had happened: the excitement, the awesomeness of losing my virginity. And the fact – or rather the assumption – that it tied me to Rivers Carillo in some mystical way.

Romantics need things to mean something. Romantics look for meaning in everything: in gestures, in words, in things unspoken. So when something this big happens, it has to mean everything – love, at the very least. Perhaps romantics with a religious background are the worst. Naïve romantics with a religious background.

Naive, flirty, romantics with a religious background. I operated on the assumption that other people thought like me, had the same values that I did. I'd been brought up to believe that sex was a dangerous, threatening thing; something that was safe only in the confines of marriage – or, if your faith was a bit liberal, a little fuzzy around the edges, as mine was, within the confines of a loving relationship. I'd been brought up to regard my body as a temple, to exercise self-respect and control. I'd been brought up to believe that my virginity was the one thing I should keep; something that I should only hand over to the right man at the right time; something non-negotiable.

So maybe when I woke up that morning feeling full of love and tenderness towards Rivers, I was merely justifying my own behaviour to myself. I woke up telling myself that I loved him – and so he must surely love me. I had to tell myself that, or else there was no justification for what I had done. That's what had motivated me as we waited for the ferry in Sausalito; why I'd flirted with Rivers again and kissed his fingers. You see, sex couldn't be the end. Our romantic idyll couldn't end that way, with bloody sheets on a squalid houseboat. I couldn't have given away my virginity as cheaply as that, just bartered it away in return for a hug and a slow dance to Bob Dylan in the cramped cabin of that horrible boat. That wasn't how the story went. Sleeping with Rivers Carillo was so big and so significant to me that it had to be the start and not the end. It had to be a prelude to something better, or else why had I done it?

I know all this now. Back then, as I woke up that morning, all that hopelessly romantic Lizzie Stephens could think was: *Today's the day that Rivers Carillo will tell me he loves me.* As if those words – those three words – were like a precious diamond on an engagement ring.

We met, as usual, secretly. We pretended to bump into each other in the food court in the basement of Macy's on Union Square. 'Hey, look who it is!' Rivers said.

'Fancy meeting you here,' I replied, my usual arch, jaunty self.

'How're you doing today?' he asked, and there was an extra note of tenderness in his voice that made my romantic little heart leap for joy.

'I'm very well indeed, thank you,' I replied and he laughed. I knew he would. It was simple to make him laugh: just a few words of very proper English were all it took. He hadn't touched me; I knew he wouldn't until we were somewhere alone. But that was okay. It could wait. It would happen.

We caught a bus and sat on the back seat – together, but not too close. It was a long bus ride, through endless streets of Victorian wooden houses. We passed close to Joanna's house and skirted a little green square. 'Look back at the view,' he told me, and I did. It was the famous view of San Francisco: a row of Victorian houses, the city skyline in the background with the Transamerica Pyramid stretching high into the sky. I was glad to see it on my last day. I would store that picture in my memory bank.

Rivers didn't say much on that journey. Occasionally he'd mutter something about the scenery or where we were. 'Haight-Ashbury,' he said at one point, and I looked out of the window to see the same type of Victorian houses, but this time painted in gaudy colours, or allowed to get tatty, and shops selling vintage clothes, second-hand records and drug paraphernalia. We skirted Golden Gate Park and drove into a coastal fog. And then we were the only two remaining passengers, and the bus stopped and we were at the beach, on the far western tip of the city. It was chilly, and we were swathed in swirling damp fog. But we were alone, and we were together, and he let me wear his jacket.

We played on the beach for a while, skimming stones into the sea that was virtually invisible behind a thick shroud of grey fog. He taught me how to skim the stones properly: standing behind me, touching me, his hand on mine, his chest against my back. This is it, I thought: any moment now, the declaration. But it didn't come. Instead he looked at my shoes.

'Are those comfortable?' he said. 'Can you walk in them?'

I was wearing trainers: jeans and trainers. I hardly ever wore jeans and trainers that summer in San Francisco. Almost every other time I'd been out with Rivers, I'd worn skirts with flip-flops or sandals or something else flattering. But that day I was wearing jeans and trainers. I had packed my suitcase and was dressed in the clothes and shoes I was planning to wear on the flight home. I emphasise this, because it's one of those 'if only . . .' things. If only I'd been wearing sandals, Rivers wouldn't have taken me on that walk. And if he hadn't taken me on that walk, I wouldn't have killed him.

'It's foggy now,' he said. 'But the fog's going to lift later today. There's this amazing path around the cliffs, right round to the Golden Gate Bridge. It's a few miles, and it's kinda rocky, but it's not too difficult. And it's worth it, because you get an unforgettable view of the bridge, especially just as the fog is lifting. It's amazing, and I think you'll like it.'

With hindsight, he was trying to say sorry. Rivers Carillo was a sleaze, but not an evil sleaze. He was probably genuinely upset by what had happened in Sausalito. He probably hadn't expected it to end like that. He probably just wanted to give me a nice day out, to say sorry; to give me a memorable end to my summer in San Francisco. He wanted to give me a treat, and his treat was to give me a chance to see one of his favourite parts of the city. He simply wanted to share a beautiful view with me. It wasn't meant as a declaration of love; I just took it that way.

It reminded me of Devon, of trudging around the coastal cliff path, following my father and his map, footsore and sunburnt but enjoying the views. Except this time there were no views. A blanket of fog out to sea on our left-hand side, crumbly cliff to our right, a dirt path underfoot, bits of spiky bushes and trees grabbing at my clothes. I was getting warm and I'd given Rivers back his jacket. He crumpled it up and shoved it in the backpack he was carrying. I followed him, keeping his strong, sturdy back in sight. Every few minutes he'd look behind him to check I was okay, or to apologise for the weather. 'It'll be worth it,' he kept saying.

The path levelled out and suddenly we were on a flat, grassy headland. A few yards away, incongruously, stood a huge, elaborate building that looked like a palace. In front of it was a sculpture – twisted bodies and a barbed-wire fence. 'The Palace of the Legion of Honor,' Rivers told me. 'It's an art gallery. And that's a memorial to the Holocaust.'

I ran in to use the loo. Stupid, the things you remember. I ran into the museum and persuaded the woman on the desk to let me in without paying so that I could use the loo. 'The restroom,' I remembered to call it. And I had always wondered – did she remember me? Did she read about Rivers's death, about how they discovered his body, and then remember the English girl, hot and red-faced, in jeans and dirty trainers, running into the museum that day to use the restroom? Was she a witness to what happened?

Beyond the museum, the path turned into tarmac and took us down into a curved road full of huge, luxurious houses. Rivers took a left-hand turn down a narrow alleyway and there we were on another beach. 'Look,' he said, and pointed around the curve of rocks to our right. Sure enough, the fog was beginning to lift and I could just make out the top of the Golden Gate Bridge, absurdly red against the grey sky. We climbed back to the dirt path, and now we could see glimpses of the sea far beneath us, jagged rocks at the foot of the cliff we were walking along. We didn't talk much; we were putting all our efforts into the trek.

And then it happened. There was a point on the path where you could – carefully – step out to your left onto a little piece of headland. We ducked under some trees and found ourselves right on the edge of the cliff. And from where we stood we had the most extraordinary view of the bridge. It was suddenly enormous, looming up bold and red from the mist that swirled around its girders. I tried to get closer to the edge, to get a better view, but felt the dirt and gravel slip under the treads of my shoes. Rivers caught hold of my arm to steady me, and then put his arm around my waist and kept it there. Looking down, I could see that the cliff dropped almost straight down – there was a ledge a couple of feet below us, and then the cliff fell down to the sea and the rocks hundreds of feet below.

Rivers had his arm around me because he was just trying to hold on to me, to keep me safe. But my romantic teenage head told me that this was the moment. I reached my arm around him and hugged him closer to me. He fidgeted slightly, but didn't pull away. I reached up and kissed him on the cheek. He looked at me, puzzled. 'It's beautiful,' I said.

'Isn't it?' he said, and tousled my hair.

What he needed to say next was, 'And so are you.' But he didn't. He said nothing. He just stood there, holding me, gazing at the bridge.

Something had to happen. I had to make something happen. I kissed him again, this time reaching around for his lips. He pulled away; I was insistent and eventually he kissed me, closed-mouthed but tenderly. I moved closer. 'Careful,' he said, and 'What are you trying to do?'

I settled for snuggling up against him. I had to say something. I had to initiate a romantic moment, and the kiss hadn't really worked. 'When will I see you again?' I said.

Rivers laughed. 'You're going home tomorrow.'

'We can see each other again, can't we? You could come to England. Or I could come back here. We'll keep in touch, won't we? This is special, isn't it? I mean, I want to carry on seeing you.'

This was his moment; the moment where he should gruffly declare his love and ask me to marry him. But he didn't. He just laughed again, a little uneasily.

I can still hear my voice getting desperate and shrill. I can still almost taste the panic I was feeling. 'I love you. I want to stay with you. I want to live with you.'

'Ha!' he said, abruptly. 'I don't think my wife would be too happy with that.'

I thought he was joking. For a split second I thought it was an awful joke. I started to laugh – and then I saw his face. He'd turned to face me, his back to the cliff edge. He was serious. 'Look, kiddo. You know the rules. You know the game. We've had fun. But it ends here. I'm going back to Indiana in September, back to my job, back to my wife. You're flying back to London tomorrow. It's been fun. I like you. I've enjoyed it. But the game is over. We won't be seeing each other again.'

Rivers was actually quite tender, quite caring as he said these words. He was trying to let me down as gently as he could, I'm sure of it. He wasn't a bad person, he wasn't evil. He didn't deserve to die. If only I could have left it there. But my whole world, everything I'd spent the last few weeks dreaming about, had just been ripped apart. My brain was muddled. Where to start? He was married. It was all a game. He didn't want to see me again. 'But we had sex!' I shouted it, as if it was irrefutable proof that he was wrong, that this wasn't just a game.

'Sure we did. And I'm sorry it wasn't better for you. But you wanted it. I didn't hear you complaining.'

'It was horrible.' I was crying now. 'The sex was horrible, but I wanted to do it again. I didn't want that to be the only time with you. I wanted you to show me what I'm supposed to do. I love you. That can't be all.'

Maybe it was that second 'I love you' that made Rivers angry. He took me by the shoulders and shook me. 'You stupid girl. You stupid little girl. You want sex? You want to sleep with me again? Here? Will this do? Now?'

He pushed me back against the tree behind us. He pushed himself against me. He kissed me, hard, forcing his tongue into my mouth. I could feel his growing erection as he forced himself on me. One of his hands was working its way into my blouse while the other held me firmly by the shoulder. I could feel his finger and thumb tweaking my right nipple, hard. He pulled his mouth away from mine and said, 'You want this, do you?'

I hit him on his arms and against his chest. I struggled against him. I slapped him around his face and he just smiled. And then I started kicking. I kicked him in the shins, over and over again, hard, just in the centre of the shin where it really hurts. And he started moving backwards, almost dancing, to get away from me. While he was off balance I pushed him, hard, with the heel of my hand, right in the middle of his chest. And he fell backwards over the cliff.

Thirty-nine

From where I sat on the edge of the cliff I could see Rivers's body on the rocks below. It was sprawled and broken and covered with blood. I had never seen a dead body before, but there was no doubt at all that he was dead. His neck was twisted around awkwardly, in an unnatural position, and half his head was smashed in. His brains had leaked onto the rocks.

The minute it happened, I regretted it. Of course I did. I'm not a monster. The minute it happened, the second it happened, the moment it happened. Even as he was falling down, down to those rocks, I wanted somehow to fly down and catch him up again. I wanted to be able to turn back time. I wanted to close my eyes and then open them again, and watch time move in reverse – watch his broken bones knit themselves together again. Rivers Carillo: one minute he was there, big and strong and alive; and then he was down on the rocks, broken and bleeding and dead. If you've ever been in a car accident you'll know a little bit what it was like. You'll know that feeling when time turns to treacle, and you're aware that something awful is happening but you can't stop it. It was a bit like that. Something awful had happened and I would never be able to stop it, and there was nothing I could do to make it better.

Seagulls shrieked. The sea rushed against the rocks, lapping over Rivers's body, lifting it slightly with each wave. I watched for quite a long time. I watched as the waves washed relentlessly against his corpse, scouring away the blood and the brains. I watched until his body eventually slipped under the sea and away from the rocky coast.

What was I supposed to do? I didn't have a phone. There was no one around, no one to report it to. And besides, what good would it have done? He was dead; his body was being washed out to sea. And no one had seen what I had done.

I picked up his backpack. I looked through it, to see if there was any evidence of me. His little Moleskine notebook and his diary – I threw them into the sea separately, skimming them, using the motion that Rivers had taught me earlier. I wanted them to soak through and disappear, just in case he'd mentioned me. I tried to throw his backpack out to sea as well but the strap got caught on a pointed piece of rock and it stayed there, resisting the tug of the sea as hard as it could. There was nothing I could do about it. I prayed, a stupid prayer, not a prayer of forgiveness but a prayer that said: *Please God, let the sea move the backpack. And please don't let me get caught.*

And then I went back to the path and carried on walking in the direction we'd been heading. I just carried on, as if nothing had happened. I put one foot in front of the other, and I counted my footsteps as I walked along that narrow rocky path, and I tried to concentrate on anything apart from what I'd just done. I felt completely numb.

The path took me right under the bridge and out onto a concrete plaza, with an information centre and some bus stops. The fog was beginning to come down again, and it was warm and muggy. There were lots of people around. There were official people, National Park rangers with uniforms and hats. I could have told one of them what had happened, but I didn't. I checked my map and my public-transport guide, and I got on a bus to the Marina District. I sat in a coffee shop while the fog descended again, and I tore up the pamphlet I had in my bag, the one full of Rivers Carillo's poetry. I stuffed it in a rubbish bin, wrapped up in the pages of a magazine. Then I got on another bus and went back to Joanna's house, let myself in and climbed upstairs to my bedroom.

I finished packing. I remember doing that. I remember getting out my plane ticket and my passport, and putting them in my handbag. I remember deciding which toiletries I'd be using the following morning and which I could pack already. I remember checking that I'd ordered the bus to the airport to pick me up at the correct time, and I remember setting my alarm clock. And then I brushed my hair and cleaned my teeth and wandered down to the big kitchen where I discovered Joanna, cooking me a surprise farewell dinner. I remember all these little, trivial things that I did, but I don't remember how I felt.

*

It was on the plane home that I became Beth. I sat curled up in my seat and I planned my future. First of all, I tried to work out what would happen to Rivers's body. I guessed that in due course it would get washed up on one of the beaches or coves around the Golden Gate area, depending of course on the tides, and I knew nothing about those. Then I worked out how long it would be until someone realised he was missing. I didn't even know where he'd been staying in San Francisco, but I assumed that his absence might not be noted for a couple of days. After all, sometimes he stayed over at people's houses.

That was when I realised about Joanna. Suddenly I realised how stupid I'd been. They were lovers. That's why I'd seen him at breakfast time at her house. She would miss him. She would report him missing. Did she know about us? Did she know that Rivers had been sneaking around behind her back to romance her young house guest from England? He wouldn't have told her; no way. But did she guess?

And who else might have known about us? The friend who owned the bookstore? The friend who had loaned Rivers the houseboat? Did he ever tell them? Did he ever say, 'I have this hot eighteen-year-old English chick who's dying to sleep with me and I need a place to do the deed'? Did the friend ever work out whose blood it was on his sheets?

And Rivers's wife, this mysterious figure back in Indiana – what about her? Was she really expecting her husband back? Did she guess what he really got up to on his summers in San Francisco, 'finding his muse'? Would she assume he was dead, or would she imagine that he'd just left her, gone off somewhere, maybe faked his own death to start a new life with someone else? Was he even married? Or had that just been a lie to put me off?

I tried to decide what I should do. For a while, I thought about changing my identity utterly. I thought about doing what I'd read about in a thriller – finding a grave or a newspaper report of the death of a baby, a girl, back around the time when I was born. I'd read that you could apply for a birth certificate that way, and then a passport, and create a whole new identity. For at least a couple of hours of my flight home I thought that was what I would do.

But I didn't want to lose my family. I didn't want my parents and siblings to lose me and have to hunt me down. I remembered my father watching a television show about some teenager who'd disappeared, years before, and his parents had spent their whole life since then dedicated to finding him. And my father had cried while watching it. He'd said, 'That must be the worst thing in the world, never to know.'

I couldn't have done that. I might have been a killer but I couldn't cause that grief to my father.

And so I did the next best thing. I made myself as different as possible. If Rivers had told anyone about me, he would have talked about a bubbly English teenager called Lizzie. A loud, flirty, fun, dramatic, silly girl called Lizzie. And so I became Beth: quiet, sensible, studious, unnoticeable, plain and dull. I became Beth, who no one would ever look at twice. I arrived home and told my parents when they met me at the airport that I wanted to be called Beth now. And they seemed pleased that I'd grown up.

I kept worrying over details in my mind. Joanna worried me. One day I'd convince myself that she knew all about us, the next day I'd be sure that she'd guessed nothing. A few weeks after I got home I got a letter from her, enclosing a bunch of clippings. First, Rivers had disappeared – they'd found his backpack and one of his shoes – so he was listed as missing, presumed dead. And then his body was found, washed up on the shore; he'd been identified by his dental records. A tragic accident while he was out walking on his favourite path. Joanna had written in her letter: 'I think you met him while you were over here. I thought you'd be interested in this.'

I was utterly unable to tell her tone of voice from that.

Joanna died about ten years ago, of cancer. It was sad, but I'd also felt a huge sense of relief. But there were still things to worry about, and every time I thought about it I found something new. Rivers's wife might have hired a private detective, or pestered the police to investigate further. DNA from the blood on the sheets in the houseboat: could they still identify it? Would they be able to match it to mine, if somehow someone were able to remember my name and to find me? Would that constitute evidence, or simply give proof that I'd known Rivers and had slept with him?

The friends who knew about me, the woman who'd let me use the toilet at the Palace of the Legion of Honor, maybe the park rangers who'd seen me looking stunned on that foggy afternoon at the bus stop by the Golden Gate Bridge: could a good detective put them all together and work out what had happened? All these things that had occupied my mind for seventeen years, all these fears and worries filling my brain; leaving me almost no room to grieve for the man I'd killed.

Forty

'He tried to rape you,' said Danny. 'He tried to rape you, you pushed him away, and he fell over the cliff.'

I fidgeted. Danny's précis of the story made me uneasy.

'He tried to rape you,' he said again, and his voice had an insistent note. It seemed that he wanted confirmation, that he needed me to assure him that the killing had been self-defence and entirely accidental. I couldn't assure him. It might have sounded like that, the way I had told him, but it wasn't the full story.

'I knew he was on the edge of the cliff when I pushed him. I could have just fought him off but I didn't. I pushed him, and I knew he would fall.'

'But he was trying to rape you.' I could picture Danny sitting there at his kitchen table, his sleeves rolled up, his tie loosened, struggling to process the information that I had just told him to make it fit within his world-view. He was trying hard to be understanding. He was trying hard to convince himself that it didn't matter that I'd killed someone. He was trying to find grounds on which he could still care for me.

So I agreed. 'Yes, you're right. He tried to rape me. So I fought back.' And thus I wiped out everything I had ever felt for Rivers Carillo. I wiped out everything I had done that made me culpable. I took away all the ambiguity in that situation on the cliff, all the tenderness and love and anger and hatred that I had felt, and the way things could have gone either way, and I denied them. I denied all those emotions. I pared it down to a few short words. Hard words, single syllables: words that washed away my guilt and made it into an acceptable story.

'You didn't tell anyone because you were scared. You were just a kid. Jesus, you were eighteen years old. No one can blame you for what you did.' Danny was warming to his theme now. He was making me into the victim so that he could still care for me with a clear conscience.

'Someone does, Danny. Someone says I murdered him. Someone killed Zoey to get back at me.'

'Are you sure that's what it's all about? There's nothing else you've done that could have caused all this?'

A weird laugh escaped my lips. 'Oh God, you're right. It must be about one of the hundreds of other people I've murdered in my life. I'd forgotten all about them.' He said nothing. He had never liked it when I was flippant. 'No, Danny. Don't worry. I've only ever killed one person. That's quite enough to wreck my life.'

'And have you any idea who's doing this?'

'Danny, I've been going over and over it in my mind, all summer, ever since I got that first letter. At one point I thought it might be you, even. That maybe you were his son, or something. And then I thought maybe it was Zoey. She looks – looked – a little bit like him, from certain angles. But obviously it's not. It can't be, because now she's dead and there's another letter. It's someone I don't know, someone I've never seen.'

'Are you sure you've never seen them? Are you sure you've never seen anyone following you?'

'Oh God, all the time.'

'What do you mean?'

'All the bloody time. Virtually every day of my life since then. But it's him I see – Rivers Carillo, or people who look like him. Younger versions of him, sometimes. I see him in crowds, I see him sitting in cafés watching me, I see him when I'm out shopping. I saw him the other day. Here, in Edinburgh. I thought he was chasing after me. I'm a nervous wreck, Danny. This thing has dominated my entire life. And it's all my own fault.'

'You have to go to the police,' Danny said decisively. 'You're going to speak to the police. You're going to give a statement about how you found the body, you're going to show them that note and you're going to tell them everything they need to know. Everything. Tell them in exactly the same way that you just told me. No one can blame you for what you did to that River guy.'

'Rivers.'

'Whatever. Now, go now. And if you need me, if you think there's going to be trouble, call me. I'll get on a train if you need me. But, Beth? This can't wait. You need to do this now.'

He was right, of course. It was the only way to end the nightmare.

*

Detective Inspector David Finlay was a tall, lean man in his forties, with thinning grey-blond hair cropped close to his skull, and clear, pale blue eyes. He was wearing chinos and a blue shirt, sleeves rolled up, no tie. He looked completely exhausted. He led me downstairs to a little room and called in another detective, a younger woman. And then he proceeded to take my statement.

I was as prepared as I could be. I had my story straight in my head. All I had to do was to tell the truth. All I had to do was to sit there and tell that policeman, with his lean, wry face, everything I had done and how I had found the body. That was the first thing I had to do. And then the questions would get more difficult, and I would need to show him the note, and to tell him about Rivers Carillo, but at least I had my story straight. I would tell him exactly what I'd told Danny. I knew what to say. And at least in that little room I would be safe, for as long as it took.

DI Finlay asked me how I knew Zoey and to describe our relationship, and he raised his eyebrows slightly when I said we'd been friends.

'Just friends?'

'Yes.' I was keeping my answers as short as possible. He wanted to know why I was in Edinburgh and how come I'd been staying with Zoey, and who else knew Zoey and where she lived. I mentioned Steve's name, and Laura and Suze, and he ticked them off on a list in front of him. 'In a moment, Ms Stephens, I'm going to ask you about finding the body. But first, I want you to tell me what you were doing yesterday.'

'All day?'

'All day, please. Hour by hour. With proof, if possible.'

I pulled out my purse. I had tickets and receipts. I always kept them – I don't know why. Any time I got given such a piece of paper, I would shove it straight into one of the sections of my purse without thinking about it. I had a pile of little bits of paper that I spread out on the table. I had the whole of the previous day, that lovely day of fun and freedom, summed up in a bunch of tickets and receipts. I had a timed and dated ticket from the open-top tour bus, I had tickets for Edinburgh Castle and Holyrood House, and a credit-card receipt from the little Indian restaurant where I'd had dinner. I had my ticket for the Josie Long show, and another one for We Are Klang's show, which was called *KlangBang*. Finlay looked closely at that ticket, at the time of the show. Eight-forty p.m.: that interested him. 'Who are they, these Klang people?'

'These three comedians. Three blokes. They do stupid sketches. They're very funny.' As I said that, I realised why he was asking. That must have been when Zoey had been killed: that was why he was so interested. I had been sitting there in that little room, nearly wetting myself with laughter, while Zoey's stomach was being hacked to bits by a madman with a knife.

'Can you prove this is your ticket?'

That was the young female detective, the first thing she'd said. I shrugged. 'I don't know. I can't remember how I paid. I think I used my credit card.'

She wrote something down. 'Can you prove you were

there? Were you with anyone? Did anyone see you? Would anyone have noticed you there?'

I almost laughed at the irony. No one ever noticed me. I'd lived half my life trying to go unnoticed. 'No. I was on my own.'

'Maybe there's something about the show you remember particularly?' Finlay picked up the questioning again.

I thought hard. Of course I remembered it; but that wouldn't help. One thing I knew from Zoey was that comedians did more or less the same show every night. Even the apparent ad libs were often rehearsed. Even if I had recited the whole show, word for word, that wouldn't have proved that I'd been there on the night in question. I twisted my fingers together and then fiddled with the receipts and tickets lying there in front of me, rearranging them so that the edges were parallel with the edge of the table. I looked at DI Finlay, at his interesting face, and then I thought of something. 'They did this thing with insults. They picked on members of the audience.' I remembered sitting as still as I possibly could, plastering a nonchalant look on my face, sending out '*Don't pick me . . . don't pick me*' vibes. 'People had to come up with the best insult they could for the guys on stage. It was really stupid, but very funny.' Finlay was frowning at me, wondering what I was about to say. 'Anyway, there was this old woman in the audience. I mean, really old, like eighty or something. And they picked on her, and she had to insult one of the comedians, this funny-looking bald guy. And she said he looked like a dead Gollum.'

So that was my alibi. The detective's mouth twitched slightly at one corner. '"A dead Gollum",' he said wryly, and wrote it down. He smiled to himself, and shook his head slightly. He looked at his colleague and she smiled too. Then Finlay scratched his chin and looked at me for a while, as if he was trying to work me out. I didn't know where to look. I was very conscious of the note in the back pocket of my jeans and I knew that soon I would have to show it to him.

He cleared his throat. 'Now, Ms Stephens, I believe you arrived back at the flat last night and found Ms Spiegelman's body.'

I nodded.

'Could you speak up, please?'

'Yes. Yes, I did.'

'And what time was this?'

'It was just gone ten. I looked at my watch as I got back to the flat.'

'I need to know everything you did and everything you touched.'

I took him through it, from the moment I'd pushed open the street door of the flats. Methodically, as calmly as possible, I told him about the key not being there, and about listening to all the phone messages as I climbed the stairs. As I spoke I had my hand in the back pocket of my jeans, feeling the note, ready to pull it out and show him. I told him how I had seen blood in the hallway, and how I'd found Zoey's body, and how I had put my hands on her stomach to try to stop the bleeding. My voice had been quiet and steady until then, but it caught in my throat as I got to that bit, and the young female detective went over to a table in the corner and poured me a paper cup of water. 'Take your time,' she said. 'This must be difficult.'

And that was when I lost my nerve. She was suddenly kind and gentle, and my throat was dry, and I'd been so strong until then. But I lost my nerve. I fingered the note in my pocket one more time, and then I shoved it deeper. I told them everything else that I'd done in that flat and where I'd left my bloody fingerprints. But I didn't tell them about the note. And I didn't tell them about Rivers Carillo. At the very last minute my resolve fled.

'So why did you not report what you found? Why didn't you call 999 straight away?' DI Finlay was definitely playing bad cop. He glared at me, his forehead wrinkled into a frown.

'Because I was scared,' I said. 'I heard footsteps. I thought the person who killed her was also going to kill me. I got scared, and so I ran.'

Finlay raised his eyebrows. 'And now you're *not* scared?'

'Of course I'm scared. But I couldn't stay running for ever.'

He was going to ask me another question but there was a knock on the door. A uniformed policeman came into the room and apologised for the interruption. Finlay went outside to speak to him, while the female detective and I looked at each other across the table. She smiled at me. 'This won't take much longer,' she said.

After a few minutes Finlay came back in, looking much happier. 'Okay,' he said, brushing his hands together as if he had finished with the whole business. 'That's it, Ms Stephens. Go with Detective Sergeant Ross here and we'll take your fingerprints for comparison purposes, and then you'll be free to go. I'm sure you'll be reassured to know that we have a suspect in custody. I anticipate that charges are imminent.'

'What?' I was stunned. 'You found him? Already? Who? Who is it?'

But Finlay wouldn't say. I was ushered out of that tiny room with my head spinning. This was crazy. Had they really managed to catch the killer so quickly? Who was it? Who the hell was it who had been haunting me all summer?

Forty-one

I walked out of the police station feeling like a zombie. I was tired and I was filthy and I wasn't sure whether I should be laughing or crying. Zoey was dead. But they had already arrested the man they thought had killed her. Who was it? Did they have the right person? Was it my stalker? Was it the note-writer? Was I safe at last? But even if they had arrested the right person, if they really had caught Zoey's killer, then maybe I was only safe for a little while. Because – what would he be saying about me? Would he tell the police why he'd done what he'd done? Would he tell them about me?

'Beth!'

The man's voice made me jump. I looked across to where the voice had come from. A tall, skinny, bearded man was standing in the doorway of an empty shop across the road, smoking. He was beckoning me over. I stood frozen to the spot for a moment. He'd been waiting for me. And then I blinked and I saw that it was Steve, Zoey's friend. He looked as dishevelled and distraught as I did. I walked across the road towards him, almost forgetting to check for traffic. I had never been so glad to see someone. Close up, I could tell that he had been crying. He held out his arms to me. He just stood there, saying nothing, and held out his arms. And I hugged him. It was a busy street, slightly run-down, away from the centre of the city, and people were walking past us – normal, mid-morning Edinburgh people, on their way to do normal things. But Steve and I stood there, the pair of us, his chin resting on my head, and we hugged each other, swaying slightly, saying nothing. His shirt smelled of cigarettes and sweat and it seemed like the most comforting smell I had ever known.

After a while he said, 'This is so fucked-up. This is so fucking fucked-up.'

He let go of me, and we stood side by side in that doorway.

'Did they tell you they've got someone?'

I nodded. I opened my mouth and to my surprise my voice was still working. 'Yes. They didn't say who.'

'It's some fucking junkie. That's who they've got. I was talking to one of the cops. He came out for a smoke and we got talking. He shouldn't have told me, but he did. I guess they were proud of themselves. They found some fucking junkie with Zoey's purse, trying to use one of her credit cards. Apparently he's trying to tell them that the bag just appeared in his doorway. That he woke up and it was there. Christ.' He stubbed out his cigarette and trod it into the ground. I said nothing. I was scared all over again. This wasn't right. They hadn't got him. They hadn't found the killer.

'You've got to give them marks for speed, I guess,' said Steve, his voice bitter. 'They were fast, I'll give them that. But this is fucked-up. This is fucking crazy. This is so fucking wrong. Like Zoey would let some junkie into the flat. Like some junkie would do that . . .' and his voice cracked slightly. 'Like he'd do *that* to her just to steal her fucking bag. Can't they see? The guy who did this must have taken her bag for some reason. I don't know. Maybe he wanted something from it. God knows. But then he dumps it. He sees some poor junkie kid sitting in a doorway somewhere, and dumps the bag on him. And the kid can't believe his luck, so he tries to use one of the cards and he gets banged up for fucking murder. This is so fucked-up. Why can't they see it?'

Steve pulled out his pack of cigarettes and offered me one. I took it. I didn't smoke, not often, but I understood why people did. You can stop time when you're smoking, or at least slow it down. It's something very controlled that you can concentrate on. You can concentrate so hard on smoking a cigarette that nothing else matters for a little while. Steve lit my cigarette for me, and I noticed that his fingertips, like mine, were still black from the fingerprint ink. He noticed something else.

'You have blood on your hands.'

For just a moment I thought he meant it metaphorically, and I wondered how he knew, how he'd guessed. And then I looked at my fingers and realised that the dried blood was still caked around my nails.

'I found her,' I said. 'I found her. But I ran away because I was scared.' That part of the story at least was becoming a little easier to say.

'Christ,' said Steve. 'Christ. You saw her. You saw what he fucking did to her.' He pulled deeply on his cigarette and shuddered. 'How are you feeling?'

I thought for a moment. I leaned back against the locked door of that empty shop. I watched a young mother with a pushchair walk past, and a brisk elderly lady with a shopping trolley. Neither of them looked at us. 'I feel dead,' I said, and I meant it. I even thought that maybe I *was* dead, actually dead. Maybe *both* of us were dead, Steve and I. Maybe no one else could see us. This was what death was like, this aimless scared wandering; this sense of not being able to get out of a nightmare.

'Do you know what I feel?' Steve knocked the ash from his cigarette with his black fingertip.

I shook my head.

'I feel angry. Fucking angry. And I'm going to go right back to talk to those detectives and I'm going to make them see sense. I am going to make a fucking scene and I will not leave until they take me seriously. We both know Zoey wasn't killed for her credit cards. We both know there's got to be more to it than that.'

I must have gasped or something. I must have made some kind of sound or gesture that gave something away, because suddenly Steve was staring at me very intently. The purple circles around his eyes had given them a curious greenish cast. 'What?' he said. 'What do you know? You *do* know something, don't you? Tell me.'

He grabbed my wrist but I twisted away from him. 'I have to go,' I said. 'I have to . . . get back. Sorry, sorry.' And I walked away very quickly down that normal, shabby, busy street. I walked away as fast as I could, and as I turned a corner I started running and then I was hurtling through the streets, out of breath and still running from the nightmare that just wouldn't stop.

Forty-two

The Fringe was still in full swing. Nothing had changed. The ugly slab of concrete concourse above Waverley Station at the end of Princes Street was as bustling as it had been all week. I was sitting on a cold metal bench by a low stone wall that encompassed a flower bed, of sorts: a compacted bed of dry soil and cigarette stubs, a few tenacious shrubs still clinging to life despite the long dry summer. I was waiting to catch a train, hiding in plain sight in one of the busiest spots in the whole city. The giant marquee that served as a ticket office for the Fringe was packed with people waiting to use the array of computer screens to buy online tickets to whichever show the critics were raving about that week. The queue at the Half-Price Hut was less choosy; people were standing there weighing up the merits of comics and actors they had never heard of, deciding which ones were worthy of three or four pounds for a cut-price ticket.

Crowds of people were milling about, bringing splashes of colour to the grey city. I watched them with a new alertness, a new fear. I watched the faces, I looked at the eyes. I wondered if he had followed me here, if he was watching me even now. I wondered what he planned to do to me next.

There were floppy-haired students from university drama societies, from Oxbridge, or Durham, or Exeter, promoting their modern-day productions of *Macbeth* or *The Crucible* or *Hedda Gabler*, as if any of it mattered. There were arty middle-aged people, *Guardian*-reader types, scarves and sandals, beards and berets, linen and corduroy. And everywhere there were groups of teenage girls in their uniform of leggings and ballet pumps, with their cheap chunky beads and their short denim skirts, their bra straps showing under their layers of brightly coloured vests and skimpy T-shirts, and their regulation ironed-straight hair. I had been one of them once, seventeen years ago, dressed in that summer's version of this bold, flirty finery, all cheap and brash and sexy and brave and innocent. And that was how everything got ruined.

Every few moments someone would walk over to me and hand me a flyer for a show. 'Are you looking for some comedy tonight?' was what some of the pamphleteers asked me. They had no idea how blackly, grotesquely funny those words sounded. I wondered when – if – they would hear what had happened; how the news would spread. I wondered if the festival would come to a huge grinding halt. Or maybe everyone already knew what had happened and they were ignoring it. Maybe the festival momentum was impossible to stop.

I let the pamphleteers give me their pieces of glossy paper, their postcards, their brochures. Just two days ago I had been doing the same thing: handing out flyers to anyone who might be remotely interested in seeing the show. I looked at the leaflets that I was handed, tried to read the words, tried to work out what the pictures meant, but nothing made sense. I put the flyers in a little pile by my side, straightening the edges so that the pile looked neat. They were just pieces of paper and cardboard. They couldn't hurt me. Everything around me was going on as it had done for the last two weeks. There were jugglers and fire-eaters and comedians and backpackers. People looked exhilarated or exhausted or confused. But no one else was as scared as I was. The world had tilted on its axis but no one else seemed to have noticed.

I checked my watch. It was time to go. I had several train tickets in my pocket, for different journeys. I looked around me, trying to make sure that I wasn't being followed, and walked quickly down the sloping path to the railway station underneath the plaza. I had bought my tickets a little earlier, working out my travel plans with great care. I had lurked around the station for a while looking for somewhere to hide, but had felt very exposed there. But now it was time to put my plan into action. I asked a guard to show me where the London-bound GNER train was. I showed him my ticket. I made a great pantomime of pointing in the direction he had shown me. I walked across to the dark-blue-liveried train. I walked up and down the train's length, seeming to take my time choosing a carriage. I got on and appeared to settle myself in a seat near a door. I took my distinctive green jacket off and I stuffed it into my bag. And then, just as the train was about to leave, I jumped off and lost myself in the crowds milling around the station. I found one of the small commuter trains to Glasgow, got on board and held my breath until it pulled out of the station. I didn't notice anyone following me.

The train arrived fifty minutes later at an ugly 1960s-style station in Glasgow. I got off, and scanned the information boards for trains to London. I couldn't see any. I started to feel panicky. I found a guard and asked him, and I thought I was about to cry. He put a kind hand on my shoulder, steered me outside and beckoned a taxi over. He said something to the driver and the next thing I knew we were driving through the busy city-centre streets. I wasn't sure where we were going. I didn't know if I could trust the driver. But just a few minutes later he delivered me to a covered road that led to a huge Victorian train station, full of dark wood and arching iron cathedral-like ceilings. Twenty minutes later I was on a train bound for London, and as far as I could tell I had not been followed.

As the train rattled southwards I fell asleep. It was a disturbed sleep, punctuated by station stops and announcements about buffet cars and refreshments. I dreamed about being chased along grey stone streets, about cobbles and steps and castle battlements. I dreamed about fire-eaters and jugglers and a man dressed as Henry the Eighth. I dreamed that I was bleeding from a huge gaping wound in my stomach, and however hard I tried I could not stop the bleeding or sew up the wound.

I woke finally when the train stopped in Manchester.

The sky outside the carriage windows was so grey it was like night-time. Rain was falling from the sky, and as it landed on the streets and the roofs of cars it bounced up again, several inches into the sodden air. I shook my head to free it from the dreams and watched the people getting on and off the train. Later, as we continued southwards, I bought coffee and a sandwich from the refreshment cart and tried to eat. Now was the time to decide what to do.

I couldn't go back to my flat. That was the first place he'd look for me. I couldn't go to my parents' house, either. I didn't want to drag them into this. Sarah, maybe – but no, it was too late. If I'd wanted to go to her house in Sheffield then I should have changed trains at Manchester. Jem? No. Not my family. Not anyone in my family. I knew that could be disastrous. I couldn't ask my family for help. It would just make everything worse. I didn't want to bring them into this whole thing. I'd already seen what he was prepared to do to people I loved.

Danny, then. Danny was already involved. He already knew the dangers. He had told me to ring him again if I needed him. He was probably expecting me to ring him. I couldn't go to his flat, I knew that. That was obvious. It was too close to mine. But he would know what I should do. He'd be able to think of somewhere for me to hide. He'd know someone or somewhere. He'd protect me when I got back to London. I knew he would.

'Hey, you.' Danny's voice was gentle and concerned. 'How are you holding up?'

'Okay, I think.'

'Where are you?'

'I'm on a train. I'm on my way back to London.'

'Oh.' He sounded surprised. 'What did the police say?'

'They've got someone. They've arrested someone already.'

'That's good.'

'No, it's not. They've got the wrong person. They found some homeless guy with Zoey's purse. They think he did it, but he didn't. They think it's just a robbery gone wrong.'

'You told them everything?'

I didn't lie to him, but I didn't tell him the whole truth either. 'Danny, they weren't interested. They just didn't want to know. And now I'm coming back to London and he's still out there somewhere, and I still don't know who it is.'

'Shhh,' he said. 'Shhh. Don't worry. We'll sort this out. I'll meet you at the station and we'll go somewhere. We'll find you a hotel or something, just till we get this all sorted out. It'll be okay. Trust me.'

I'd forgotten how hot London had been that summer. As I got off the train at Euston it was as if the city had saved up all the heat that I had missed while in Edinburgh, and it hit me with it in one hot blast. The air was thick and stale. It stank of burgers and coffee and body odour. It was the tail end of the rush hour, and I carved my way through the crowds on the platform heading for the station concourse. I was looking for Danny. I was looking for his tall figure, his cropped head and his reassuring dark eyes. He'd be in his suit. Or he'd be in his shirtsleeves with his tie loosened, his jacket slung over his shoulder or one arm. He'd be there, waiting at the right platform, waiting for me to emerge from the crowd. He'd be standing right there, solid and safe, and he'd hug me and tell me everything would be all right.

But he wasn't there. I scanned the crowds. The train was ten minutes late. He'd had plenty of time to get there. There was no reason for him not to be there. Every man in the crowd who was tall and dark-haired was Danny for a moment, and then they weren't. He wasn't there. I walked further out onto the concourse, looking around me, checking I wasn't being followed, desperately hunting for Danny. I dug in my bag for my phone and pressed redial. 'Where are you?' I asked, my voice frantic.

'Where are *you*?'

'I'm here. I'm standing right by the information booth. You can't miss me.'

'*I*'m standing right by the information booth.'

I heard crackly sounds behind him, then the distinctive sound of a station announcement in the background of the phone call. There was no station announcement at Euston at that moment.

'Danny, you're at King's Cross, aren't you?'

'Of course I am.'

'I'm at Euston. I told you. I told you I was coming in to

Euston. I caught the train at Glasgow. Danny, you're at the wrong station.' I was close to tears.

'Shit. Sorry. No worries. I'm not far away. I'll be with you in five seconds, okay? Don't move. Stay exactly where you are.'

I did, for a while. I stood there in the middle of the crowded station and I tried to stay calm. I imagined Danny running at full pelt along Euston Road. It wouldn't take him long. He'd be here in minutes. But people kept pushing past me. All sorts of people. People and people and people. Faces in the crowd. People staring at me. A businessman with grey hair, combed over a bald spot. A smart black woman, all crisp and professional in her suit and high heels. A woman with an Arab headscarf, a guy in an old army jacket and with a dark beard, a young mum with a pushchair – they didn't stop. They came straight at me. I felt myself being pushed one way and another. I felt as if everyone in the crowd had decided between them to push me around. Everyone seemed to be heading straight towards me, hitting me with sharp-edged briefcases and umbrellas, rolling pushchairs over my feet. Everyone was the killer.

I fought the rising panic. Danny would be here soon, I kept telling myself. I felt in my courier bag for my keys, knowing I'd feel safer with a weapon. As I pulled them out of my bag and made a fist with them I realised there were extra keys on the ring. They were Zoey's keys, the keys to Zoey's flat, to that haven of calm and security in Clapham. She had given them to me the night before she'd left for Edinburgh. She'd known something or guessed something; she must have done. She knew I'd need somewhere to hide. Without leaving any time for thought I darted through the crowd, onto the escalator and made my way down into the dark, fetid embrace of the Underground.

Forty-three

Zoey had never seemed to care much about her own personal safety. She was bold and brave and she said what she thought, and she took risks. Of all the women I knew who lived alone in London she was the only one without a whole series of bolts and locks on her front door. Just a Yale lock. Just a solid wooden front door with a Yale lock. I let myself in and pushed away the pile of letters behind her front door. I slammed the door behind me, and despite everything I felt comparatively safe for the first time since it had happened. I felt like I had come home.

The hallway, with its deep blue-green paint, was dark even in the daylight. I flicked the light switch and all the fairy lights lit up, reflecting in the distorted antique mirrors that hung along the wall. Her dark red studio room was snug and inviting. I threw down my bag and kicked off my shoes, and slumped onto the bed. I looked around me at the shelves filled with books and CDs and DVDs, the pictures and ornaments everywhere. Even without her – even now she had gone – this room was still full of Zoey. You would never have been able to say the same thing about my flat. I ran my fingers along the spines of the books, all alphabetised and themed. There was a book lying on the small table next to her bed, a book of David Sedaris essays, and it suddenly seemed important to me to put it back on the shelves in its rightful place. But I couldn't find the gap. She had a particular order to her books, everything in the right place, and I couldn't find out where the book was supposed to go. I told myself it didn't matter, but it did. I found myself crying tears of frustration.

On one of the shelves there was an old black and white photo from her parents' wedding. What on earth could it possibly be like to lose a daughter? Parents weren't supposed to have to deal with the death of their children. I wondered whether they'd been told yet; whether the police had notified them and whether they were flying over to sort things out. I wondered if I should get in touch and introduce myself, or whether I should just slink away into the background: the woman who had caused their daughter's death.

I ran myself a bath. I wasn't sure if I should. It seemed weird, taking a bath in Zoey's flat, but I was dirty and smelly and I wanted to wash away everything that had happened, and I felt safe and at home there. I poured scented bubbles into the tub, and ran it as hot and deep as I could stand it, and I lay in that bath for twenty minutes or more. I thought I could hear my phone ringing, over and over again. The sound seemed to be coming from miles away, from another city, another life. I tuned the sound out. I tried to empty my mind. I wanted to fall asleep and slip under the hot water and leave everything behind. I even thought about slitting my wrists. I got as far as picking up Zoey's razor, which was in a pot at the end of the bath. It was one of those weird disposable ones with the razor part encased in a white block of shaving gel. I gave a grim laugh. No good at all for my purposes.

I pulled on Zoey's thick, luxurious bathrobe and I gathered up my dirty clothes from the bathroom floor. I noticed a couple of T-shirts pushed into the corner by the laundry hamper. I picked them up and looked at them. They'd been worn. They needed washing. Zoey must have dropped them last time she emptied the hamper. I gathered them together. *I'll put them in the machine with my clothes*, I thought. And then I realised. What was the point? She was dead. She didn't need those T-shirts. She wouldn't wear them again. What are you supposed to do with a dead person's dirty clothes? I buried my face in them as another wave of grief shuddered through me. And then I did the only constructive thing I could think of doing. I went into the tiny kitchen area, found some Persil capsules, and stuffed the whole lot – my clothes and hers – into the washing machine. It was the least I could do for her.

I looked in her wardrobe to find some clean clothes to put on. Again, weird, I know. It felt odd, but she had given me her key for a reason. She had told me to make myself at home, and I was desperate. I just wanted to feel clean and halfway normal again. I pulled out a faded black vest top, an old pair of jeans and a red V-neck sweater with holes in the elbows. Despite the heat of the day I felt cold. I put them on. They fitted well. They felt soft and comfortable and familiar. Zoey and I: we were so alike and yet so different. I could have been her. I could have been like her if my life had been normal. And now she was like me. Now she was dead instead of me. Now she was dead and it was my fault.

It was when I went across to the mirror on the wall of the bed-sitting room to comb my wet hair that I saw it. There was a large envelope on top of the bookshelf immediately below the mirror. The envelope was A4, manila, the same size and colour as my Rivers Carillo file. There was a note scrawled across the front of the envelope, in the loopy foreign-looking writing that I recognised as Zoey's. 'Dear Beth,' it said. 'If you're here, then it probably means something bad has happened. Please make sure the police get the contents of this envelope.'

What did she know? What had she guessed about me? I fumbled with the flap of the envelope. I reached in and pulled out some sheets of paper, maybe twenty in all. It was white A4 paper, laser-print quality, nothing special or particularly distinctive about it. Each sheet seemed to have been folded in three at some point, to fit in an envelope. I turned them over and as I read the top sheet I started to shake. I recognised the handwriting immediately.

To the murdering bitch. Does your new friend know what you did?

And the next one: *I'm outside right now, watching you.*

And again: *Don't think you can escape me, you murdering bitch. I know where you're going.*

And: *One day I'm going to get back at you, but not yet.*

*

I was sitting on Zoey's bed with the letters on my lap. I was counting them. It seemed really important to count them. My first count was eighteen, and then next time I made it twenty; and then I counted them again and this time I couldn't remember which order the numbers came in. I couldn't work out what these letters meant. I knew what the words said, but I didn't know what they meant. My brain felt a little bit like it did at the start of a migraine. My brain could not process the information in front of me. How come Zoey had these letters? Did she write them? Had she been sending me the letters all along? Were these the ones she hadn't got around to sending? But they were folded, as if they'd already been sent. Had she intercepted them somehow? Had she been trying to keep away from me? Had she been watching out for me, trying to keep me safe? Had she known all about it from the start? I couldn't make it make sense. I couldn't fit the pieces together.

From where I was sitting I could see out into the hallway. There was one of Zoey's antique mirrors directly across from me. I looked up, looked at the mirror and it showed me my reflection, distorted. My face was all out of shape and looked horrific, like a gargoyle. I couldn't work out whether it was really me or not. It made almost as little sense to me as the letters did. And as I sat there, staring at the mirror, trying to work out what was going on, I saw some movement in the corner of the mirror. Someone was there. Someone was outside in the hallway.

I clutched the letters to me, and picked up one of Zoey's ornaments, a big red 1970s glass vase. Slowly a face appeared around the door frame. It was a man's face. I screamed and I nearly jumped out of my skin.

He jumped too. He put his hand on his chest as if to slow down his fast-beating heart. 'My goodness,' he said, in a posh voice. 'I thought for one moment that you were Judith.'

I recognised him, I thought, but my befuddled brain was not working as fast as it should have done. 'Judith?' That was all I could think of to say.

'You would have known her as Zoey.' He came towards me with his hand outstretched. He was fortyish, with fair hair that fell into a floppy fringe over his forehead. He was wearing smart lightweight trousers and an open-necked blue shirt. I stood up, put the vase down and shook his hand.

'I know you,' I said. All of a sudden I had realised where I'd seen him before. It was the polite Englishman that I'd seen on the Royal Mile, the one who came to Zoey's show, the one I ran away from. I felt the hairs on the back of my neck start to prickle. 'What are you doing here?'

'Sorry,' he said. 'I startled you.'

I ignored that. 'What are you doing here? How did you get in?'

'I had a key. I let myself in. I never did introduce myself properly, did I? I'm Edward Moore.'

'I'm Beth,' I said, no wiser. 'I'm – I was – a friend of hers.'

'I know,' he said. 'I know who you are.'

Edward Moore said those words very precisely, with a

lot of weight. *I know who you are*. What did he mean? Who was he? Why was he here? What did he know?

'I'm glad I've found you here, anyway,' he said, pleasantly. 'I wanted to say sorry to you.'

'What do you mean?' I was starting to back away from him. Something indefinable about him was giving me the creeps.

'It must have been dreadful for you, finding her like that.'

He looked concerned and sympathetic. There was nothing threatening about his face or his body language, but all at once I was aware of how tall he was, how he was looming over me. 'What do you mean?' The same question I had already asked.

'Finding her body. It must have been awful for you.' And then he looked closely at me, at what I had in my arms – the pile of letters. 'But maybe it wasn't entirely unexpected?'

'Who are you?'

'You know perfectly well who I am.' And with that he did become threatening. His sympathetic smile, his pleasant face, had been replaced by a blank mask.

'No, I don't.' My memory was whirling around, trying to place his face, his name, somewhere in my past, trying to place him in San Francisco all those years ago.

'Of course you do. I can see you've found my letters.'

'You wrote these?'

'Of course I did.'

'Why?'

'Because she was a murdering bitch.'

The world flipped around. *She*? 'What do you mean, *she* was a murdering bitch?'

'Judith. Zoey, as you knew her.'

'You wrote these to Zoey?' I felt as if the whole world had suddenly fallen off its axis.

'Yes.' He smiled. 'Oh, I know. You got caught up in it, didn't you? I think I dropped off one or two of them at your flat, or when you were with Judith. That's why I addressed them so carefully. "*To the murdering bitch.*" So she'd know they were for her.'

Edward Moore's voice was so calm and reasonable. He was smiling a dreadful smile, revealing teeth that were long and yellowish, with receding gums. His diction was so perfect, such correct English with such a stiff upper lip.

'I don't understand. Why was Zoey a murdering bitch?'

He'd been leaning over me but suddenly he stepped back on his heels. He put his hands in his pockets and pursed his lips. He seemed to be weighing up his options. There was something ominous about his implacability. I wondered if his final conversation with Zoey had been anything like this. I was scared. I darted sideways and tried to get around him, but he simply put out his left arm and grabbed my right shoulder with a strong hand. He grabbed it so hard that I dropped the pile of letters and they fluttered to the floor. He pushed me backwards and I slammed into one of Zoey's bookshelves. He pulled his right hand out of his pocket. There was something shiny in it. I opened my mouth to scream, but that strong left hand was instantly clamped over my mouth, digging into the flesh of my cheeks. The shiny thing in his right hand became a knife – a flick knife, I think. He was just holding it casually, like an extension of his hand.

'Now, don't be stupid,' Moore said. 'You're just trying to change the subject. You weren't supposed to be here, you know. You shouldn't have been here. I came here because Judith has some things of mine, some things she took, some things that I want back. But in fact I'm glad I found you here. It's good to talk to someone about Judith, someone who understands. It's good to speak to you because you know all about it. I think you're the only one. You've seen the notes. You know why I killed her.'

His right hand, the hand with the knife, was between us now. He was holding it at stomach level, and all I could think about was how he'd torn Zoey's stomach apart. I was trying to bite his hand but I couldn't get my teeth into it. His hand was so big that it covered my entire mouth, and all I could do was to nip harmlessly at the fleshy part of the palm. His hand was so big that it was partly covering my nostrils as well, and I was struggling for breath.

'I had to kill her.' His voice was still soft and beautifully spoken. 'You know why. I'm sure she told you about me.'

I couldn't speak. I could barely breathe. I shook my head to tell him no, and also to try to shake him off, but he just squeezed my mouth harder.

'I did love her, honestly. But she was a bitch. A murdering bitch. She killed our child. I ask you, what man could stand for that?'

Christ. This was crazy. Zoey, a child-killer? What was

he on about? I couldn't clear my head. I was panicking. I could feel bile rising in my throat. I was going to choke.

Moore leaned his forehead against mine. It was an intimate gesture. It felt almost as though he was going to kiss me. I would have kicked him in the shins, my favourite self-defence move, but I was pinned against the bookshelf and it was cutting into the back of my knees, cutting off my circulation, making my legs go numb.

'Please tell me I'm right,' he said, and his voice was gentle and pleading. 'What man can stand for that? It's wrong, killing a child. She said it was just a foetus, that she wasn't ready yet. She said it was just a surgical procedure, that she had every right to do it, but she didn't. That was *my* child she killed. So I had to kill her. You do see that, don't you?'

I could taste the skin of his hand. I could smell his scent, sharp and lemony and old-fashioned. His hair was in my eyes. He was crying, and I could feel the tears on my skin. And I could feel his knife, digging into me, just above my navel. This was how I was going to die. Finally I knew. If I hadn't been so terrified I would have been laughing. A mad knifeman was about to kill me, and it had absolutely nothing to do with Rivers Carillo.

Suddenly there was a loud noise. A clicking, mechanical sound, like someone at the door, but it came from the kitchen. He – the knifeman, the killer – looked at me, as if I'd somehow conjured the noise. It was the washing machine; that was all it was. It was the washing machine moving into a new phase of its cycle. But he didn't know that. And as he looked at me, puzzled; as he tried to work out what the noise was, who was there, I grabbed his hand, the hand with the knife. I twisted it, a sudden sharp movement. I twisted it savagely towards him, and then I felt his hand over mine and he was helping me, he was guiding the knife. There was a sharp stabbing motion, and all at once there was warm liquid all over my hand. I clutched my stomach with my hand but there was no wound. And then I realised that his left hand had fallen from my mouth. He had the knife in his own stomach, and he was jagging the weapon from side to side. There was a gaping wound. His blood was all over his shirt, his trousers, all over me. And then he gave a strange gurgle, and he fell forward onto me.

I tried to save him. Frantically I pressed my hands against his stomach to try to staunch the blood, as if that would save him, save Zoey, save Rivers Carillo. But it didn't work. Zoey's husband died a long and painful death.

Forty-four

Danny was frantic. He'd been ringing me over and over, desperately trying to get hold of me, to see if I was all right. He had dashed down to Euston to meet me and he hadn't been able to find me. He'd had announcements put out over the station tannoy for me, about me, appealing for help to find me. He'd asked at the information booth. He'd reported my disappearance to British Transport Police and was about to talk to the local police station too. He had been out of his mind with worry, he told me.

All that time, all those missed calls. It wasn't until after I'd dialled 999 and called for an ambulance and the police to come to Zoey's flat, and I'd sat there with blood on my hands for the second time in two days, that I had thought to call him.

Danny came racing over to Zoey's flat and he hugged me. He was annoyed and he was worried, and he was caring and he was cross. He pushed the hair out of my face and he sat with me and held my hand as I told a uniformed policeman and then a pair of detectives all about Zoey's husband, and how – and I knew this; I knew this for sure, I wasn't making this up – how it was his hand that had twisted the knife in his own stomach.

And I wasn't quite sure why, or how, but they seemed to believe me.

And later, quite a lot later, several hours had gone by. We were still at Zoey's flat and then DI Finlay arrived. He had flown down, he said. Part of the investigation. He mentioned Steve's name. Steve had something to do with it. But I still couldn't work out what Finlay was doing there. And then I had to tell the story all over again, to DI Finlay, and while I was talking I couldn't remember where I was, what city I was in. There was blood all over the floor and my clothes were covered in blood and so were my hands and it felt like déjà vu. And then I remembered the note, but it was only when I reached into the back pocket of my jeans, as I tried to think of a way to explain why I'd taken the note from Zoey's body, that I realised they weren't my jeans at all. They were Zoey's jeans. My jeans were in Zoey's washing machine, still with that note in the pocket.

While I was talking to DI Finlay, while I was trying to remember who was who and where I was, I looked up and saw my face in the antique mirror, all twisted and distorted. And that's when I remembered how the world had flipped around when Zoey's husband was talking to me. I realised that I didn't have to mention Rivers Carillo at all, because he didn't matter. He was nothing to do with anything. None of this was connected with him at all. It's weird how you can see things completely the wrong way around.

*

Later, Danny took me back to my flat. I had another bath and went to bed. It was nearly morning and I had never been so tired in my life. But despite that I lay awake, my brain turning and turning, trying to make sense of things. It was nothing to do with Rivers Carillo. It was nothing to do with me. Those were the facts that I kept coming back to. The notes I got? They'd been for Zoey, not me. The note at school – the day we had lunch together. *Give this note to the lady when she comes back from lunch.* Vicky had misunderstood. She'd given it to the wrong lady. *Remember*, that note had begun. *Remember, I'm watching you.* Why 'remember'? That should have been the clue. It was the first note. How could I remember anything if he'd never told me anything before?

The comedy night in Southampton: no one had followed me down there. Zoey's name was on the bill. He knew she was performing there. He waited, watched us arrive; noted the car. She'd been in my flat when the third note arrived. *Murdering bitch*, he had written on the envelopes, so that Zoey would know they were addressed to her.

Zoey must have been out of her mind with fear but I had never noticed. I was too self-centred, too self-absorbed. My fear, as it turned out, was a selfish emotion. I got caught up in someone else's screwed-up life and because of my fear, or because of my paranoia, or because of my guilt, I assumed the whole thing centred on me. Two extreme ways of dealing with fear: I, with my imaginary threat, had been scared of ghosts and shadows.

Zoey, with her real threat, had been defiant and careless and bold.

'She was fucking stubborn,' said Steve. He'd known, it turned out. He'd known about the letters. He'd known at least some of the story. The two of us were having an early-evening drink in the upstairs room of a pub near Piccadilly Circus where later a bunch of comics would perform at a charity night in Zoey's memory. 'She was so fucking stubborn. She was fierce about it. "Why should I change my life because of him?" she said. The more letters he sent, the angrier she got. And the more risks she took.'

Steve had been with Zoey when one of the notes had arrived, just before she left for Edinburgh. Eventually he'd persuaded her to tell him about them, about the abortion, the real story of her marriage. He'd tried to make her go to the police. He suggested that she should think about changing her material, stop doing jokes about her husband. That was why they'd fallen out, why Zoey had claimed Steve was 'clingy'. That was why she'd given me the keys to her flat, not him.

'He didn't abuse her physically, I don't think, but he was an emotional abuser. They met in the States and everything was fine, apparently, but once they moved back over to England, he turned into a fucking monster. He tried to belittle her, to make her feel small and worthless. She knew she couldn't bring a baby into that relationship, and that's why she had the abortion. And then things got worse. She said the notes started soon after she left him and started doing comedy again, over here. And of course, Zoey being Zoey, the worse things got, the more bitter her jokes got. Apparently he would turn up at gigs and watch her from the back, and she would just get fucking angry and stubborn and refuse to compromise even one line of her material. I guess you have to admire the stroppy bitch. Except that's how she got herself killed.'

None of this has changed anything I did. I still killed Rivers Carillo. But now I'm learning to live with it. I'm not scared of him any more. I'm not scared of any avenging angels. It won't happen. It's over, it's in the past.

I've told a few more people what I did because I owed some people some explanations. I needed to build some bridges and form some normal human relationships. I invited my older sister Sarah down to London for a weekend, to stay at my flat. She was so surprised to get the invitation that she claimed she nearly fainted when I asked her. I invited Jem round for dinner while Sarah was staying with me. After the meal, while we were all sitting around comfortably enjoying each other's company, I told them the story that I'd told Danny. Jem said 'Shit' and 'Oh my God, that's fucking awesome.'

Sarah hugged me hard, and cried, and said, 'I always wondered what happened to you over there.'

'Now you know,' I said. And it was all right. They didn't freak. They didn't hate me. They didn't judge me.

I didn't tell my parents. That would have been a step too far, and it would have hurt them far too much. But I've been to see them a few times recently and my mother has told me how happy I look. She asked me if it was because of Danny.

Danny. I could give you a happy ending. I could give you Danny and me in love, together for ever, but it wouldn't be true. Danny was too nice to me after it all happened, and he asked too many questions: how I felt about it, was I okay, did I need anything?

I treated Danny so badly. I took him for granted. I dangled him on a string and I used him when I needed him, and then I didn't even think to tell him where I was on that final evening, when he was searching for me at Euston. I was snug in Zoey's flat, lying in a bath, and I didn't even remember to phone Danny to tell him that I was okay. I didn't even answer his phone calls. I was off in my own little paranoid self-centred world.

Everything I ever felt for Danny was a muffled emotion: a vague fondness, goodwill, a general feeling of warmth. I took advantage of his feelings for me, of his good nature and his kindness and his sensible normality. Sometimes the kindest thing you can do for someone is to let them go. Danny deserves someone nicer, someone good, someone who won't take him for granted. He's moved away now; he's found another flat. Jem bumped into him recently and said that he seemed okay. I hope he finds someone nice, someone who will love him properly.

Steve asks questions too. Maybe he asks too many questions as well, but they're interesting ones, and because he seems to know something about darkness it's somehow easier to answer them. We've been seeing quite a bit of each other recently, and it's good. It feels strange, though, as if we're betraying Zoey in some way. Sometimes it seems as if Zoey's still in the room, and that it's not right that Steve and I are going on with our lives without her, and it's not right that we're finding comfort with each other. And sometimes I wonder if I'll ever allow myself to be completely happy, completely at ease in a relationship.

Because, whatever happens, Rivers Carillo will always haunt me. I'm not scared of him any more. I'm not scared of his ghost, and I'm not scared of being caught. But I'm scared of myself. Sometimes I get that same old urge: an urge to blurt out the truth. Sometimes I wonder if it's time to let go, if I could possibly tell Steve the truth.

When I was eighteen I killed a man. No. Tell it properly. When I was eighteen I murdered a man and got away with it. I'm a murderer. I murdered Rivers Carillo. I kicked him and he fell backwards over the cliff. I stood on that clifftop in San Francisco and I fought off Rivers Carillo. But he wouldn't have raped me. He was too sensible. He would have stopped sooner or later. He was only trying to scare me, to scare some sense into me. I pushed him and he fell. That's true. I pushed him over the cliff, and when I did it I was scared. I was pushing him away, and he fell over the cliff.

Onto a little ledge just a few feet below.

The second time I pushed him, I meant to kill him. He was lying there, on that ledge, looking up at me, pleading for help. I think he'd broken his leg or twisted his ankle. He couldn't get up. He was lying there, and he needed my help. And I pushed him again. This time he fell onto the rocks below, and his skull cracked open and I knew he was dead. I knew he was dead because I murdered him.

Why did I do it? I wish I knew. But there is no 'why', and that's the thing that scares me most of all, more than anything. I killed him for no reason. I could say that I saw red, or that I saw my chance, or that I was covering my tracks. Or maybe that I figured I could do it and no one would ever know. I had the chance to kill someone and no one would ever know. I hated Rivers Carillo, and I had loved him too. He'd made me feel wonderful. He'd made me feel ridiculous. Maybe I saw a big red button and just had to push it. Maybe the imp of the perverse sat on my shoulder and told me to do it.

So that's it. That's why he's been haunting me all this time. Now you know. Now you finally know. And I deserved it – I deserved every single little bit of fear and self-loathing that I've felt over the last seventeen years. I deserved it. I murdered a man and got away with it, so instead of the law doing it I have had to punish myself.

What would Steve say if I told him? I have no idea. And it doesn't matter anyway, because I never will. I will never let go. I've kept the secret for so long. I've kept the secret for seventeen years. I think I will probably keep it for the rest of my life. And I think Rivers Carillo will probably haunt me for the rest of my life, too. He's been doing it for seventeen years. Why would he stop now?

Acknowledgments

Many thanks to my agent Luigi Bonomi and my editor Nikola Scott. I couldn't have done this without you.

I would like to thank every comedian I've ever worked with and every promoter who has ever given me a gig, including – but not limited to – Shaun Almey, who gave me my first-ever gig; Lynne Parker and Funny Women; Nick Doody; Steve Hall and We Are Klang; all at Pear Shaped; my fellow survivors of *that* gig – Ashley Frieze, Jeff Lane, Gareth Richards, Sophie Johnson and Chris Mayo; and of course the wonderful Logan Murray, who taught me most of what I know about stand-up.

Thanks to my family, as always. And finally, thanks to all my friends – both real-life and on-line – who kept me going with support and encouragement.

ALSO AVAILABLE IN ARROW

Grievous Angel

Jane Hill

When Justine Fraser found herself on an exchange programme in America, she had no idea that the quirky Nicky Bennet – a brief, steamy fling – would, years later, turn out to be one of Hollywood's biggest heart-throbs. Sexy, moody, outrageous, Nicky is to die for, and when he goes missing, his enigmatic suicide note spins the media into a frenzy.

When Justine sees the note in the paper, she immediately knows that it is the one clue to solving the mystery of his sudden disappearance. Slowly piecing together the fragments of Nicky's life, she sets out on a road that can only lead to betrayal, violence and revenge, discovering that the man she is looking for might turn out to be an entirely different person from the one she fell in love with . . .

'A new voice in psychological suspense fiction' *Daily Mail*

'By turns playful and poignant, sexy and sinister, Hill's darkly comedic portrait of a woman scorned packs a captivating surprise' *Booklist*

ALSO AVAILABLE IN ARROW

The Murder Ballad

Jane Hill

Stumbling headlong into a passionate fling and impromptu marriage to music star Trey, Maeve's life is about to change beyond recognition. Trey wants to whisk her off to his country house in North Carolina and Maeve follows her him without a backward glance.

But when she first lays eyes on her new home – a dilapidated old cabin in the middle of nowhere – she begins to feel uneasy. Nothing quite matches up to what she's been led to expect and, below the surface, a dark secret lies buried, a passionate and deadly love affair and an age-old murder that has never been resolved. Too late, Maeve realizes that she is all alone in a strange country, sharing a life with a man she hardly knows . . .

'A new voice in psychological suspense'
Daily Mail

'A sensational new addition to the psychological thriller shelves'
Daily Record

ALSO AVAILABLE IN ARROW

Suffer the Little Children

Donna Leon

When Commissario Brunetti is summoned to the hospital bedside of a senior pediatrician whose skull has been fractured, he is confronted with more questions than answers. Three men – a Carabinieri captain and two privates from out of town – have burst into the doctor's apartment in the middle of the night, attacked him and taken away his eighteen-month old baby. What can have motivated such a violent assault by the police?

But then Brunetti begins to uncover a story of infertility, desperation, and an underworld in which babies can be bought for cash, at the same time as Inspector Vianello uncovers a money-making scam between pharmacists and doctors in the city. But one of the pharmacists is motivated by more than thoughts of gain – the power of knowledge and delusions of moral rectitude can be as destructive and powerful as love of money. And the uses of information about one's neighbours can lead to all kinds of corruption and all sorts of pain . . .

Praise for Donna Leon:

'*Through A Glass, Darkly*, like all her work, has the exuberance of a Puccini opera.' *Independent*

'A joy from start to finish.'
Evening Standard

arrow books

ALSO AVAILABLE IN ARROW

Bloody London

Reggie Nadelson

'Artie Cohen is the detective New York deserves: smart, wounded, emotional, haunted, and not as tough as he thinks. Reggie Nadelson's Cohen books get better and better.' Salman Rushdie

As New York basks in a fine Indian summer, no one notices the feral teenagers in Central Park, or the homeless living by the river. Certainly no-one connects them to the Russian gangsters buying into respectability on the East Side, or to the dead Englishman in the swimming pool . . .

Thomas Pascoe, a super-rich, elderly investment banker, is found gorily murdered on the day he was due to return to London, floating in the pool of the most exclusive apartment block in town. As head of the 'co-op' for the luxury apartments, where the residents own the shares, Pascoe had his say in who got to live in them, and who didn't. Could this be a motive for his murder?

'Artie Cohen is the latest in a long line of slick, wise-cracking American private eyes. A worthy successor to Raymond Chandler and Dashiell Hammett, he is a Philip Marlowe for our times.' *Daily Mail*

'Superlative storytelling, with writing so good that you hardly dare turn the page in case, between times, it goes off the boil. Rest assured it doesn't . . . Disquieting, timely, terrific.' *Literary Review*

arrow books